# TORN HEARTS

A Chance and Choices Adventure
Book Five

# Lisa Gay

Copyright © 2018 Elisabeth Gay
All rights reserved.

ISBN-13: 978-1-945858-11-6

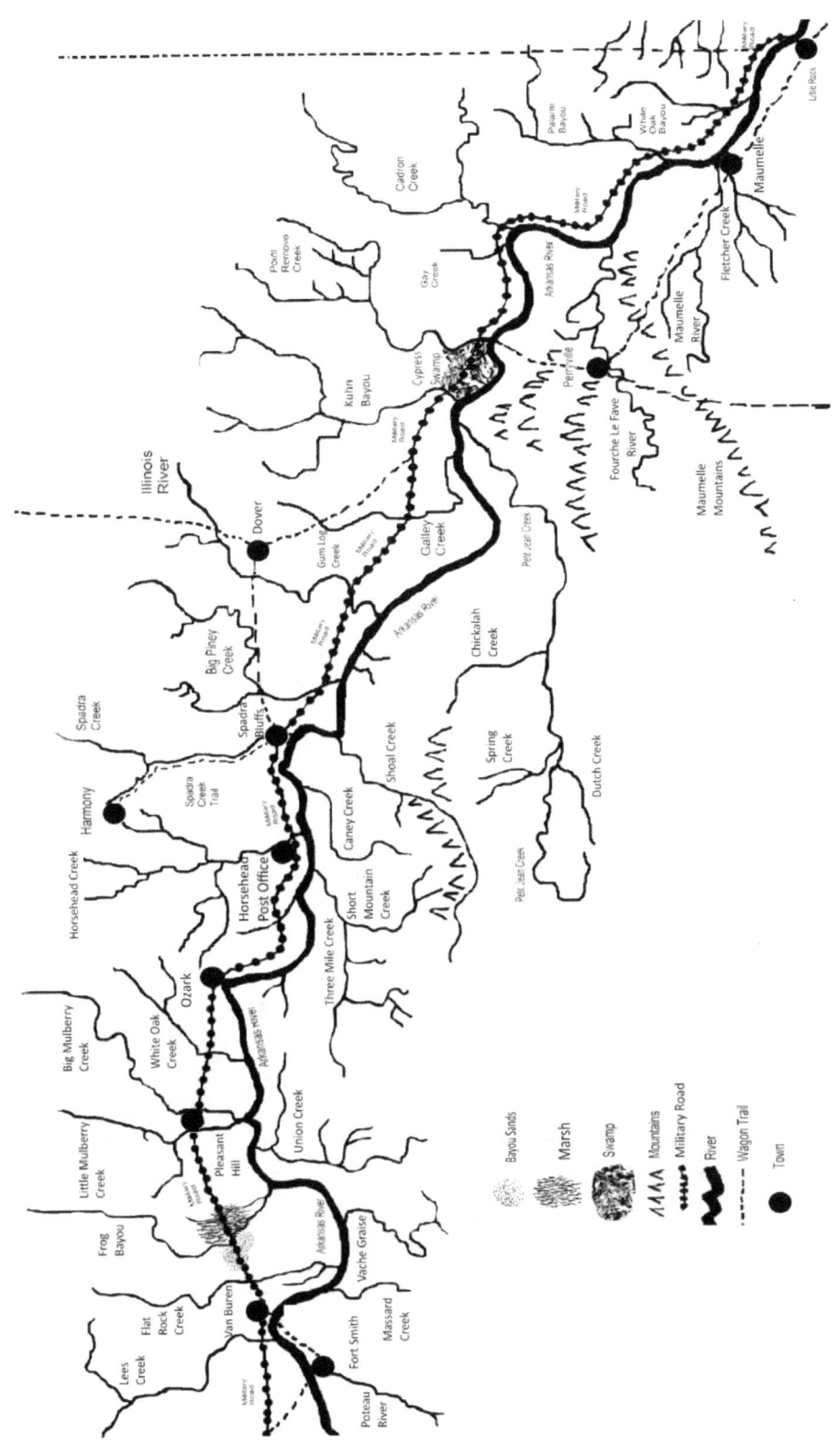

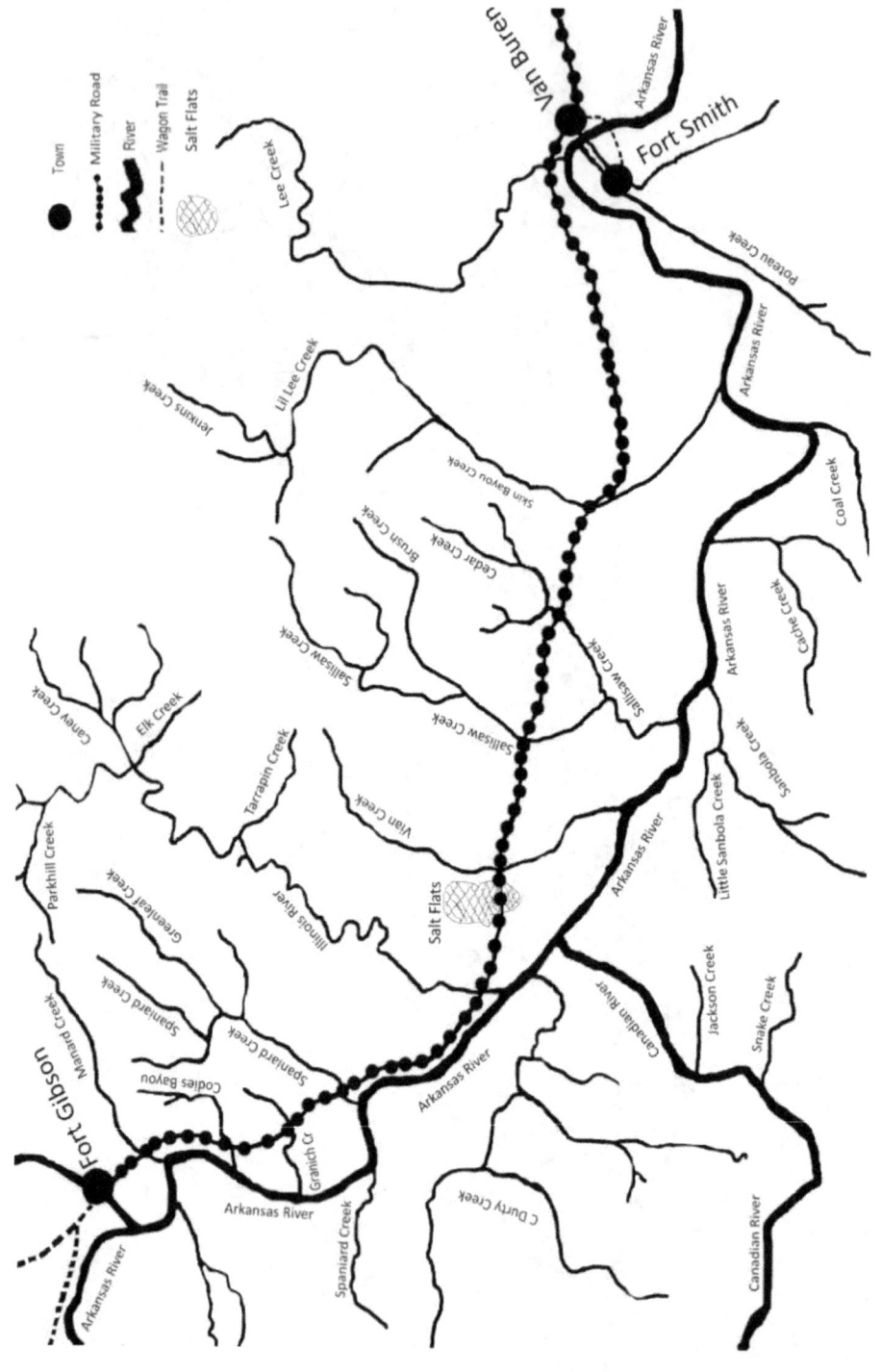

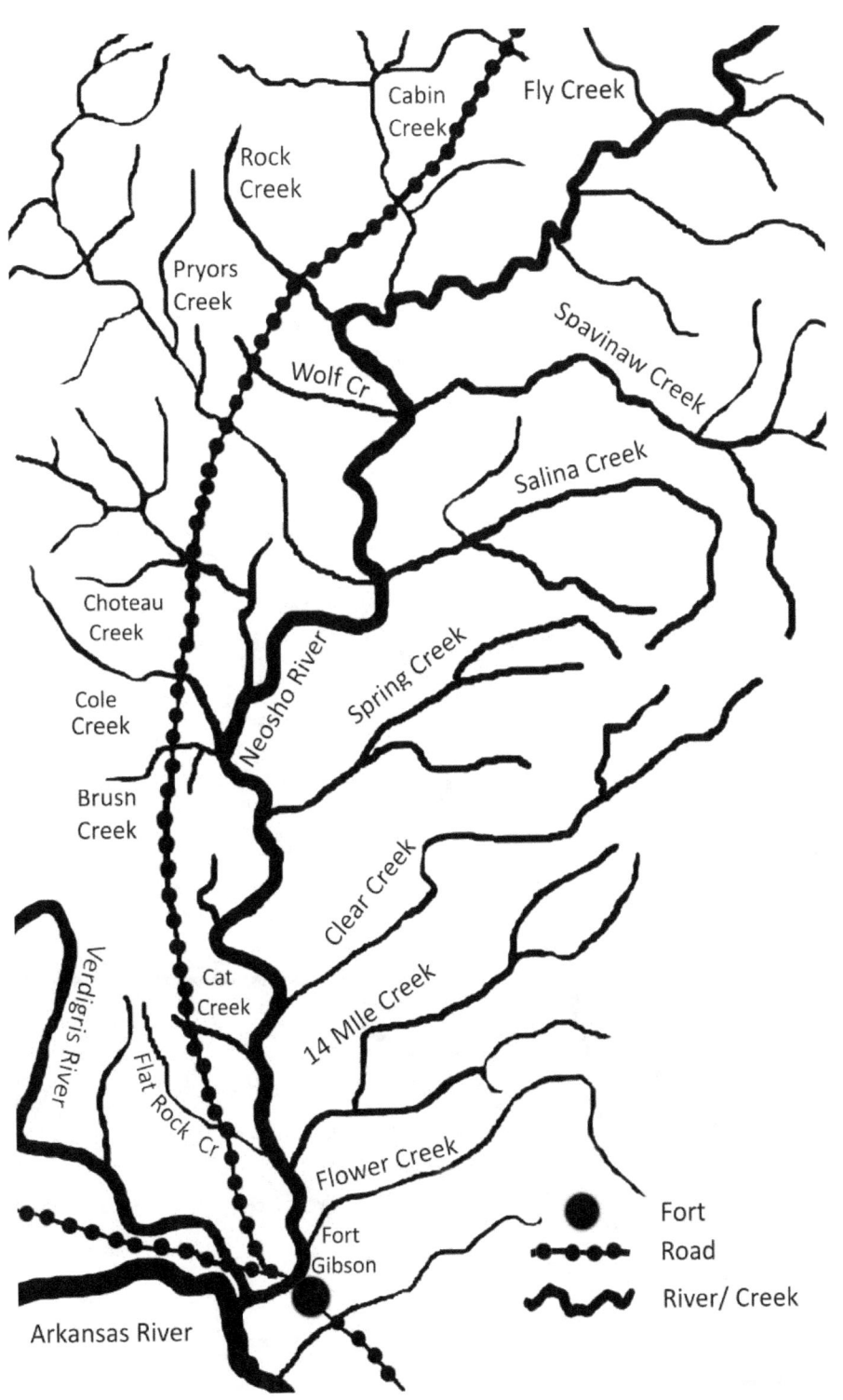

Fly Creek

Cabin Creek

Rock Creek

Pryors Creek

Spavinaw Creek

Wolf Cr

Salina Creek

Choteau Creek

Neosho River

Spring Creek

Cole Creek

Brush Creek

Clear Creek

Verdigris River

Cat Creek

14 MIle Creek

Flat Rock Cr

Flower Creek

Fort Gibson

Arkansas River

● Fort

●–●–●–● Road

〰〰〰 River/ Creek

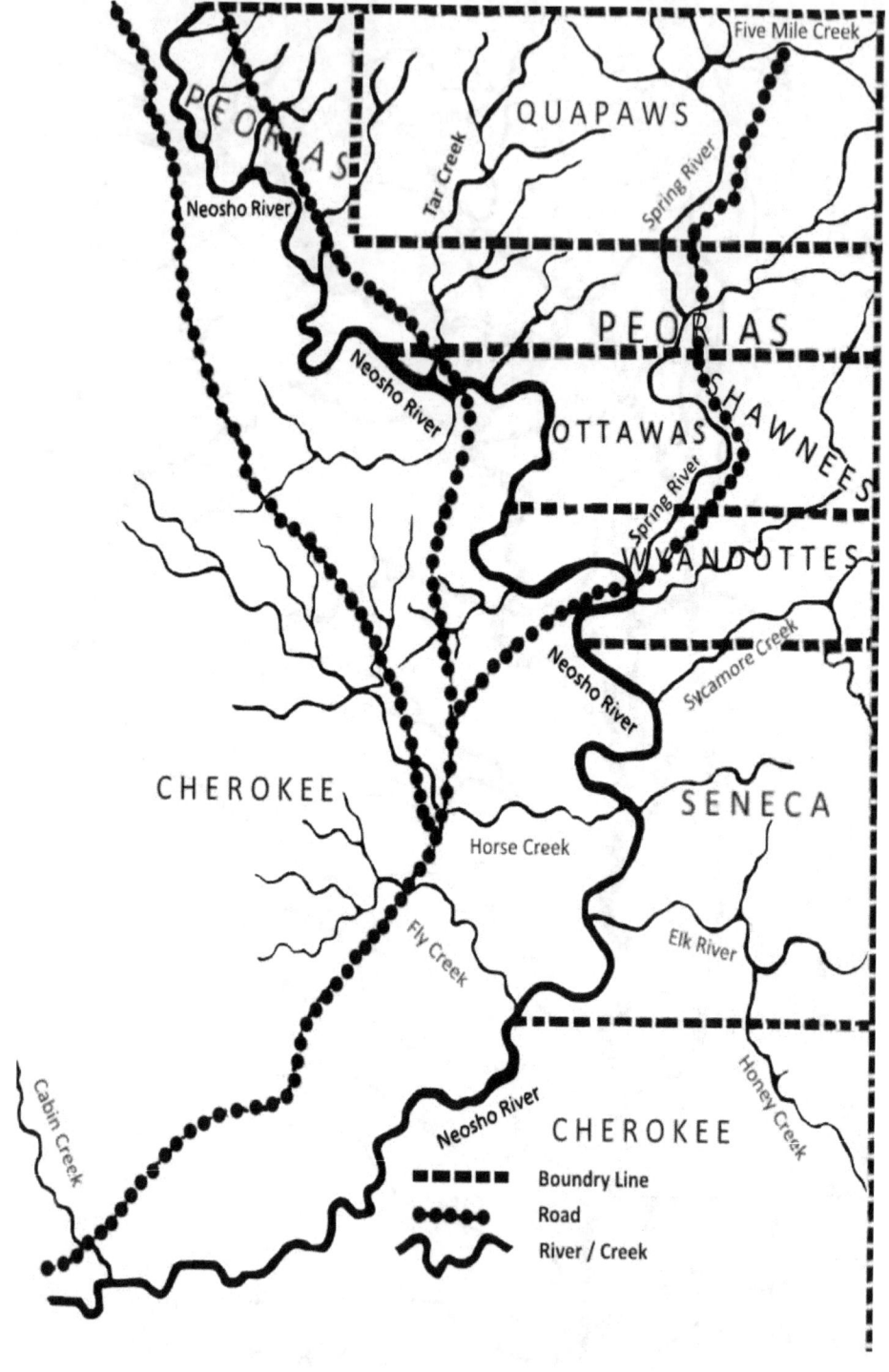

Those involved in these incidents:

**Place of Origin – Alexandria, Virginia**

Micah Clemont - His Honorable Justice of the United States Supreme Court

**Place of Origin- Dover, Arkansas:**

John Clark – Clerk of the Court and Justice of the Peace

Madeline Clark – John's wife

Robert Clark – John's brother

Gertrude – town resident (Gertie)

**Place of Origin – Eighth District**

Rufus Knapp - Warden of Arkansas Penitentiary

**Place of Origin – Fletcher Creek**

Theo – Roscoe's alternate identity

Abraham – Noah's second alias

Lily – Ann's second alias

Matt –while in Maumelle, stopped mugging of Esther

Morris – helped stop mugging

Katie – Morris's wife/operator of the Fletcher Creek Underground Railroad segment

Justin – Sally's ex-boyfriend / Matt's son

Carmen – Justin's new girlfriend / Morris's daughter

**Place of Origin – Fort Gibson**

Colonel Howland – Commander

Private Dennis

Private Morris

First Lieutenant Saunders

Elizabeth Saunders – First Lieutenant Saunder's wife

Lieutenant Jackson

Lieutenant Olson

**Place of Origin – Fort Smith**

Hank Butterfield – Butterfield Gang Leader

Roy Butterfield - Butterfield Gang /Hank's brother

Edith Atwood –Hank and Roy's sister

Richard Atwood – Edith's husband /Judge

Mr. Butterfield – Hank, Roy, and Edith's father

Mrs. Butterfield – Hank, Roy, and Edith's mother

Clarabelle– childhood friend of the Butterfield family

**Place of Origin – Frog Bayou**
Vincent Young

**Place of Origin – Harmony**
Ann Williams – oldest sister – Noah's wife
Stephanie Yates – middle sister – Eli's wife
Sally Williams – youngest sister
Eli Yates – Stephanie's husband
Tom Yates - Eli's father/owner of Yates
Mercantile
Hattie Yates – Eli's mother
Chris Williams- Ann, Stephanie, and Sally's
dead father
Emma Williams - Ann, Stephanie, and Sally's
dead mother
James Williams –Chris Williams' brother
Smithfield Wyman – sheriff/livery owner/
blacksmith (Smitty)
Mara- Smitty's wife
Earl – man, temporarily running Yates
Mercantile
Clara – Earl's wife
Joe – Saloon/Inn Owner
Zachariah Eggleston – previous travel
companion

Clyde Eggleston - Zachariah's father
Patty Eggleston - Zachariah's mother
Lawrence Gridley – doctor (Doc)
Nellie Gridley – Doc's wife/nurse
Laura – Doc's daughter
Horace – friend previously shot while tracking
Butterfield Gang
Betsy – Horace's wife
Eyanosa – Noah's stallion
Dusty – Williams' former horse
Samson – Williams' former horse

**Place of Origin – Indian Territory**
Noah Swift Hawk – Ann's husband
Arabella – Noah's former horse

**Place of Origin – Kuhn Bayou**
Minnie Eggleston – Zachariah's wife /previous
gatekeeper of Kuhn Bayou Bridge
Harry Pitts – Clerk of Court Kuhn Bayou /alias
of Harold Le Barron

**Place of Origin – Little Rock**
Daniel Hall – Judge of State of Arkansas
Martin Harrow – livery owner

Dollie Harrow – Martin's wife

Edwin Snow - stable hand at Martin Harrow's Livery

Miles Cornish– Captain - U.S. Army

Melvin Hatcher– Private - U.S. Army

Candace Daniels – mugged by Roy Butterfield (Candy)

Marie - Stephanie's alternate identity

Dr. Luke Smith – Noah's first alternate identity

Harold Le Barron – Harry Pitts' alias/associate clerk of the court

Sally's injured mules:

Beauty – injured side

Mule 4 – injured eye

Mule 7

Mule 8

Noah and Ann's injured mules:

Honor

Justice

**Place of Origin – Maumelle**

Esther Knapp– mugged by Roy Butterfield

Murray Strong – Esther's brother

Noah's mare

## Place of Origin – Perryville

Adeline – innkeeper

Raymond – a local farmer

Sebastian De La Cruz- found on the road

Lola Davis – Sebastian's girlfriend

Sargent – Raymond's horse

Mateo – Sebastian's horse

Honey Dew – Lola's horse

## Place of Origin – Pine Bluff

Roscoe Bacon – founder of Bacon's Trading Post

James Bacon – Eli's alias as Roscoe's nephew

Nancy Bacon – Sally's alias as Roscoe's niece

Roscoe's donkeys:

Little Jenny – miniature donkey

Little Jack – miniature donkey

Big Jenny

Shaggy

Spot

Blanco

Chocolate

Smiley

Honey

QuickSilver

Roscoe's mules:

King

Ace

Rose

Hector

Molly

Jumper

Blue

Chief

Diamond

Redeemed

Roscoe's goats:

Bella with two kids

Fancy with two kids

Billy


**Place of Origin – Pleasant Hill**

Innkeeper

Innkeeper's wife

Peter – Innkeeper's son


**Place of Origin – Unknown**

Charlie- Butterfield Gang member

Pete- Butterfield Gang member

Gus Hutchinson - Butterfield Gang member

Ben Rowe - Butterfield Gang member

Al - Butterfield Gang member

Arnold Buzzmann - Traveling Resupply Business co-owner & second owner of the injured mules

Solomon – a runaway slave

Hannah – Solomon's wife

Moses – Solomon and Hannah's oldest son

Asa – Solomon and Hannah's second son

Eleazer - Solomon and Hannah's youngest son

# ONE

The commanding officer of the Little Rock Arsenal strode across his office, turned on his heel, and fired a question at the soldier in shackles. "What in the Sam Hill did you accomplish?" Captain Miles Cornish didn't really want an answer. He was furious that the soldier had deserted his post as their cook. Miles had suffered months of much less than savory meals.

"As it turned out, I didn't accomplish anything."

"Don't give me flippant answers. Where are they?"

"I wish I knew."

"You expect me to believe you're not protecting Sally's family?"

"I don't know where they are. You can keep me in the stockade until I rot, and I still won't know where Noah and Ann are."

"How dare you speak to me in that tone!"

"My life is over. I don't care what happens."

"That's not true, but I can make you wish it was. Buck up and get your attitude straight!" Heavy persistent knocking at the door interrupted them. "Enter." Captain Cornish stood inches from the young private's face. "Get to the mess hall, and fix me something worth eating."

With the short chain between his legs, the young man shuffled across the room with his head hung low. Captain Cornish watched his favorite cook. *Women! Sally made a perfectly good man lose his mind!*

The door opened. Judge Daniel Hall stood in the doorway. "Wait a doggone minute! Aren't you Melvin, that soldier who ran off and tried to warn those heathens?!"

The soldier's brows furrowed. "No, sir, I had no intention of warning anybody about anything, but I was trying to find them." He waited for the judge to move. "Captain Cornish ordered me to prepare him a meal. May I go?"

The judge looked at the officer across the room. "Does he know anything helpful?"

"No."

Judge Hall stepped out of the doorway and into the office. He closed the door behind the unhappy private. "What do you plan to do about this now, Miles?"

Miles heaved a sigh.

## TWO

Much closer than Judge Hall realized, Noah tended to the injuries of two women the outlaw, Roy Butterfield, had shot. *Why did I ever think we could get Roy all the way to Little Rock? Now, people are injured. Some are even dead, and I don't know if I'll be able to get back in time. I just can't let these women suffer, not when we let Roy get away. He's dead now. Still, I wish I'd killed him when we first had the chance.*

When Noah left Maumelle, he was five hours behind the men already walking back to the Fletcher Creek hideout. Well trained by his Indian father, he didn't need to travel slowly to

4

follow the trail. He figured he could still get there first if his horses could keep up the pace.

The men ahead weren't aware of Noah Swift Hawk's Quapaw heritage. He had dyed his skin black with walnut husks and was pretending to be a runaway slave. Because of his high cheekbones, narrow nose, and the blue eyes he had inherited from his white mother, the men ahead of Noah already guessed he wasn't a slave. However, they were helping folks in the Underground Railroad, so they went along with the ruse.

That wasn't why Noah didn't want the men to know he had gone to Maumelle. He wanted them to believe that they had solved their problem on their own. They had, mostly. He had intervened behind their backs, but only enough to prevent his scared and worried friends from being reckless. If he could get home first, they would believe they were capable of taking care of themselves, and then Noah and his family could move on.

It was dangerous for him to remain so close to Little Rock. He had pushed his luck for the last two months, while his family had taught the Fletcher Creek community how to live in the woods. In exchange, his brother-in-law's broken ribs and fractured ankle had time to heal.

That morning, Noah's wife, Ann Williams, had left before anybody else was awake. She hoped the people of Fletcher Creek would think she and Noah were helping other travelers. After all, they had been taught the procedure and assigned the task while they hid at Fletcher Creek. Noah and Ann, however, planned for her to wait for him at the lower springs.

Noah crested the northern ridge of the valley where a hidden community operated a segment of the Underground Railroad. *Ann will be lying on a blanket, her black hair curling around her face, and those beautiful green eyes full of love. And her breasts...* His desire mounted as he thought of Ann while he descended to the small clearing on the slope of the mountain. *I've never made love with her at the lower springs.* Noah saw her. "My wife!" *We'll never be here again. If they get there first, we'll say we were helping some travelers.*

"My husband, I'm so glad you're back. Why do you have another horse?" Ann asked.

"I'll tell you later."

Even with no spare time, Noah got off his horse and kissed Ann passionately. They shared their love on the blanket beside the mountain springs.

Immediately after, as they quickly got ready to descend to the small cluster of cabins below, Noah explained, "I earned the horse helping some people. We need to hide her. We'll have to leave Fletcher Creek tomorrow and pick her up on our way out."

"She's carrying a big bag. Should we at least unload her into the wagon?"

"Yes. She trotted all the way from Maumelle."

The people in the cabins in the valley didn't see Noah arrive, hide his new mare, or carry a bundle into his family's tent. "I have something very important that everybody needs to know."

Roscoe, their sixty-year-old friend, helped Noah take the bundle off his shoulders. Noah laid it in the middle of the tent. By the light of their lanterns, they watched him open the bundle.

"That looks just like Mama's music box." Ann's fourteen-year-old sister, Sally, picked it up. Theirs had been ruined when the Butterfield Gang had riddled their home with the powerful bullets of the newly imported twenty-round revolvers Mousier Lefaucheux of France had recently invented. She examined the bullet hole. "How can this be?" She pressed the carved box to her heart. She was grateful that none of her family had been hurt. Still, it had devastated her when their deceased mother's music box had been broken and then stolen.

Noah laid out a vest and shirt then brought out a pair of boots. He removed a long, slender knife from its hiding place inside the boot seam.

"You shot Ben?" Ann's other sister, Stephanie, asked with horror.

"No, it wasn't Ben, and it wasn't me." Noah brought out a bundle of letters addressed to Roy's executed brother.

"Roy was in Ben's clothes?" Ann assumed only Roy could've had the clothes and letters to Hank Butterfield.

Noah slid the shiv back into the boot. "Yes, but I don't know how he came to be in Ben's clothes. Edwin was with Matt and Morris when they saw Roy robbing a couple in an alley. The three of them tackled him, the gun went off, and shot the woman before flying out of his hand toward her. She picked up the revolver and shot Roy nineteen times before she collapsed. Roy Butterfield is very dead.

"The sheriff locked them up until after the investigation. That's why they didn't come home. They'll be here soon. You can hear all the details from them. A month ago, Roy robbed a different couple in Little Rock. He killed that man and almost killed his wife. After the others left, I fixed that woman's wound. That's why I have the books in the saddlebag.

"The same way I did with Sally's mule, I repaired a large amount of damage to the back of the woman who killed Roy. That's why I have the new mare. I'm hiding it, so the people here won't know that I followed them. We need to get going, so if everybody agrees, we'll tell them tonight and leave tomorrow."

"The water's too high," Ann replied, "It's not safe to cross right now."

"But everybody's going to ask where the new horse came from. You know Justin asked me not to go with them. What if one of them gets mad that I lied and decides to tell Judge Hall about us?"

Stephanie tucked her long, blond hair behind her ear. "If it won't hurt Eli, it's fine with me."

Eli looked into his wife's blue eyes. "I'm fine, Stephanie. I'm healed enough. I'm ready to go."

Sally knew the young man of Fletcher Creek who she had fallen in love with was no longer interested in her, and she didn't want to watch Justin court somebody else. "If we can get across, I've no reason to stay."

Noah rolled up Roy's clothes. "We'll get across."

When the rescuers triumphantly arrived, everybody gathered outside to listen to the stories. Matt's youngest child sat in her rescued father's lap and listened with fascination to everything that happens to the body of a dead person. "Paw, you're so brave."

Noah listened for clues that they suspected somebody had intervened. He hadn't done much anyway. Matt and Morris, along with Edwin, were the real heroes. The unsung hero was Morris' wife, Katie. She had taken a huge chance when she had brought home travelers in The Underground Railroad.

After the men had reported all the happenings in Maumelle, Noah was sure. He announced, "We're leaving in the morning."

Katie spoke up. "Let us make a wonderful farewell breakfast for you."

Noah accepted. "That would be nice." He was ready to move on but glad they had been there for the last two months. Because they had, the people of Fletcher Creek had everything they needed to survive and thrive. The people who had become their friends would never again be desperate, and they knew it. In addition, Noah and his family had been able to completely restock their supplies.

After everybody was asleep, Noah got his mare and unloaded the books. He put his new horse in the corral where she'd be safe for the night. Before anybody was up the next morning, he moved her to their exit path.

As breakfast was prepared, Noah and Roscoe created a barrier that protected the items stored in one wagon's front from the rear section where they could carry Roscoe's goats.

The young man, who had rejected Sally, found her alone. "May I talk with you for a minute?" Justin held her hands. "I want to apologize for behaving the way I have. You're a wonderful and beautiful woman, but I can't leave with you. My family needs me, and I don't think I'd be able to live up to your expectations. Besides, you can do everything. You don't need me, but Carmen does, and she doesn't have any expectations about how I should live. I'm sorry for making you think I would go with you."

"Don't be sorry. I enjoyed what we shared, and I completely understand how much a family means to a person. I made the same choice. I think you're right that Carmen needs you, but don't believe that she has no expectations. You should talk with her about what both of you want."

"May I kiss you goodbye?"

Sally stepped into Justin's arms. "I'll always remember you."

After a long kiss, he whispered, "I'll remember you too." They walked back separately.

The morning meal was excellent and full of warm companionship. As the people leaving harnessed their mules, Katie told Ann, "I'd be happy if you stayed, but I understand. You have your reasons to move on. I can never tell you how much I appreciate all of you. You saved us."

Six happy people left the Fletcher Creek Hideout with two fully-stocked wagons, six of the mules Noah and Sally had cared for while they'd been in Little Rock, and the ten mules, ten donkeys, three adult and four baby goats that Roscoe had brought from Pine Bluff.

# THREE

Noah stood on the Little Rock side of the creek. He pushed a long branch into the tumultuous water that roared past. He stood up and ran his fingers through his short hair, dyed as black as the walnut husks had stained his skin. He looked at Ann. "I can't touch the bottom."

He knew this was the consequence of flaunting his disregard for Judge Hall's orders to stay away from the woman he had illegally wedded. The previous fall, Judge Hall had annulled Noah and Ann's interracial marriage. The judge had also sentenced them to hard

14

labor rebuilding the Cadron Ferry and had warned them that he would have them flogged and give them a year of hard labor if he found them together again.

Noah and Ann had refused to give up their love. When Judge Hall had found them reunited he was fit to chew iron and spit nails. He became Hell-bent on punishing the disdainful Indian and the white woman who had willingly become his wife.

They had not been able to flee Little Rock by the easy road. Now, the family had to cross Fletcher Creek to remain in the Underground Railroad. Roscoe set the signal that notified the next person that they legitimately needed help. "We don't know if we can trust whoever is on the other side. And how on Earth is anybody going to get us across?"

Ann stared at what looked like an impassable barrier of muddy water. "Whoever's over there is taking as much of a risk as we are. Besides that, they're the only hope we have."

An arrow plunged into the soil beside them.

"Get down!" Noah flew over Ann. They hit the ground together. Then, he noticed a thin line fastened onto the arrow. He drew it across the creek and found a heavy rope tied to the other end. "Look at this." He reeled in the attached set of leather straps that could circle a wagon, along with its accompanying harness configured to slide over an animal's legs and then hitch over its body. "With this, I think we can cross over." *What a relief! I absolutely can't let anybody be injured.*

Roscoe wrapped the thick rope around the tree where he had set the signal. "Even swimming, the smaller mules teamed with bigger ones should be able to pull the wagon. Eli, I need you to get the rope tight."

Even though he was only eighteen and five years younger than Noah, Eli was the strongest of the group. He liked being appreciated and pulled the rope taut. "What about the miniature donkeys and the goats?"

Ann contemplated a moment. "We can fit only the goats in the wagon. The donkeys will have to walk."

16

"Let's do it." Noah checked the rope's knot.

Ann, Stephanie, and Sally harnessed the large donkeys they had selected to pull the first wagon then crammed the goats into the rear. Ann told her youngest sister, "Sally, come with me and Noah."

Noah directed the donkeys to cautiously take them into the churning water. The rope and harness worked perfectly. Splashed and drenched, they exited into a narrow space between the bushes.

Sally noticed a large brown rectangle in the green undergrowth. "What's that?" She unfolded the crisp white paper inside the container made of black walnut. "There's instructions in here. I guess we won't be meeting our guide. I don't blame them for hiding. As Ann said, they're taking a big risk." Sally read the note silently.

Roscoe strapped in a donkey. *I'm worried about animals not attached to a wagon.*

The donkey strove across the torrent of cold water. Noah helped it exit on the east side.

Roscoe exclaimed, "Fantastic!" He, Eli, and

Stephanie strapped mule, after donkey, after horse into the harness until they had sent most of them to Noah, Ann, and Sally.

Across the wide roaring stream, Noah was too far away to even see the color in Eli's brown eyes. He yelled to get Eli's attention, "Attach Little Jack next!" He turned to the girls beside him. "Put on your leather gloves. We'll probably have to pull him."

Eli fastened a miniature donkey to the harness. "He's ready!" The donkey had seen the others cross with no apparent difficulty. He waded in, seemingly without concern. In the deep water, the current swept his hooves out from under him. He swung into a horizontal position. His eyes shown white with fear.

"He's drowning! Do something!" Sally screamed.

"Pull faster," Noah commanded.

As Little Jack brayed and splashed frantically, the female miniature donkey started toward the water as if to help. Roscoe grabbed the tiny animal before it could go into the creek and disappear with the current.

Across the creek, they drew the rope as fast as they could. Even so, Little Jack's head went under. *I'm not letting our animals come to any harm either.* Noah wrapped the rope around both hands. "Run!"

In only a moment, Little Jack reached the shallow water. Roscoe hollered, "Stop!"

Noah hurried back. He helped the donkey stand in the current and then struggle out.

Roscoe stood beside his thirty-inch-tall donkey, still on the eastern side of Fletcher Creek. "That's not going to work for this one. She's smaller and not as strong. We'll have to rope her into the harness and wrap the rope around the wagon. We can draw her up when the water gets deep."

Eli considered, *I should be the last one over, but we just spent months at Fletcher Creek, so my broken ribs and ankle could heal. My bones can't take the punishment.* "Roscoe, you have to come last."

"That isn't a problem. I'm still plenty strong."

Stephanie said, "Two in the wagon and one

to untie the rope. We don't have anybody to drive."

"We don't need to. You and Eli, get in the wagon." Roscoe moseyed over and yelled, "We have a plan!"

Noah listened to their strategy. "Set it up!"

Drawn by the cart, the tiny donkey walked into the creek. Eli and Stephanie reeled her in as the water got deeper. She didn't have to swim, but she did as the wagon pulled her along in an upright position.

Roscoe threaded the lifeline through the harness ring where the pull rope attached. He requested help from the being he wasn't entirely sure was available or trustworthy. *If You're there, please get me safely across.* After only a few steps, the current swept Roscoe under. His mind screamed, *You didn't do it!*

Tethered at the other bank, Roscoe sped downstream. He squeezed his eyes closed, but muddy water went up his nose and filled his mouth. Before he had time to even try to get his head above the cold water, the rope reached its end and drew him to the western shore.

Noah hauled Roscoe up the bank. "God, thank You for getting us safely across."

Roscoe gathered the rope as they walked up the creek side. "When I went under, I thought God was letting me drown, but He did what I asked."

"A dead person can't praise Him. It wouldn't have made sense for Him to let you die." Noah suddenly stopped. "Hold on for a minute." He pried a piece of bark from a tree. He licked it. *That's what I thought.* "These are Allspice trees. Have you ever tasted any?"

"No." Roscoe gnawed a piece. "This tastes great. Let's harvest a lot."

"And pick plenty of leaves to rub on us. They'll help keep the bugs away."

When the two men returned, Ann read them the directions from the box. "Take from this creek as much water as you'll need for two days. Do <u>NOT</u> drink any water you find until my message that the water is safe. Leave the rope and harness in this box. Follow the orange cloth strips. Remove the markers as you go. Do <u>NOT</u> stray from the path. At the end of this section, you'll find another box. Put the cloth strips inside. Follow the instructions."

"It's a good thing we already filled everything." Eli placed the rope back into the wood box. "God, keep us safe. Let's go." *I sure hope Pop will go west. If not, this family's gonna rip apart.*

They headed toward the orange cloth that Sally had spotted while the rest of their caravan had crossed the creek. They had officially started on their way back home to Harmony, Arkansas.

# FOUR

A pileated woodpecker drilled holes into the hundred-year-old oak holding the orange flag that Sally untied while standing on the wagon seat. "I'm glad we went back to using our real names."

Ann held up her hand, dyed as black as Noah's, and looked into Sally's hazel eyes. "Having been three different people, it's gotten confusing as to who I am. I'm happy to be Ann again."

"Unless some situation arises that requires us to hide our identities again, I'm glad to be Noah."

Stephanie thought, *if he has to, I hope Noah*

*will hide behind his blue eyes as an entirely white man other than Dr. Luke Smith like he did in Little Rock. That was a fiasco, and I hope that dye wears off soon, so he doesn't have to pretend to be a slave anymore.* What she said was, "I agree."

The day grew hot as they followed the flags and threaded between the trees that allowed wagon access. Sally brought up the increasing stench. "It smells like Kuhn Bayou Swamp."

"More like urine," Stephanie stated her opinion of the disgusting smell.

Noah looked around. "We can't be in a swamp. There isn't any water."

Eli, however, heard a familiar sound. "I hear frogs, and it's so humid. There must be water somewhere." A loud splash made everybody turn. "What in tarnation?!" Eli exclaimed.

The back, neck, and head were all that was visible of the mule, Molly. She stretched her head up, curled her upper lip, and heehawed in fear. The whites of her eyes grew large as she thrashed. "Calm down," Noah ordered in a forceful voice. He made sure he didn't join her as he grabbed the mule's halter. "God, help me save Molly!"

24

Roscoe commanded, "Get the goats back in the wagon. Gather all the unharnessed animals between the wagons. Noah, don't let go of my mule!" Roscoe sprinted away.

"She'll be under before you get back." Noah's muscles bulged as he held the struggling mule. "You're the strongest, Eli. Help me!"

Eli lay on the solid ground at the edge of the sphagnum moss growing in the water concealed below the surface of the bog. He seized the other side of Molly's halter and pulled up. "How was I supposed to know the path was so narrow?"

Roscoe returned and heard the comment. "I'm not blaming you or anybody else. We can use this rope, but don't put it around her neck. It'll strangle her."

Molly again tried to swim through the rotting plants below the thin layer of green. Instead, she sank halfway up her neck. She jetted her nose into the air, brayed frantically, and continued to sink. Noah grabbed the rope from Roscoe's hand. "Eli, attach that side.

Roscoe, fasten the middle to the back of the wagon." Noah tied his end of the rope. He yelled so the girls could hear, "Do you have them all?!"

As she led the last two goat babies into the wagon, Ann saw that her sisters had gathered the rest of their animals. "We're ready!"

"Get going! Her nose is barely above the bog!"

Ann – along with everyone else – had just learned to hug the trees that had the strip of orange cloth and to go straight from one to the next. "I'll walk in front of the team."

Stephanie steered the second wagon, towing Molly through the entangling bog. "Is it working?"

"She's coming." Noah pushed plants away.

"Keep creeping along," Roscoe told those guiding the wagons.

Eli tugged upward. "If she hadn't thrashed so much, she wouldn't have sunk so fast. We need to teach all of them to do what we tell them."

"Let's concentrate on this." Noah carefully

placed his feet. "Here she comes. Barely move forward. She has to get situated."

"You can do it. You'll be all right. Keep coming." Roscoe attempted to comfort Molly as she fought to get onto the solid ground. He removed a scraggly string of moss from Molly's eyes. "The step up is too high. We need to find a place that's shallower. Keep moving."

Making sure she knew where she was stepping, Sally navigated the edge of the bog. "Please, God, help us save her." She and Roscoe held the men keeping their hands on Molly. Sally told her sisters, "We're doing it. She's almost out," even though Molly wasn't any closer to salvation than before.

Noah touched Molly's side. "Lean over." Instead, she brought her leg forward, which hindered her extraction. "Lie on your side." Noah reached over and applied pressure toward him. "Lie down."

She did not. The wagon dragged Molly past the pink azaleas that had grown on the thin surface of the bog, tricking them into their current dilemma. Noah repeated the command. "Lie down."

Something in the floating mass of rotting plants fastened to Molly's leg. She fell onto the bank. The rope dragged the kicking mule out on her side. "Thank you, God." Noah hollered, "Stop!"

Roscoe drew Molly a bucket of their water. "After finally getting across Fletcher Creek, you'd think we could get at least a mile before disaster struck."

Sally brushed rotten, stinking plants off the mule finally laying motionless on the firm land. "It wasn't a disaster. We got her out. If we hadn't, that would have been a disaster."

Ann joined the group beside Molly. "Can't we ever have any luck? Why is it one disaster after another?"

"You see?" Roscoe put his arm across Ann's shoulder, "I'm not the only one who thinks so."

"What?" Ann asked.

Roscoe explained, "Sally says this wasn't one."

Ann reminded them of the prejudice that –in her mind– had created their current difficult situation. "We had to cross a flood with two
28

wagons and thirty-five animals all because of that idiot judge, and now we almost lost Molly. I call that a disaster. Why does he even care what we do? He'll never see us again. Noah is a wonderful person, but Judge Hall is too stupid to see that. All he sees is an Indian. Because of him, Eli was injured, we had to hide for months at Fletcher Creek, and now we've had to place ourselves into the hands of some unknown person to guide us through this extremely dangerous bog. I despise the man. Judge Hall is the one who ought to be whipped, not Noah or me. But that's what he'll do if he catches us."

"But we made friends at Fletcher Creek." Sally thought of the young man of Fletcher Creek with whom she had fallen in love. The memory of Justin brought her pain.

"I still despise him," Ann replied. "I felt so defeated after our farm was burned down. Now, I'm mad as a wildcat. I want to chew him up catawampusly." She knelt and stroked Molly. "I'm sorry this happened to you. You have my permission to kick Judge Hall all the way to Hades."

Once again underway, Eli admired Stephanie's sleek body and swaying hips while she led the mules in front of him. *Umm. Umm. I love that woman.* Then, just beyond her, something different caught his attention. "Look at that swamp rabbit. It's staying on top."

Stephanie watched the animal. "And look at those plants it ran past." She stopped to look at a metallic-green sweat bee stuck on the sticky hairs of a pink flowered, short-leaved sundew. "Remember that plant book Mama had? We read about carnivorous plants. I think this is one of them."

Sally pinched her nose and squatted at the edge of the smelly bog. She spoke in a nasal tone, "Let's watch. Too bad it's caught such a pretty bug."

"Stephanie, you remember everything you've ever read. Did that book say orchids grow in this kind of place? I'd love to see some." Ann joined her sisters to watch.

"I think it did," Stephanie replied.

Much later in the day, they saw a double strip of orange cloth with another wooden box below it in a grassy field. Stephanie opened the container while Sally untied the orange strips. "What's it say?" Sally asked.

Stephanie read, "Since you have animals, tie this rope around the clearing. You don't want them to wander and drown in the bog. When you leave, put the rope back in the box. If you want to go west or north, tie an orange cloth on the branch above. If you want to go south, tie the blue cloth."

Sally tied an orange marker.

To keep the horses, donkeys, and mules contained, Ann and Noah started stringing the rope around the clearing. Eli and Stephanie put all the animals into the large glade to graze. The animals would get most of the water they needed from the grass, so they gave them only a small portion of the water they had brought.

Noah told Ann, "This rope won't keep the goats in. We should stake them and move them around until dark then put them in the wagon for the night."

"I'll get some tent ropes and spikes." Ann left Noah to finish tying the provided rope around the clearing.

When they had the goats secured, the rope corral constructed, and the meal ready, there was still enough daylight to eat and clean up. The last fifteen minutes before the sun set, Eli read to them out of the Bible they had brought from Harmony nine months earlier. Then, since it was his turn, Eli spoke the nightly family prayer. "Heavenly Father, we praise You for helping us save Little Jack and Molly, but mostly for protecting Noah and Ann from capture and for healing me after the wagon wreck. Continue to keep people and animals safe, send us to the places You want us to go, and to the people You want us to help. I ask in the name of Jesus, Amen."

They laid out their tarps, blankets, and down pillows in the only available space. Noah snuggled next to Ann and stroked her raven-colored hair, which she had cut short the previous winter. "There's nothing like lying with my lovely wife under a wagon."

The night passed uneventfully. At first light, Roscoe checked on his animals. *They're all safe. They look plenty rested and happy enough.*

Ann walked over. "I'll stake the goats on the grass until it's time to leave. I'll also shovel out the wagon."

During the night, someone had hung an orange cloth just beyond the clearing. "How did somebody do that without me knowing?" Noah felt uneasy. *If somebody can sneak that close, I might not be able to keep our family safe.*

Noah took down the strip above the box and then drove directly toward the next marker. The land changed as they carefully weaved through the forest. When they saw a foot-wide outcropping of stone that rose a few feet above the ground for several yards, they stopped for their mid-day meal. Noah recognized the rock. "I can knap arrowheads out of this and also sharpen knives with it. We should take some." He picked up and packed several large chunks of novaculite.

Eli added a few smaller stones. "I want to make arrowheads too. I'll probably ruin a lot of them. I definitely need more practice." After the meal, they again followed the markers west.

Their guide impressed Noah. Noah was a

well-trained Indian hunter, but he had not once seen or heard whoever was setting the markers ahead of them. Their guide could mark two different safe paths through terrain made dangerous by deep moss bogs and undrinkable water. The previous night, they had been led to what was probably the only clearing able to accommodate their large number of animals. They had also been taken across streams at easy fords as they had weaved through the forest, all without their guide revealing his identity.

# FIVE

The markers brought them to the Maumelle River, flowing northeast from the southern range of the mountains ahead. Sally found another instruction box.

Roscoe asked, "What's in that one?"

Sally read the paper, "You can drink the water of this river and the water on the other side. Lash the ash logs to your wagons, and you'll float. It's hard to judge the current, but you'll certainly come out on the other side far downriver. It's raining in the southern mountains. Cross today." Sally put the note and all the markers they had collected into the box.

35

Ann looked at the broad river. "It'll be dark before we get across. Maybe we should wait until morning."

Noah remarked, "If this person said, 'go today,' it's because we won't be able to cross tomorrow."

Roscoe concurred, "You're both right. There isn't much day left, but we should cross today. We don't have time to argue. We need to get started."

Eli drove to the stack of logs. "There's no crossing harness to help us."

Sally had an idea. "We can give Little Jack, Little Jenny, and the goats a sedative and then put them all in the wagon together. If we tie more of the animals to the front of the wagon harness, they can help pull, and they'll be safer too. We'll have to let the rest swim free then look for them on the other side."

"You think they'll all follow?" Stephanie asked.

Roscoe said, "We'll drive them into the river. The only problem is Sally's mules. Mule 4 still can't see very well. It's one thing for Beauty to walk beside her to help her, but I doubt she can direct her friend while swimming."

Noah decided. "We'll put them in the harness."

"But their skin is still so fragile," Sally protested.

Noah told her, "In the middle of the group, it shouldn't be too hard on them. I'll start a fire."

Roscoe wondered if one of them would ask God to get them safely across, and what would happen if they didn't. When they had the sedative ready, both the wagons had an ash log attached on each side. Sally and Roscoe gave the knock-out potion to all their little animals.

Noah harnessed Mule 4 and Beauty with eight other sturdy mules and donkeys. "I should ride Eyanosa in front of them. The animals will do better if one of them is swimming in front."

"I can bring up the rear on Redeemed." Stephanie felt sure the previously ornery mule she had trained would do what she asked.

"Stephanie, I want you safely in the wagon," Eli held out his hand to help her onto the wagon seat.

Roscoe offered, "I'll come last on King."

Trusting in their own planning, Noah rode his horse into the river. Following him, the mules pulled the wagon with Ann, Sally, and the sleeping animals. As they had been told, when the swimming mules dragged them into the deeper water, the wagon floated on the logs. Behind them, Roscoe drove in the animals that didn't follow into the river on their own volition.

Halfway across and quite a bit downriver, Sally looked out the rear of the bobbing wagon. Eli and Stephanie still hadn't left the shore. *If they don't come now, they'll still be in the river after the sun goes down. I hope they can hear me.* She yelled with every drop of power she had, "Come now!"

The second wagon started in. Behind it, Roscoe and King entered. *We didn't pray. We'll find out if that makes a difference.* They were all in the river in the light of day, but the sun was close to touching the Maumelle Mountains in front of them. The water swept the mules making their way on their own past the wagons then downriver to the north.

Ann reached the western shore. The bank wasn't as shallow as she had hoped. *The last thing I need is to be unable to get out of the river.* She cracked her whip in the air. "Giddy up!" The mules pulled hard. Their hooves sank into the soft mud, but they dragged the wagon out as the sun kissed the mountain ridge.

Sally had cared for and then purchased four of the mules injured in the blizzard earlier that spring. Noah owned two more of them. All six completely trusted Sally. Her unharnessed mules and Noah's had stayed close to her. "Follow me," she commanded. The mules ascended behind her. "That was a long swim and a strenuous climb. We need to let the animals rest."

Still in the river, Eli heard Roscoe holler at the animals in front of him, "Go! Swim faster!" Eli urged the animals pulling his wagon with the same words. Those weren't commands they had taught the animals, but Eli didn't want to be in the river in the dark, and he felt compelled to urge them on.

The tip of the sun sank out of view as loose

animals emerged from the river south of Ann. In the red twilight, the rest still swam for the far shore. Noah had stayed close to Ann. *Ann and Sally are safely out of the river.* "I'll get the animals to the north."

Twilight faded into night as Eli and Stephanie pulled out of the river with Roscoe right behind them. To recover the animals that had made it across upriver, Roscoe rode south. He passed Ann and Sally on their way to join the others farther to the north.

Roscoe told them his plan, "I'll look for another box with instructions. I'll gather the mules I saw get across before the rest of us."

"Don't go too far looking for the box. I'm sure Noah can get us home from here." Ann said, "We're going north until we get to the other wagon then we'll build a fire. Come along the river and look for it."

Before she was out of the river, Stephanie had seen Noah pass the place where she set up camp. Eli got the tired animals unhitched. It wasn't long before Ann and Sally arrived and let the animals with them join the herd.

Ann stacked firewood. "I'm making a big fire, so Noah and Roscoe can find us."

"What are you cooking tonight?" Eli asked.

Sally handed Eli two large cast iron skillets. "Cornbread with bear crackling, fried bear sausages, and fried potatoes, along with some of the greens we collected at Fletcher Creek."

Stephanie climbed out of the wagon with a bag of roots and a jar. "And hot sassafras tea with honey."

Riding on King, Roscoe arrived an hour later with the mules he had found. The already grazing animals neighed and heehawed greetings to the new arrivals. The animals that had ridden across asleep still lay in the wagon, oblivious to everything.

Noah didn't know how far he had to go or how many animals he had to find. When he arrived in camp one mule short, everybody was concerned. Roscoe fretted. "What if Rose didn't make it?"

Noah offered, "I'll look again."

"I don't want you to go back out. Maybe she'll find us on her own," Ann replied.

Roscoe brought up his other matter of concern. "When the goats and donkeys wake up, they may hurt each other if they're crammed in there together. Help me get the goats out." Roscoe opened the wagon cover, climbed in, and passed out the kids. Eli removed the back slats and attached the exit planks at the rear. He and Noah pulled the adult goats down the smooth boards. They left the donkeys in the wagon with the cover open and the walkboards in place.

## SIX

Roscoe opened his eyes with the sun. He hoped Rose had found them and went to find out. The mule wasn't there. However, Little Jack and Little Jenny were out of the wagon, grazing with the herd. The kids didn't seem to be suffering as a result of their forced sleep. However, in the dark, Roscoe had staked them too far from their mothers, and they hadn't been able to nurse. Roscoe moved the mother goats, Fancy and Bella, to their babies. The kids immediately gulped milk. Roscoe looked at the river. *How did that happen? It never rained a drop last night.*

43

Ann woke. She didn't know the goat babies had just started to eat. She pushed them aside to milk the goats in the chilly morning air. The kids pushed back in for another drink. Ann eventually won enough battles to get a quart of milk. She carried it to the fire where Roscoe fried eggs. "Is the coffee ready?" Roscoe picked up the pot with the hot pad. Ann held out her tin cup. "Did you find a box?" She heard the fast-moving water and turned her head.

"Yep, the note said, 'I hope everybody got across safely. Leave the logs. Go through the gap by the Big Rock. It's the highest peak slightly to the northwest. You're on your own from there.' Here's a drawing." He pointed to the arrow indicating the gap.

Noah arrived with his cup. "That won't be a problem." He carried his steaming coffee away.

Ann joined him next to the rising river. "It's a good thing you didn't listen to me."

Roscoe called out, "Eggs are ready!"

Noah sat cross-legged next to the fire. "I'm glad we came over. We'd be blocked this morning."

44

Eli added to the conversation when he and Stephanie arrived. "It's still raining over the mountains. I hope the river doesn't overflow its banks."

"Did Rose get here?" Stephanie asked.

Roscoe replied, "No, and none of you asked your God to help before we started across. You should've gotten Him to help us." He added, "I hope Rose didn't drown because you didn't."

Sally heard the comment. "God doesn't punish people who forget to pray. You're right that we should have, but don't blame us. If God made you think about it, maybe you were the one who was supposed to pray. As for Rose, maybe she doesn't know where we are. What if we make a lot of noise?"

*He's their God. He wouldn't have put thoughts into my head.* Roscoe put eggs on their plates. "We shouldn't do that. No telling who may hear. I went south all the way to the box. I didn't see her. She's got to be north."

"We'll have to stay close to the river to look for her. We could become trapped if the river gets too high and floods the valley. We should

45

get going," Ann picked up her fork, "as soon as we're done eating."

They gobbled their breakfast. Stephanie gulped the last pint of goat's milk before she rolled up everybody's bedding and shoved them in their designated places.

Sally sat in the driver's seat of wagon one. Ann perched in the other. They quickly picked up to a trot. Instead of going northwest directly toward the gap in the mountains, the wagons jiggled and bounced along beside the river.

Noah, Eli, Stephanie, and Roscoe rode their favorite animals: Eyanosa, Ace, Redeemed, and King. Stephanie called out weakly, "Eli?"

He rode to her. "What do you need, honey?"

"I'm so tired." She slumped and slid off Redeemed. Eli jumped off Ace. He knelt beside his unconscious wife. "Stephanie?" He tried to wake her. The whole family gathered around. "What's wrong, Noah?" Eli pleaded, "Help her."

Noah felt her pulse and listened to her breathing. "I think she's sedated."

"How did that happen?" Sally glanced

inside the animal wagon. "The kids are asleep too. Stephanie drank a lot of milk, but why did the kids not go to sleep until now?"

Roscoe looked at the sleeping goats. "The babies weren't staked close enough for them to nurse last night. I moved them over this morning."

"That explains why they gave me such a hard time when I was milking their mothers."

Eli carried Stephanie to the wagon and put her on the stack of mattresses. "Now, we know not to drink milk after they've had the sedative."

Sally cracked the whip to get moving. After an hour at a trot, they were much farther downriver than Noah had gone the night before. Suddenly, the mules shifted their ears.

"They hear something," Roscoe announced.

Neighing and braying, their mounts galloped ahead. They let the animals direct themselves. Soon, they heard a mule frantically calling for help. During the night, after the exhausted mule had finally gotten to the far bank, it had collapsed. Too tired to move, the rising water had washed her into a tree where underwater roots had captured and pinned her under the low limbs that hung over the water.

"How can we get her out?" Eli asked.

Roscoe looked over the area. "We'll have to get her to swim back into the river and around the roots. Then, we can pull her to the bank."

For a moment, Rose's feet lost contact with the riverbed. She tried to swim but couldn't get her leg out from behind the root. Her eyes pleaded for help.

"We'll have to pull her. Tie the rope to King and Ace." Noah climbed onto the roots. "The branch is scraping up her head."

*They're doing it again. One of them needs to ask God to save my mule.* Roscoe did not do as urged.

Every time Rose writhed, the roots shook and threatened to knock Noah into the river. Eli warned him, "Come back. There's no hope."

Noah sat in a loop of the root and tied the rope around his chest. "If I go in, pull me out." He continued toward the mule. "Focus on me and calm down." He climbed to the lowest root. The water was six inches from Rose's head as

48

Noah fed the line around her neck and front leg. He tried to get the rope around her other front leg but couldn't reach, so he lowered his body into the river.

Ann and Sally arrived. Ann pulled her wagon to a stop and then ran to the riverbank, "Don't try it!"

Noah's head went out of view. A second later, his head popped up on the upstream side of Rose. Ann silently prayed, *God, protect Noah.* The water pushed Noah hard against the mule. He looped the same rope that prevented the forceful water from pulling him away around Rose's front legs and body. He tied a knot that wouldn't tighten and strangle her or untie under duress.

Noah tried to pull Rose away from the bank. Going back into the river was not a direction the mule was willing to go. With her leg caught in the root, she couldn't move that way anyway.

Ann screamed, "Get out! You can't save her!"

Sally stepped in front of Ann. "You're making it harder for Noah because he's worried about you being afraid. He needs to concentrate. Besides, you know he won't give up if there's any hope at all." Ann knew her sister was right. She clamped her mouth shut. *God, please help Noah. He won't stop until he's saved her.*

Noah again tried to get Rose to move. This time, he felt the tension on her leg, went back under, poked around, and saw that the mule's hoof was trapped. He came back up and took another breath before he went down again. He pulled up on Rose's knee and got ahold of her foot. It slipped out of his hands. Mule flesh ripped as her leg went back into the trap. Again, Noah went up for air. The water circled Rose's head. *I'm running out of time.* He descended again, raised her leg at the knee, grabbed her hoof, and attempted to pull it above the root. His lungs begged for air. With Rose's hoof still in his hands, he put his feet on top of the root and fought to straighten his legs. Her hoof came over. Noah shot to the surface.

*Now, if I can get her to turn and swim away from the bank, I can get her out.* "Come on, Rose. Go out. You can do it." With his feet on the underwater branch, he pushed her head against the current. She grudgingly moved out. He wedged himself between her and the tree, pushed against the root, and shouldered her. Rose took a step to the side. "Go out!" Noah pushed harder. Rose took another step. She stood almost parallel to the flow of the water. Suddenly, the water sent her shooting toward the roots with Noah in between. *I'm done for!* He sidestepped.

*On, no!* Ann threw her hands over her eyes.

Rose tried to stabilize. She stepped backward then slammed into the tree, just barely clipping Noah. The movement away from the bank brought her head out from under the overhanging limb. With her head and foot free, Rose calmed considerably. Trying to turn the mule, Noah pushed against her neck. Rose absolutely was not going back into the river.

"Back her out," Eli suggested.

Noah pulled the rope as he climbed away from the bank. Unfortunately, the root didn't extend far enough into the river. He got back into the water, put his feet against an underwater root, and pushed her chest with his back. As Rose stepped back, Noah moved out. Suddenly, the water snatched the mule and pulled her into the current. The rope instantly pulled Noah under.

Ann screamed, "No!"

Eli ordered, "Prepare King and Ace. The ropes are going to jerk them hard." They faced the two mules upstream as the slack quickly drew out.

"We should have tied the ropes to the wagons." Sally grabbed the rope and ran. She wrapped it around the axle just behind the wheel, looped it through itself, and then stuck the handle of her knife into the loop.

*Snap!* The wagon lurched but absorbed the jolt that would have certainly yanked King and Ace off their feet. The line around Noah jerked tight.

Unable to get to the surface, Noah swirled. *God, why didn't You stop me? I've given up a life with Ann to save a mule. Forgive me for what I've done to her and all the other things I've done wrong.*

He could hold his breath no longer. *Take me to You.* Still underwater, his lungs involuntarily inhaled.

*The rope. Too constricting. No air.* More importantly, no water could get into in his lungs. Eddies carried Noah to Rose. He grabbed her tail. With all his strength, he pulled his head above the water. With one hand, he struggled to loosen the rope around his chest. With the other, he tightly clutched Rose's mane.

King and Ace drew Noah and Rose toward the shore. Ann instructed Eli and Roscoe which way to drag the mule and man. *Show me a place where we can pull them out.*

Sally called out, "You have to get them out faster! A creek is about to block us!"

*There's no way he could've held his breath this long.* Ann strained her eyes, searching for Noah's head above the water. She saw it. A black bump on Rose's back. She cried with relief. *I need to see to direct Eli and Roscoe.* She quickly wiped away the tears.

Almost to the inflowing water of Bringle Creek, Rose and Noah got their feet on the riverbed. Ann dashed into the water. Sally splashed in, right behind her. They got on either side of the man one loved as a husband and the other as a brother. "Thank You, God!" the girls chanted while they helped Noah to the wagon. Sally kissed his cheek and then left.

Roscoe helped Rose onto the dry land. *I didn't hear one single prayer.* Rose fell to the ground. *I'm not sure if God helped us or not.*

The collision with Rose and the rope around Noah's chest had bruised and gouged him. Ann tended to him. "My heart is going to stop. I know you can do so much, but you scare me to death."

Noah defended himself, "I didn't know that would happen."

"That's the whole point. Things happen that nobody thinks will happen."

During the seconds Noah had thought he was drowning, he had wished he'd been more careful. "I'm sorry. I know you're right, but she looked at me and begged me to save her. I couldn't just watch her die."

"You're such a compassionate man. I know

you want to make everything right. That's one of the things I love about you. It's just that you take such potentially disastrous chances. I don't understand why the consequences to me aren't as important to you. What if you had died?"

"It is important to me. I believed I'd be successful. I didn't think you would have a bad consequence, and I knew if I didn't act, Rose would drown. I can't let a sure death happen."

Ann finished wrapping Noah's chest then kissed him. "I understand. It scares me because I don't want anything bad to happen to you, and selfishly, I don't want to lose you. I'll try to be braver about your bravery if you'll try to not be so brave."

"I'll try to be more careful. I really appreciate you talking to me rationally, even when you're extremely upset. I don't know how you do it. Let's go."

They checked on Rose. "How is she?" Noah asked.

Roscoe informed him, "Her leg is cut up, the top of her head is rubbed raw, her side is bashed, and she's exhausted. She can't even walk. I don't know if she can get into the wagon. Even if we did rearrange everything and got her into the wagon, I don't know if she'll make it."

"The river is still rising," warned Sally. "Do whatever you need to do, right now."

"Rose might be able to take a few steps when we're done." Ann climbed into the wagon. "Let's make space."

Eli placed Stephanie on the soft mattress he moved to the floorboard in front of the driver's seat, exactly where he had lain with his ribs broken.

Sally passed supplies. "Do you think Rose is too tired and won't try to stand inside the wagon?"

Noah felt determined to be more careful. "If we can get her in the wagon, I suggest we put her out and not take a chance. Besides, it might help her recover."

"I'll get what's left from yesterday." Roscoe uncorked a jug and poured the liquid into a bucket. Rose drank it down.

Since they needed to get away from the

rising river, they quickly made space and then drove the wagon to the exhausted mule. It took all of them, but they managed to get Rose on her feet.

She tried to take a step. Ann said, "Look how her legs are shaking." They shoved Rose's rump to help her up the planks, pushed in from both sides to keep her from falling over, and forced her into the wagon. They immediately helped her lie down. She was too exhausted to care when they laid the still sedated baby goats around her.

Eli sat in the driver's seat with Stephanie at his feet. The search for and retrieval of Rose had brought them past the gap. Eli prayed, "Stephanie's unconscious. She can't even try to swim if we get trapped. God, please get us to the mountain gap."

Since the miniature donkeys and adult goats now walked, they progressed too slowly. Before they could exit the valley, the water overflowed the riverbanks and spread across the flat river basin. Eli panicked. "We can't get there! Stephanie will drown!"

On Eyanosa, Noah carried Ann from the lead wagon to the wagon Eli was piloting. "Ann's going to get in with you and tie empty jugs to Stephanie. Stay on this ridge of high ground."

Ann stepped into the wagon. She emptied all five of their gallon-sized jars of honey into a ten-gallon tub then ran the rope through the finger loops on the bottlenecks. "Take this, Eli." Ann passed the string of jugs out the front. She knelt over her sister with a knee on either side and fed the rope under her arms. "How can I tie this, so it won't slip off, and it keeps her head above the water?"

"You drive. I'll tie the rope. This is a good plan, Ann. First, I'll put her buckskin pants on under her dress and the shirt over the dress top." Eli tied two loops and then slid them up Stephanie's legs. He fed the rope back through the loops before he ran it up to and around an arm. He tied it and then went around her chest. He knotted it again before looping and securing the rope around her other arm. He fastened the part of the rope with the jugs to the loop around

58

her upper body. "That should stay on and keep her upper body above water. I'm so glad you thought of this."

"Of course, Eli. I love my sister. I don't want to take a chance any more than you." The lead wagon blocked their view of the gap. "I hope we're almost there. I doubt we have five minutes." Ann tried not to focus on the water approaching the slight rise on which they rode.

Only Sally saw the view ahead. She stopped and scurried to the rear. "To go west, we have to cross the water from here."

Noah trusted Sally. "Looks wide, but the water's not moving fast on this floodplain. We'll have to chance it. I'll ride ahead on Eyanosa."

Roscoe rode over. "No, you won't. If I die, it's no loss. If you die, what will Ann do?"

Sally said, "It is too a loss. You'd better not die."

"I don't want to die. I'm going to be very careful. Besides, I don't think it's deep." Roscoe added, "I wish we still had those ash poles." This time, he thought, *if You care, help us.* He told Sally, "Keep an eye on King's legs. If the water gets above his knees, holler. It'll soon be too deep for the goats." He urged King into the water toward the gap only two hundred yards away, unfortunately, on the other side of an unknown depth of floodwater.

The caravan sloshed in. Sally monitored every step King took while they rolled along. The water rose up his legs. It also neared the floor where Stephanie lay. "Take the reins, Ann. I'm going to move Stephanie." Eli picked her up. "Put the mattress on the seat." Ann did so. Eli laid his wife on the mattress, only two feet higher than the floorboards.

Little Jack, Little Jenny, and the goats walked in water just lower than their backs. Noah rode Eyanosa beside them. "Six inches more and they'll be swimming."

"We're almost halfway," Roscoe called back.

Several yards farther, Sally informed them, "We can't make it. It's too deep."

Ann already had ropes in her hand. "Tie them to the wagons like we did with Little Jenny crossing Fletcher Creek."

Noah got the rope. "Roscoe, try to go all the way across while we tie them on."

By the time Roscoe returned, the donkeys were roped at the sides of the lead wagon and the goats to the rear. "I got over with King walking in the deepest section, but barely coming back. It's even deeper now. The deepest part's not far, and then it gets shallower. We need to go now and move fast."

Noah commanded his horse, "Eyanosa, follow." He stepped into the lead wagon. "Eli, pull the goats up to the wagon when the water gets too deep. I'll get the donkeys."

"Forward ho!" Sally told her team.

Noah and Eli pulled the swimming animals to the wagons. Ann kept an eye on Stephanie while the wagon rolled into the deeper water. Soon, it overflowed the floorboards. Ann asked, "How much farther 'til we pass the deepest place?" Noah relayed the question to Sally, who passed it on to Roscoe.

"Almost there," he answered, "fifty feet, maybe."

Sally stood on the floorboards with her feet

in the river. Noah told her, "Stay above the water. Stand on the seat." He had already tied the rope holding the donkeys, so he walked to the rear to tell Ann the same thing. She was already on the seat with Stephanie.

Ann saw him. "If it gets much deeper, we'll find out if these wagons will float without the ash trees."

"These wagons are heavy. If the animals have to swim, they won't be able to pull them if they don't rise off the river bed."

Six inches before the water reached the seat top, Roscoe hollered, "We're coming out!"

Sally called out, "Much obliged, God!"

Noah untied Little Jack to descend with the water. He let Little Jenny down a few inches at a time. Eli untied both ropes. He held one in each gloved hand and let the ropes slowly slide out as they came up the shallow slope of the Maumelle Mountains.

## SEVEN

At fifty feet above the river, just before entering the ravine north of Big Rock, Roscoe saw an artesian spring venting water from the ridge to their right. He decided they were out of danger. "We're safe. Let's prepare the mid-day meal."

Stephanie had no idea what was happening, but Eli did. He brought her next to them to include her while they watched a family of chipmunks perform acrobatics at the water playground. Eli sat with Stephanie's head in his lap and stroked her hair. "How much milk did she drink?"

Sally lounged beside her family. "The pitcher was over a quarter full. She drank all of it."

"We should milk the goats and throw it away before the kids eat again." Ann went for a stool.

Sally got one too. "Let's squirt it on the ground. How will we know when all the sedative is out?"

Roscoe told her, "We'll have to let the kids nurse and see what happens. They've missed a lot of meals." He examined the sky through his spyglass. "It's not raining down south anymore. The sky is clear as far as I can see. We should set up camp here. It's a beautiful place, we have good water, and there's plenty of grass. Right here, we're also shielded from view."

"I like Roscoe's plan." Sally carried her milking stool to the wagon.

Eli kissed his wife's forehead. "That's fine with me. I don't like carrying Stephanie on the floorboards."

Ann returned the other stool to its place in the wagon. She heard something and cocked her head. "Is that a pig squealing?"

Sally whispered, "I'd love to eat a pig."

Roscoe encouraged them, "I know a good recipe."

"Eli, you want to go hunting?" Noah hoped Eli's ankle felt healed enough.

"First, let me tighten this ankle wrap."

Noah got his weapon of choice. "Get your bow too."

Planning to shoot the pig with arrows, and not use loud guns unless they had to, they sneaked toward the squealing. Ahead, they heard pigs rooting for bulbs and fighting about which of them was going to eat the delicious treats. Noah was about to ask their Father above and the animal spirit below for permission to have a pig. Before the words started out of Noah's mouth, Eli whispered, "My God in Heaven, we ask for permission and help to kill a succulent pig to roast and eat, and that the rest of the herd be prolific and not suffer from the loss of the pig You give us."

Noah finished with, "Amen! Let's try for that red one." Several yards away from each other, they inched forward. When they were both in position behind trees that provided enough cover for them to get to their knees, they signaled, rose, took aim at the good-sized red male, and let their arrows fly.

*Foosh.*

*Foosh.*

Two arrows streaked toward the pig doomed to be food for humans.

*Thwap.*

*Thump.*

The target dropped. The rest of the herd scattered.

Noah dropped his bow. He grabbed a branch above and pulled his feet up, barely in time to avoid the sharp tusks of the charging swine.

Eli cried out, "Help! Noah, I need you!"

Unable to see if Eli had gotten out of the way, Noah feared. *Oh no, Eli's been gored!* He dropped to the ground and ran. Eli hung from his hands. "What's the problem?" Noah asked.

"I don't want to drop on my ankle."

"I thought you had a pig tusk through you."

Wincing due to his bruised chest, Noah held

Eli around the thighs and lowered him to the ground.

"Sorry about that. I wanted you to get here before I had to let go. Much obliged, brother."

"I understand. I wouldn't want to get my ankle injured again either. Let's go look at it."

They hurried over and examined the arrows. Noah offered his opinion, "Both perfect shots! Clean into both sides of the heart. We're good together. You want the skin again?"

"It might be fun to tan it." They buried the pig's innards. Eli tied the legs with the piggin strings he always had around his hat while Noah found a sturdy branch. Eli said, "We should have asked Roscoe to come."

They raised the pig to their shoulders. "You're right. I enjoy hunting with you, and I didn't think about it. We'll ask next time."

They returned to the wagons victorious. Eli slid the pig into the washtub Ann had emptied when she'd refilled the honey jugs. Roscoe had the fire going to cook cedar poultice for Rose's and Noah's injuries. "We can prepare a pit and cook the pig overnight."

Noah dragged the pig-filled tub close. "Wouldn't it be easier to remove the hair before we skin it?"

"I think so." Eli went to the wagon. "Roscoe, where's that giant cleaver of yours? I want to cut off this beautifully ugly, hairy, tusked head and keep it as a trophy. Then, I'll de-hair and tan the skin. Back in Pop's store, I read that pigskin is bumpy and thin but very tough. I hope the skin is as red as its hair."

*He'll find my money in there with the kitchen utensils.* "I'll get it." Roscoe still had the hundred dollars Eli had paid him to feed and house them while they'd hidden at Pine Bluff that winter. That money, along with the coins that had been in his sales box, and another hundred dollars he had received when he had sold Bacon's Trading Post, were all anybody knew about. He believed it would be safer if nobody knew he also had the seven thousand, seven hundred and fifty dollars that he'd saved during the twenty years he had run his store. Roscoe rummaged through his bag. He handed Eli the cleaver and then carefully closed the bag.

*Wham!* Eli decapitated the boar with one mighty chop. He set to skinning while Sally and Ann crushed dried jalapenos and prepared garlic cloves, onions, and the last of the mealy apples from the previous fall.

After Eli washed the body, Roscoe stuffed the vegetable mixture inside and rubbed the outside with spices. He put it back into the cleaned washtub with potatoes and honey.

Noah had started to dig the pit. With his injured body, he didn't get far before Ann took the shovel from him. Once the pit was deep enough, they pushed the fire into the hole and added the wood Noah and Sally had gathered. When the bonfire had burned to coals, the large rocks inside the pit were superheated. They placed the tub into the hole with the hot stones and coals, put another washtub upside down over it, laid a cloth over it all, and then covered everything with dirt.

Waiting commenced. Eli scraped the remaining bits of flesh from the pigskin, Roscoe tended to Rose, and Stephanie slept. Ann decided to read the letters that had been written to a person from their past, Hank Butterfield, the leader of the outlaw gang. With the letters given to Noah in Maumelle, Ann lay on the blanket beside Stephanie.

Noah climbed into the wagon. "Sally, come here." He opened the saddlebag full of the books he had acquired when he had gotten the letters. He extracted a small pouch. "Edwin sent something." Noah handed Sally the green velvet bag dispatched from the young stablehand who had taken them to their first stop in the Underground Railroad.

Sally opened the pouch and poured a ruby necklace into her hand. "It's beautiful. How did Edwin get this?"

"I hope this doesn't upset you. Just like Hank's letters, it was one of Roy Butterfield's belongings that Edwin claimed after Roy was killed. There isn't any way to return it to its rightful owner, or even know who that would be, so he wanted you to have it."

"Do you think these are real?"

"I do, and I want to tell you what Edwin said."

70

"I'm listening."

Noah pointed to the large, heart-shaped, ruby pendant. "Edwin said, 'This stone reminds me of your sister's lips. I never got to kiss them.' Edwin kissed the stone and said, 'If she ever needs a kiss, there's one right here for her.' Then he put the necklace into the bag and handed it to me. I told him I would give it to you and tell you what he said."

"Things don't work out for me when it comes to love. I guess it doesn't help that he never even knew my real name. Edwin is such a sweet boy, but I don't love him. Still, it's nice to know that he's out there loving me and that I have a kiss if I ever need it."

"Want me to help you put it on?"

"No. I'll put it where it's safe. I appreciate you bringing it to me." Sally slid the bag with the ruby necklace into the medicine bag she had made when they had been hiding at Pine Bluff. She put her medicine bag back into its place in the wagon.

Noah moseyed to Rose. "How is she, Roscoe?"

Roscoe finished wrapping the leg that had been captured by the root. "I think she'll be fine. If she wasn't going to make it, she probably would've already died. If she's not lame, she should be able to walk tomorrow." Roscoe passed the kids to Noah and Sally, who carried them to Fancy and Bella. The mother goats nudged and tried to wake the kids to nurse.

Sally walked over. "I think the mamas are upset. We should hide the babies until they're awake."

They didn't want to put the kids back into the wagon in case Rose woke up, so they put them where the mothers couldn't see them, but Roscoe could keep an eye on them.

Noah looked at Ann's slender, shapely body on the blanket. He lay beside her and kissed her closed eyelids. Ann opened them and looked into the blue eyes of her husband. Softly, he said, "Oh! Might I kiss those eyes of fire, million scarce would quench desire; Still would I steep my lips in bliss, and dwell an age on every kiss; nor then my soul should sated be, still would I kiss and cling to thee: nought should my kiss

72

from thine dissever, still would we kiss, and kiss forever; E'en though the number did exceed the yellow harvest's countless seed; to part would be a vain endeavor: Could I desist? Ah! Never. Never."

"And I could forever dwell in the passion of your kiss." Ann pulled his head to hers to accept and give a blissful kiss.

Though Noah felt the words expressed the feelings of his heart, he had memorized and quoted a poem of Lord Bryon. He thought about letting Ann believe that he had said those words from his own mind, but he confessed, "I practiced until I could say those words, but I could never express the emotion until I was saying them to you. They came out of a book of poetry I got for you."

"Noah, my husband, I know that you meant every word, and I love you for saying them to me."

"I want you to know that I feel exactly that way about you." They lay in each other's arms on the blanket in the field with Stephanie beside them.

Sally saw one of Bella's babies get to its feet. "Everybody, one of the kids is awake." Because Ann had pushed them away from their mothers that morning and had taken most of the milk, the kids were not as sedated as Stephanie. They regained consciousness and called for their mothers, who replied to their hungry kids to come and nurse.

Twenty minutes after the kids had eaten, Roscoe commented, "I guess the milk is all right now."

Ann replied, "I still think we shouldn't drink any yet." She and Noah left Stephanie on the blanket and joined the three beside the fire.

They weren't accustomed to so much spare time. Noah decided to see if he could knap the stones he had gathered. "Eli, I'm going to try to make a knife blade from this novaculite. Last winter, you chipped that chert into a nice blade. Do you want to try making arrowheads?" Noah wanted to include their friend. "You want to try, Roscoe?"

"That sounds like work. I'll check our mules."

74

Sally went with Ann to watch Noah and Eli. She asked her sister, "Have you given a name to the mare Noah earned in Maumelle?"

"Our mules, Honor and Justice, are a pair. I want to make the mare a pair with Eyanosa, but I don't know how to speak Noah's Indian language. I don't know what would be right."

Sally wanted Ann to clarify. "Since Eyanosa means 'big both ways' are you going to name your mare 'narrow both ways?'"

"Not that! Just something that would go with it."

Roscoe retrieved the animals that had strayed too far before he went to check on Rose again. He found her sitting up. "Rose is up. Help me remove the cover and the side boards. We need to get her out."

In a minute, the way out was open. Rose stood in the wagon on steady legs. Her eyes looked clear and calm. Roscoe led her forward and down the planks at the side. As soon as she was on the ground, Roscoe let her go. She nuzzled all the people around her then trotted to her herd and chomped on the grass.

As they prepared the evening meal, Ann spoke of the man who had attacked Noah and the other Butterfield brother who had set her crops, house, and barn on fire the previous spring. "I want to read one of these letters Noah got after that woman killed Roy. It's only four years old, but it's almost worn away. Hank must have read it many times. Roy had the letters. He probably read it too."

Sally replied, "All right. Go on and read one."

"April 18, 1836

Dearest Son,

Your father and I miss you and hope you're doing well in Dover. I hope you're finding what you're looking for and are happy. Your father's been working hard plowing without you. He's getting it done with the help of Roy. Roy's getting so big and doing a good job helping. I've had so much to do with your sister. As usual, she's always fussing about how she looks but we're working hard weaving and baking a lot of bread. Every time I smell the bread cooking I think about how you'd come running into the house from the field. You'd slam open the door and say give me a big piece of that bread. It smells so good. I'd give you some with jam. You always gave me a big hug and said much obliged Ma. I sure miss you son. Your father is as strong and healthy as ever. He misses you too, but he would never say it. I know he loves you even though he never told you and I think he's proud of you too. I've always known how smart you are. I'm sure you'll become a great man and change the world for the better. I'm sending this letter with your brother. Give him a good meal and plenty of food to get back home. Come visit us soon.

Love Ma"

"I'm thirsty," Stephanie informed them.

"You're awake!" Eli jumped up.

"What happened? I feel like I've slept a year."

Eli handed her a tin cup of spring water.

"The sedative got in the goat's milk. Sally said she saw you drink a lot. The kids got knocked out too."

"I didn't want to waste any. More water, please." Stephanie held out her cup.

Eli took it. "Are you hungry?"

"Yes."

Ann went to prepare a plate of food.

Stephanie asked, "What did I miss today?"

Sally spoke one concise but confusing statement. "Rose and Noah almost drowned, then Noah and Eli killed a pig, and we're cooking it in the ground, and Rose is in the field, and you can see that Noah's right there." She added, "Oh, and I own a ruby necklace."

"What?"

"I guess we'd better elaborate," Noah replied. They told Stephanie everything that had happened in more detail. Noah explained why none of the others had known about the necklace until Sally had announced it to Stephanie. "I didn't tell anybody because it was a private gift and message from Edwin to Sally. If she wants to share, that's up to her."

"There isn't anything to tell. Edwin likes me and gave me a necklace from Roy's box of probably-stolen items."

"Can we see it?" Ann asked.

Sally slowly drew the sparkling red jewelry from the velvet bag. Stephanie examined the stones. "It's beautiful. Put it on."

"Help me," Sally requested.

Stephanie walked behind Sally, placed it around her neck, and closed the clasp. Sally's cheeks were as rosy as usual, as well as her lips that matched the color and shape of the pendant. The red hues harmonized with her short chestnut-colored hair curled around her face.

"Sally, you're so lovely!" Ann exclaimed.

Eli whispered to Stephanie, "Nobody is more beautiful than you." However, they could all see that Sally was going to attract the men.

Sally wore the necklace as she read 1 John 1:1-2:2, the evening's Bible verses. "That which was from the beginning, which we have heard, which we have seen with our eyes, which we have looked at and our hands have touched –

this we proclaim concerning the Word of life. The life appeared; we have seen it and testify to it, and we proclaim to you the eternal life, which was with the Father and has appeared to us. We proclaim to you what we have seen and heard, so that you also may have fellowship with us. And our fellowship is with the Father and his Son, Jesus Christ. We write this to make our joy complete.

"This is the message we have heard from Him and declare to you: God is light; in Him there is no darkness at all. If we claim to have fellowship with Him and yet walk in the darkness, we lie and do not live out the truth. But if we walk in the light, as He is in the light, we have fellowship with one another, and the blood of Jesus, his Son, purifies us from all sin.

"If we claim to be without sin, we deceive ourselves and the truth is not in us. If we confess our sins, He is faithful and just and will forgive us our sins and purify us from all unrighteousness. If we claim we have not sinned, we make Him out to be a liar and His Word is not in us.

"My dear children, I wrote this to you, so that you will not sin. But if anybody does sin, we have an advocate with the Father – Jesus Christ, the Righteous One. He is the atoning sacrifice for our sins, and not only for ours, but also for the sins of the whole world."

Roscoe stopped her. "People actually saw, heard, and touched Jesus? And what you read is what they heard Him say?"

"Yes," Sally replied.

"And Jesus said we're deceiving ourselves if we say we haven't sinned, but He says He'll clean us up?"

"Yes."

"I need cleaning up, but I don't think it's up to somebody else to do it. I made my own messes. It would only mean something if I clean myself up." Roscoe got up and walked to his bedroll.

Sally closed the Bible so as not to distract Roscoe from what God had him thinking about.

In the morning, they dug up the most melt-in-your-mouth meal they had ever eaten. The pig was young enough that it was tender but old enough that it dripped grease and juices that had cooked into the vegetables. They stuffed themselves and still had plenty left in the washtub, which they covered and loaded into the wagon. Even though they sealed it well, the mouth-watering aroma floated in the air. As they prepared to get on their way, Ann read the next letter to Hank Butterfield.

"December 15, 1837

Dear Son,

Please come home right away. It may be the last chance you'll have to see your father. He was chopping wood when the axe slipped and hit his leg. It was a nasty injury and now it's as red as a beet. Doc says its gangrene and he needs to cut off his leg. Your father says he can't be a man with only one leg and won't let him do it. He says he'll get better if we just let his leg heal. I told him he'd be a man no matter if he has two legs, one leg, or no legs. Roy is trying to do all the work, but he's just a boy. He and Edith are so worried about your father. If you come here, it would mean so much to us and I'm sure your Pa will tell you how proud he is of you and that he loves you. He's been thinking about dying and talking about how you always helped him so well. Come home. We need you.

Love Ma"

As they left, Stephanie said, "He was worse than I thought. He wouldn't even go see his dying father."

They followed the stream that had cut the gap, listened to the warblers in the sycamore trees, and enjoyed the pleasant spring air. Noah asked, "When we get to Perryville, should we go straight through?"

Eli answered, "First, we need to get there. Even taking the time to keep a constant lookout, it'd be much easier and faster on the road. If we hurry home, and Pop will come with us, we can go west this year. Isn't that what you want, Noah?"

# EIGHT

While Noah and the Williams sisters looked up at the Maumelle Mountains looming before them, Captain Cornish jetted up from his comfortable chair in Little Rock. *I'm tired of a civilian telling me what to do with my soldiers. I've wasted too much of my time and that of my men.* He slammed his hands on the leather desktop. "Judge Hall, I have all the respect in the world for the law and its enforcement, but I will not send even one more soldier to look for Noah Swift Hawk and Ann Williams. I shouldn't have allowed my men to be drawn into this in the first place. I have a miserable young soldier

84

who no longer has the heart to fix an enjoyable meal because he met Sally Williams, and you've forced her to run away and hide with her family. If this is so important to you, YOU find them. I'm not doing it."

Daniel Hall stormed out of the room. He slammed the door. *I need somebody with a stronger incentive and the stomach to eliminate them.*

# NINE

Noah Swift Hawk and Ann Williams arrived at the edge of the dangerously-exposed road. As far as Ann could peer with her spyglass, the way looked clear. "Maybe nobody is looking for us anymore. It's been more than two months since we escaped Judge Hall."

Eli stated what he wanted to do. "It's been tough getting through the forest. Let's take the road. We can stop again before we reach the top and scout out the other side."

*Everybody's tired of the hard traveling. Taking the road would save time. Getting caught is only bad for Ann and me. If we get caught, I'll say I forced*

*Ann to go with me.* Noah agreed, "We should put the little animals in the wagon, in case we need to run."

Roscoe contemplated the ridge that rose ahead of them. "That's a steep slope. We'll need to use the strongest animals."

Sally compressed her spyglass. ""Do you think my big, strong patchwork mules are healed enough?"

"No." Roscoe advised, "They've been healing well since you sewed them up, but this would be too hard on their fragile skin."

With a new set of animals, Ann and Sally kept the wagons at a steady pace. Eli and Stephanie rode ahead. Noah and Roscoe repeatedly hung back and then caught up. Just before the ridge, they all stopped.

Ann waved. "Noah, come here."

Noah rode to the parked wagon. "I'm here."

"Sit by me for a minute." Noah put a foot on the wagon floor, stepped into the wagon, and sat beside Ann. She wrapped her arms around him and laid her head on his shoulder. "Last time I was on this mountain, I was headed the other way looking for you. My heart felt as frozen as the deep snow. I was so afraid I wasn't going to find you. I felt completely miserable. Now, I'm here again, but we're together, and I'm ecstatically happy. I can't help thinking how different life would be if I hadn't found you, and how grateful I am that God has allowed us to be together. I love you, my husband."

"I love you too. You know I felt the same miserable way, and I'm as happy as you are that we're together. God has been good to us."

With a happy heart, Ann replied, "Yes, he has, my love. Now, find out if it's safe ahead."

"Take this while I'm gone." Noah handed Ann a Lefaucheux revolver. She strapped the gun belt around her waist. Noah went into the back. "Just in case," he put a box of rounds on the floorboard before he got back on Eyanosa. "Come with me, men."

The three women waited with the stopped wagons. Ann and Stephanie kept their spyglasses on the men. Sally watched their rear.

The men rode up the mountain, tied their

rides below the ridge and then crawled in the ash tree leaf litter on the southwestern slope. The earthy smell of moist dirt and leaves filled their nostrils. Roscoe's hand touched something. "A morel mushroom! They're so tasty." He glanced around. Scattered across the forest floor, the tops of others poked out from under the leaves. "I rarely find these. I want to get all of them." Moving up the hillside, they popped the mushrooms from the ground and tossed them into the sacks they always carried.

At the ridge, the men lay in a patch of tall, red cardinal flowers. As a young warrior-in-training, Noah had learned to be patient. Therefore, not moving or making a sound, they listened to rose-breasted grosbeaks singing in the distance. They lay so still that flashes of iridescent green zipped and dipped above them. Hummingbirds came to court, drink nectar, and eat the tiny bugs on the cardinal flowers. The men changed their focus back and forth. They surveyed the opposite side of the ridge and watched the small, red-throated birds attempt to entice the duller green females.

"Look there." Roscoe pointed at a glint of light. The hummingbirds whooshed away. The men focused on a spyglass pointed toward Perryville.

Eli moved his looking tube away from his eye. "We need to make covers for our spyglasses. The same thing could have given us away if that person down there wasn't looking toward Perryville."

Roscoe suggested immediate action. "One of us has to go back and get the wagons and animals off the road. It'll take some time to get here, but it's better to move to safety now."

Since he wanted to be sure Stephanie was safe, Eli slid backward. "I'll go." Slithering on his belly until he was well below the ridge, he made his way back to Ace.

Only Eli came back to the wagons. Stephanie asked, "Is somebody there looking for us?"

"Somebody's there, but probably not looking for us. To be on the safe side, we need to move the wagons and animals. I'll look for a place on this side. Ann, would you look on that side?"

Ann got off the wagon and jumped bareback

onto the donkey, Blanco. She rode into the forest. They didn't want to lose any of their animals or have their location given away by one of them being in the wrong place, so Stephanie and Sally tied all the rest of the animals onto four lines before attaching them to the backs of the wagons.

Roscoe and Noah continued to watch the watcher. He never looked toward the mountain. Roscoe remarked, "Clearly, he's thinking whoever he's looking for will be coming from Perryville."

Noah speculated, "He might be a bandit. I wouldn't want him to shoot somebody or rob them."

"He's too well-dressed to be a bandit. His hair is neat, and he looks clean. Besides, we don't know what's going on. Maybe we should let things happen as if we weren't even here."

"But we are, and God put us here for a reason."

As they reasoned through possibilities, two dots appeared far down the road. The person hiding from view came to attention. He studied the approaching people. When they were close enough for him to be sure, he picked up his rifle but continued to wait.

"He's gonna shoot them," Roscoe stated.

"It's best not to do anything. If we shoot him, we may be doing the wrong thing."

A swarthy-skinned man with a muscular physique approached with a woman whose well-formed body sat in good horse-riding posture, as if well accustomed to the saddle.

The people riding were almost to the man behind the trees. As Roscoe said, "I think he's letting them pass," they saw the rifle flash. The man's body jerked backward off his horse. His companion jumped off her horse and threw herself over his body before Noah and Roscoe heard the shot. Her back heaved with her sobs over the dead man.

Noah and Roscoe expected to see the murderer rob the couple. Their assailant stepped into view. The woman rose to her feet and screamed at the man. When the man was in range, she slapped him across the cheek, beat on his chest, and then slapped him again. He tried to stop the attack while the woman clawed, kicked, hit, and inflicted pain every way she could.

"I don't think he's going to hurt her."

"Me neither. They know each other." Roscoe continued to watch. The man got away from the woman, yelled back, and pointed to the horse. He tried to pull her to it. She fought him every step. After several minutes of fighting, the man walked to his hat, which she had knocked to the ground, and removed the piggin string. He grabbed the woman and forced her to the ground, tied her hands and feet, and then threw her over her horse. She rolled herself off. He screamed a few choice words and then left her on the ground while he went into the woods.

The woman rolled to the body in the road and lay beside it. In a minute, her attacker came back with his horse and a rope. He picked up the woman again, flung her over her horse, tied her on, and then started back toward Perryville. He led the horse with the thrashing woman secured in place, along with the man's horse. He left the body in the road.

"Maybe he's alive. I'm going down. I'll help him if I can. Bring the wagons." Noah dashed down the slope. *If he's alive, he needs help fast.* Noah jumped on his horse. Eyanosa realized the command was to go as fast as he could, and he obliged. Since they had the advantage of going downhill, they covered a lot of ground in a short time.

Roscoe arrived at the wagons just as Ann and Eli returned. Ann filled with fear. "Where's Noah?"

"He's fine. We don't need to hide. We need to move on quickly, though. I'll explain as we go."

Roscoe related what they had seen. "He's probably already dead, but Noah went to see if he could help."

Irritation rolled through Stephanie's mind. *He still thinks he's a doctor.* Her thoughts shifted. *In a second, we'll be going downhill. This is how Eli was almost killed.* Stephanie hadn't forgotten the past accident, and she didn't forget to ask for the most powerful help possible. "God, please let the brake work."

Even though they had many mules tied to the back, they still feared they would lose control of the wagon just as they had when they had escaped from Little Rock.

Eli applied the brake. With relief that all was well, he let off the pressure. They had the medical supplies they needed to get to the injured man. Eli allowed the wagon to roll with the mules at full gallop.

As his family came down the mountain, Noah knelt beside the man and felt for a pulse. *Weak but present.* Noah examined the bullet wound. *Looks like it went between his heart and lung.* "Thank You, God." He rolled the man over. *It's still inside. I should drag him off the road. The shooter might think wild animals dragged him away. Hopefully, he'll forget about him.* He pulled the body into the woods.

*I have to bring up the blood volume.* Noah put his canteen to the man's lips and poured. The man swallowed. He continued to pour water into the man until the flask was empty. He opened his medicine bag and removed the long awl he had made from the antler of the elk he and Ann had killed at Pine Bluff. He slid it into the hole. The awl clicked against the bullet. Noah pulled it out to see how deep the ball had traveled. *I can get it.*

Noah made an incision at the wound then used the awl to guide him through the cut. He found the bullet wrapped in a piece of the man's shirt and vest, put the tip of his knife under the metal ball, and then slid it up the awl and out. Then, with the knife and awl, he made pincers. He pulled out the cloth and leather. The man's intact heart moved what little blood he had to his lungs. As the injured man breathed, a nick that hadn't been visible bubbled air and blood into a foam.

Noah probed until he found the small vein that the bullet had severed then pinched it shut. The bubbling stopped. *I need to cauterize this.* Once he had found the bottle of matches in his saddlebag, he returned to his patient, lit a match, put it out, and then tapped the vein.

*Sizzle.*

Blood still oozed. Noah lit another match. He let it burn longer and then held it against the vein.

*Sizzzzzzzzzzle.*

Noah examined the wound. The stench of cooked human flesh rose into his nostrils. *The vessel sealed.* He covered the hole. As the sun went down, Noah waited for his family to come down the mountain. He looked through his spyglass. *There they are.* He stepped onto the road when the lead wagon got closer.

Stephanie jumped off the wagon. "You aren't a doctor, Noah! You could have killed him!"

Noah didn't understand what was going on in Stephanie's mind, but he knew her reasoning was wrong. "He'd surely be dead if I had done nothing. At least by trying to save him, I gave him a chance. I don't know why you keep saying I shouldn't help people."

"You haven't gone to medical school," she informed him.

"So, I'm only qualified if I went through the white man's training, but not if I went through the Indian man's medical training?"

"Well, I didn't mean that."

"What did you mean, Stephanie?" Ann snapped. She wanted to be on good terms with her sister, but she could tolerate no more of Stephanie acting like Noah wasn't good enough. She and Noah had gotten too much of that already.

"I don't know what Noah knows."

Roscoe wondered, *how will God handle Stephanie's continual concern over Noah's qualifications? That is, if God cares. He probably won't even fix the problem. When I was fifteen, I begged Him to send Margaret back to me, but He didn't care one iota about my broken heart.*

Eli stepped into the conversation, "Honey, please talk with me." He led her away from the others. "Do you want to destroy this family? Remember, on my birthday; you said that it was all of us together, no matter what?"

"But he keeps acting like a doctor."

"Please, trust Noah. He knows what he's able to do. Why don't you believe that he's able to give medical treatment?"

"I don't know about Indian medicine or even what training he got as an Indian."

"But he knows. What do you think he's trying to do? Do you think he has any objective other than helping?"

"I believe he wants to help and thinks he can."

"Then stop telling him his ways are wrong or inferior and let him help."

"I'm not telling him he's inferior."

"Yes, you are. Every time Noah's given medical care, has it been the right thing or not?"

"It's been the right thing. I know he wants to make things better. I don't know what I'm thinking." They walked back to the others. "I'm sorry, Noah. I don't think the ways or knowledge of Indians is inferior. I'll trust that you know what you're doing."

Changing the subject, Eli told them, "We should move on, in case the shooter comes back." He helped Noah get the injured man into the wagon. Noah climbed in to continue to provide care. Now that he had the medical supplies, he stitched up the hole created by the bullet and his incision.

Long before the sun would be up the next day, they crossed the Fourche La Fave River on the public bridge. In Perryville, they went to Adeline's Inn. Roscoe told the others, "I'll go back to being 'Theo' and rent us five rooms."

Noah looked out the cover. "Perfect. We'll get the wagons into the barn and take care of the animals."

Roscoe entered the inn and read the conspicuous sign. **Knock on the door under the stairs.** He went over and knocked.

"Just a minute," Adeline opened the door hatch she kept barred on her side.

"We need five rooms and shelter for thirty-eight animals and two wagons."

"One dollar and eighty-five cents for the rooms. Put your animals in the corral. Give them feed if they need it. Pull the wagons into the barn. That'll be five more dollars."

Roscoe handed the woman nine dollars. "Put the rest toward baths and food in the morning."

Through the door hatch, Adeline handed out five keys attached to wooden fobs with numbers carved into them. She gave Roscoe a sixth key. "This is the key to the barn."

"Much obliged." Roscoe went to the barn. "Put the animals in the corral. We can lock the wagons in the barn." He gave Ann, Sally, and Stephanie a room key, kept one in his pocket, and handed the last one to Noah. "I'll help you get him into a room."

They drove the wagons into the barn and put the goats in a stall. All the mules, donkeys, and horses went to the corral. Ann filled the water trough for the goats and gave them hay while Sally, Stephanie, and Eli took feed to the corral. Water was already there, so they locked the barn and found their rooms.

Ann put her bag and Noah's bag in their room and then looked for Noah. Down the hall, a door stood open. She peeked in. Noah washed blood from the man but waved her over. "I should stay here tonight to keep a watch on him."

"I agree. I hope he'll be all right."

"I think he'll recover. Which room is ours? I'll go there in the morning."

"Room 4. I love you."

"Love you too." Noah closed the door.

## TEN

Quite a bit of liquid unavoidably spilled before Noah had gotten most of two canteens of water into the man with a hole in his chest. The unconscious man moaned as Noah removed the damp clothes. After Noah verified that only a clear fluid had seeped into the bandage, he put his ear to the man's chest. The man's heartbeat was strong. He didn't seem to be struggling for air, but his lungs sounded raspy.

*I'll keep watch over him.* Noah drew the sheet over the injury and then pulled the overstuffed chair to the bed. In the soft chair, he fell asleep.

Late morning found all of them asleep. The

man with a hole in his chest woke. *Pain.* He moved his hand to his heart. *A bandage? What happened? I was riding with Lola. Now, I have pain in my chest.* He opened his eyes and looked around. *I'm in a bedroom. Who is that?* He feared. *If I've been shot, maybe Lola was too. What if I've gotten her killed?*

He didn't know where he was or what was happening. "Mister, wake up." He spoke loud enough to wake the man, but not too loudly. The man in the chair became alert. The injured man asked, "What happened? Is Lola all right?'

"I think so. She was fine when the man who shot you tied her onto a horse and rode away."

"It must have been Raymond. He claims that he loves her. If he didn't kill her right then, I don't think he will."

"He ought to know shooting you isn't going to get her to love him."

"She doesn't love him. Lola chose me. She told Raymond she was leaving. He told her she would love him if she'd just get to know him. Lola let him know that she didn't want to and wasn't going to marry him." The injured man tried to sit up. "I have to help her."

"You almost died, and you've lost a lot of blood. You need to rest and recover. If what you say is true, she'll be safe while you heal."

"He might take her away. I won't be able to find her."

"He thinks you're dead. He has no reason to leave. If you kill yourself, you'll never be able to help her."

"Will you get her?"

Noah thought about Ann. *If Raymond kills me, what would be Ann's consequences? That man already shot somebody he knew. He wouldn't hesitate to shoot somebody he doesn't know.* "No. I have a family."

"Then I'm going." The man sat up. "Where are my clothes?"

"I guess you have the right to get yourself killed," Noah tossed the man's clothes onto the bed, "but do you have the right to get Lola killed by trying to save her when you aren't strong enough to be successful?"

That stopped him. His first thought had been the fear that he had gotten Lola killed. "Is life as a captive better for her?" He lay back and turned his face away.

104

"I'll get you something to eat." Noah left the man to his thoughts and sorrow. He walked down the stairs to the main hall where Adeline served dinner.

Noah requested, "Give me a plate of food, eating utensils, and a pitcher of water I can take to my room."

"Of course," Adeline went off and fixed the tray.

Noah expected to find the man dressed and on his way out. He still lay in the bed. "Sit up, and try to eat."

The man drew himself up. "I'm Sebastian."

Since Noah's skin was still somewhat dark, he decided to use the name he had used when he had pretended to be a slave. "I'm Abraham." Noah put the pillow behind Sebastian's back then handed him the tray. "You've lost a lot of blood. You need to drink as much water as you can." Noah poured a glass of water and then handed it to Sebastian, who drank the water straight down before passing it back. Noah filled it again. He knew the man felt miserable, was in pain, and worried about Lola. He let Sebastian eat without talking.

They heard a knock on the door. Noah was afraid the person outside would call out his name. He quickly opened the door. "Sebastian, this is my wife, Lily." Ann knew that Noah, therefore, would be Abraham.

"Hello. I'm glad to see you're alive and eating."

"Pleased to meet you, Lily," Sebastian turned to Noah. "You have a beautiful wife, and I won't."

Ann looked at Noah. She knew the man who'd shot Sebastian had taken a woman. She assumed the man meant that he was either married to or had wanted to marry the woman who had been kidnapped. Ann wondered if Noah was going to try to rescue her.

Noah told her the answer before she asked the question. "I told him that I can't help him."

Ann knew how it felt to be kept from the person she loved. "Does she love you?"

"She told me she does," Sebastian replied.

"She does. I saw how she acted when Sebastian was shot."

"Wait until you heal, and then get her. Next

time, be careful. Don't ride in plain view." Ann heard another knock on the door.

Noah again opened the door. "It's Nancy." He thereby notified Sally to resume her alias as Nancy Bacon, Roscoe's niece.

From the hall, Sally asked, "How is he?"

Ann spoke to her sister from inside the room, "He's alive and awake."

Sebastian pleaded with the woman he couldn't see, "Nancy, help me rescue my woman. She's being held captive." He planned to find a way to save Lola, whether or not the people in the room wanted to help or liked him asking the woman in the hall for help.

Sally assumed Noah was already making plans. "When are we getting her?"

"It would be very dangerous. I'm thinking about the consequences to the person who matters the most in my world." Noah took Ann's hand in his.

"I appreciate that you thought about what's best for me. I love you, Abraham." Ann laid her head against Noah's shoulder, thereby, informing her sister which names they were using.

Sally stepped into the room and shut the door behind her. She looked at her sister. "You're willing to leave a woman as a captive of a murderer?"

"Attempted murderer but that makes no difference. The intent was there," Ann replied.

"And kidnapper," Sebastian added.

"He's dangerous, and I don't want the people I love to be hurt," Ann explained.

Sally argued, "I wouldn't be able to live with myself, knowing I'd left a person to a horrible fate when I could have helped."

Ann defended her point-of-view, "I don't want to either, but we don't know what's going on or what we'd be getting into."

Noah offered a compromise. "Let me go and find out what's happening. I won't do anything. I'll just come back. Then, we can decide what we should do."

"Perfect! We'll plan well and execute perfectly," Sally replied.

"Promise you won't do anything," Ann demanded.

"I promise. I'll only get information."

"I like you, Nancy." Sebastian then explained where he thought Lola was confined.

Noah took both women out of the room when he left. "Don't go back into the room with Sebastian until I'm back."

"We won't. I'm glad you'll at least find out what's happening." Sally hugged her brother-in-law.

Noah headed to the farm. The two women went to tell the rest of the family what they were planning. Adeline didn't know Roscoe. Therefore, as Theo, he went to the dining room to get six helpings of whatever she was serving.

## ELEVEN

Noah observed the farm through the spyglass. Raymond left the house, went into the barn, and then returned to the house. He came out again, went to the woodpile, and split logs before returning to the house. Noah saw goats, a cow, and three horses in a corral. In the yard, chickens pecked in the dirt. Every time Raymond went into the house, he moved toward the right. Noah relocated and looked into the house again.

A woman stood inside the room. Noah sneaked closer and timed the trips. The man was never more than thirty minutes outside.

Raymond again left the house, so Noah sneaked close and heard the sound of dragging. He assumed the woman was chained and pacing. The man came back into the room. "Let me go, Raymond. You can't make me love you."

"I told you to stop saying that."

"How could I love a murderer and kidnapper?"

"I'm not a murderer."

"What do you call it when you shoot a man in cold blood?"

A door slammed. Footsteps stomped across the porch. While wood was walloped at the far side of the house, Noah took the opportunity to look into the front room. A glass of milk sat on a table. *I wonder if that's goat's or cow's milk.* Noah had an idea and left.

"Stephanie, when you drank the goat's milk, did it taste different?"

"I drank it fast, but I didn't notice anything."

Noah explained his plan, "We need to travel on. Everybody goes tonight. When the man looks for who stole Lola, our family won't be suspected because we would have been gone before she disappeared. So nobody knows that he's alive, Sebastian will need to be sneaked to the wagons. After we're gone, I'll circle back. I'll give the goats and the cow just enough sedative to sedate them overnight. The sedative will be in the milk when they drink it the next morning. It'll put them to sleep. I'll get the key, unlock Lola, and take her away. We'll catch up with you."

None of them wanted to desert the woman, and they thought Noah's plan would work. "You'll need to get away fast," Roscoe told him, "Use their horses."

"You make some sedative. I'll ask Sebastian about the horses."

Sally and Roscoe went to the wagon, got ingredients, and rode out of town. Ann arrived at the room after Noah had asked about using the horses.

"They're mine and Lola's, but I don't have a bill of sale. Leave them if you think that's better."

"Are either of them able to pull a wagon?"

"Both of them are. They're farm horses."

112

Ann added her addition to the plan, "I need to go with you. Lola may be afraid if she wakes up with a man she doesn't know, but she may not be scared of a man and woman together."

Sebastian picked up a scarf from the pile of clothes that Noah had thrown on the bed. "Take this scarf. Lily, you wear it. Lola will recognize it. Draw her attention to it, so she knows it's a signal."

Noah wasn't letting Ann within bullet range. "You can come, Lily, but only if you stay far away from the house. We'll meet after I get her." Noah and Ann left to wait in their room until the others returned from their assigned tasks.

As he had in Little Rock, Eli resumed his alias as James Bacon, Roscoe's nephew. Even so, he stayed outside the store. He didn't want the shopkeeper to recognize him from his visit the previous fall.

As a woman named Marie, Stephanie went into the store to buy peppermint sticks and licorice —she told herself they were for indigestion— as well as flour, cornmeal, and beans. She noticed a medical kit with surgical tools, dental tools, first aid items, bottles of liquids and pills, small billows with a tube attached, and even bone cutting saws. There was also a trepanning set for drilling holes in a skull and a urological tools set. Stephanie placed her finger on a small booklet with the title *Treatise on the Diseases of the Chest and on Mediate Auscultation* by R. T. H Leannec, translated from French by John Forbes. "What's this about?"

The store owner picked up the walking cane beside the pamphlet. "It goes with this." She took the cane apart. "The man I got it from said the booklet explains how to use this to hear inside a person." She made a portion of the cane into a stethoscope. "Inside the rest of this cane are," she placed fourteen small bottles on the counter as she named them, "quinine, digitalis, blue mass, laudanum..."

"How much? How did you get them? Are they defective or anything?" Stephanie asked.

"I traded them with a man who was down on his luck and his supplies. The cane is ten dollars. It comes with the pamphlet. The surgical set is thirty-five, the urological and trepanning set are twenty dollars apiece."

Stephanie didn't have much money, but she wanted to let her sister and brother-in-law know that she had thought about them the previous night and was going to stand behind them. "I want to buy the cane." The woman packaged the food and the cane. Stephanie paid and then left.

Outside, she loaded everything into the cart she had built under Eli's supervision while at Fletcher Creek. As they walked back to Adeline's Inn, Stephanie showed Eli the cane and told him about the other medical kits. "It's too much of a coincidence that all this medical equipment is here. When I saw it, I knew God had put it here for Noah, and He's telling me to believe in Noah."

"It's wonderful that you want to give this to Noah. You should tell him about the rest."

At Adeline's, Stephanie went to Ann's room and knocked on the door. "Just a minute," Noah slipped on his pants and shirt then stepped out of the room. Stephanie stood at the door, leaning on a cane. "Is everything all right? What happened?" he asked.

"I'm fine. This is a gift for you."

"Much obliged, but I'm not ready for a cane yet."

"I think you are. May I come into your room and show you?"

Noah cracked the door. "Marie wants to come in."

"Give me a second." Ann slid on her dress. "Come in."

Stephanie and Noah stepped into the room. "I want you both to know that I've thought about what Noah said. I believe in you, Noah. I got this for you today." She took the cane apart, placed all the little bottles on the dresser top, and then put together the hearing device. "It's called a stethoscope." Stephanie handed Noah the copy of *A Treatise on the Diseases of the Chest and on Mediate Auscultation*. "That means using a tool to help you hear inside a person. This booklet tells you how to use it." Stephanie demonstrated the same way she had been

116

shown. "Listen to my heart, Noah." She put one end to her chest and the other end of the tube to his ear.

"Oh, my! I can hear very well!"

"Did you hear my heart say that I love you, and I'm sorry?" Stephanie asked.

"I think I did." Noah opened his arms. If Stephanie wanted to let him hug her, she could step over. She did.

Ann stood beside them and put her arms around her husband and sister. "This is a very thoughtful gift. That you gave it means a lot to me too." After they held each other in a moment of forgiveness, Ann said, "Let me listen." She listened to Noah's heart then to Stephanie's heart. "This is wonderful!"

"They also have a surgical kit with dental tools, a urological kit, and even tools to drill holes in a person's head."

"How much are they?" Noah asked.

"Thirty-five for the big set of surgical instruments and twenty for each of the others."

Noah looked at Ann. "Should I go look?"

"Absolutely." Stephanie may have had doubts, but Ann believed in Noah completely.

Noah put on his boots.

"I'll go back with you," Stephanie told him.

*It would be good for them to go alone. Even after all the time we've been together, I don't think they've done much individual talking. Maybe part of the problem is that Stephanie doesn't know Noah well enough.* Ann encouraged the two to go on. "I'll stay here, in case the others get back first."

As they went out the door, Stephanie asked, "What medical training have you received?"

Noah peeked over the railing. All was clear. He started the story as they sneaked down the stairs. "Shortly after we're born, our parents take us to Grandfather. He throws the totems to discover our destiny and how to train us. There were two of us together. Two totems landed between us. The one for medicine was closest to me, and the one for warrior was closest to Nikiata. Many years later, Grandfather told me he saw the totems like this, but the mother of Nikiata had wailed and wailed, insisting that the totems were in the range of both of us and that the medicine totem was for her son."

Noah opened the inn door and carefully

looked outside. He waved Stephanie out onto River Road then resumed the tale, "Grandfather had agreed that both totems were close to both children. He trained Nikiata. Others trained me as a warrior, but Grandfather knew the truth, so he trained me secretly. He told me I could never be their Mystery Man. However, the Great Spirit had ordained it, so he followed his instructions. When he was training Nikiata, Grandfather would look for him. When he couldn't find him, he taught me directly. When he did teach Nikiata, I hid and listened. I think I learned more. I watched Nikiata. Many times, I saw him do things that showed a lack of understanding, but I also saw him shoot the eye out of a Flycatcher."

They paused at E Street. Noah asked, "Do you think it would be better to stay off the main road?" He looked up the street. "I think we should." He turned left onto E.

Stephanie followed. "Then it was better for you because you got to be trained as a medicine man and as a warrior. You're an excellent tracker and hunter."

119

E street ended. Noah stood behind a tree. "I'm glad it happened. I know more than I would have if it hadn't."

Stephanie stood behind Noah. "You know, I doubt anybody would even think twice about us if we just walked to the store. We probably look suspicious, slinking around like this. Was the medicine man your mother's father?"

"No. Medicine men, actually Mystery men, are called Grandfather, out of respect." Noah started up Magnolia Street.

Stephanie walked beside him. "Why did you leave your home?"

"I wasn't able to be whole. I couldn't watch Nikiata do stupid things, and another person in my village was very bothersome. I felt I had to get away."

They drew near the store. Stephanie slowed. "Who was bothersome?"

"Just a bully."

"I don't believe you were bullied." Stephanie stopped at the corner of D Street. "Somebody's coming up the road."

Noah pulled her behind a boxwood hedge

and put his finger over his lips. A young man went past carrying a pail of ale. Noah waited until he was out of view then followed D Street. "I wasn't, but she bullied everybody she could."

"A woman ran you away?"

"She wouldn't leave me alone."

"I guess she wanted to be your mate?"

"Yes, but I didn't love her. I don't like her at all. She wouldn't understand that I wasn't going to marry her. Like this man who took Lola. You can't force somebody to love you." They turned onto Pine Street.

Stephanie asked, "Was there any woman you loved?"

"I've never loved anybody but your sister."

At the corner of Pine and C Street, Noah looked into the store from the edge of the large picture window. "Eli and I just walked over here, and I went right in." Stephanie stepped around Noah and went into the store. She notified the shopkeeper, "I brought somebody to look at those other medical items."

Noah followed her in. He casually asked, "What can you tell me about these?"

"The man said they were the finest money could buy. I don't know about medicine, so I can't tell you more."

"Did he give you any books?"

"He had some, but I didn't take them."

"Do you have books of any kind?"

"Heavens, no! Who would buy a book?"

"I would. Without the books, the tools are less useful. Still, I could give you fifty for the lot."

*I doubt anybody else will want this. I've had it for months. Still, I'd like to make a little.* "Sixty dollars," she countered.

"If you also give me a box of rubber erasers and four bottles of lavender-scented water."

"Sold."

"Wrap the erasers and toilet water together, so I can carry them." Noah counted as he handed silver dollars to the shopkeeper.

The woman put the money in a bag, tucked it into her bosom, and then went to get the erasers and scented toilet water. *Strange combination of items.*

Noah toted the urological kit, the surgical

equipment, and the trepanning set. Stephanie carried the package of erasers and scented water in one hand and the set of dental tools in the other. She started back to the inn by the direct route, C Street. She resumed the conversation, "What is it about my sister that you love? When did you first love her?"

"I think I loved her when she walked into the room at Doctor Gridley's house, but I didn't realize it at the time. I knew that she was a woman who would try to save the life of a person she didn't know, would trek through the mud, and then sit in a pool of blood to do it. She got people, who barely knew her, to do what she wanted without using fear. She even came back to find out how the unknown person she had saved was faring. I also thought she was the most beautiful woman I had ever seen. The forest lives in her eyes.

"I knew something was there the night she poured tea for us in your sitting room in front of the fire. I watched her pour tea into Tom's cup. Something happened inside me. I knew beyond any doubt that I loved her the night the farm burned down. She cared first about everybody else, even if it meant her death. That's when I knew I wanted to keep her in my life."

Stephanie listened to what Noah thought made her sister loveable. She heard qualities of character. She thought about Noah not wanting to watch an incompetent person and not being able to do anything about it. He wanted to do what he had been trained to do but had not been allowed to do so. She hadn't been allowing it either. Stephanie realized she should let him. They turned right onto River Road. "May I see your plant drawings when we get back?"

"Of course, I would love to show them to you." When they got back, Sally and Roscoe had returned with the sedative. They were in the room with Ann and Eli. "May I show them to you later?" Noah asked.

"Yes." Stephanie put the rest of the items beside everything Noah had placed on the dresser. "I'm glad we got to talk." She hugged her brother-in-law.

Roscoe saw what Stephanie and Noah had

bought. He raised his eyebrows. "You bought all these medical tools together?"

Stephanie answered, "I saw all this at the store. I realized that God wants Noah to have these tools, and He wants me to get my attitude straightened out."

Roscoe found it impossible to believe. "God couldn't've put all this there for Noah. So many things had to have happened to get them there."

"It wouldn't have been any harder than gathering all those ravens and sending them to run the Butterfield Gang away from our house." Sally asked, "So, what's our next step, Noah?"

"Nobody was in the dining hall, but I don't know if we can get Sebastian out to the wagon unobserved." Noah knew the plan was to sneak him out.

"He's in the wagon," Sally informed them. They all looked at her. "Noah taught me how to be stealthy."

Since none of them had seen her get him there, Eli replied, "I can see that."

"We should settle up and leave," Ann stated.

Roscoe agreed, "We won't have to pay for another night. All the animals have rested. They've eaten their evening meal of hay and oats and had all the water they want. We've all eaten and rested, so let's pack up, pay the innkeeper, and head north."

Soon, they were all at the wagons without Adeline seeing any of them. Adeline hadn't seen Roscoe or Sally on any previous visit, so they went to the bar. Adeline recounted the tally, "Five rooms for one night, five baths, and fourteen meals. What you gave me last night, plus two dollars and twenty-nine cents."

Roscoe gave the woman the money.

Sally asked, "How much for a gallon of vodka?" Roscoe turned his head and stared at her.

"One dollar and eighty-five cents or six gallons of 100 proof bourbon whiskey for two dollars."

"I'll take the whiskey." Sally handed over two small gold coins. Adeline left.

Roscoe asked, "Why do you want alcohol?"

"I've been thinking about witch hazel. A

person soaks the twigs in alcohol to make it. Abraham said the parasite medicine he made at Fletcher Creek would've been better if he'd soaked the walnut husks in vodka, and other medications are made that way as well."

"I'm very glad to know that's why. I thought you'd taken up drinking." Roscoe took the corked keg Adeline brought from the cellar.

Eli and Noah had the wagons ready and all the animals tied on, except the goats. They didn't need prodding. They had learned to ride. Ann waited for Roscoe to load whatever he had on his shoulder. "Raymond may be as dangerous as the Butterfield Gang. We better pray for safety. God, if we need another flock of birds or something equally unlikely to protect us, have it ready. I know You've already got a plan in motion. Do whatever You have to do to keep Noah, the rest of us, and Lola safe. You know how worried I am. Help me be brave. I ask in the name of Jesus. Amen." Ann turned to her sisters, "Ride until you get to the place we stopped when we were going the other way."

Noah added, "We're taking Sebastian's and

Lola's horses. He shouldn't get any reward for attempting to kill a man or holding a woman hostage." He hugged Sally. "We love all of you."

Stephanie handed Noah the canteen of sedative. She wrapped her arms around him. "I love you too."

"I'm very happy about that." Noah took Ann's hand and headed toward Raymond's farm.

# TWELVE

At the edge of town, Noah told Ann, "I'll make sure nothing's changed at the farm."

"I want to come with you, just to see. Tomorrow, you can come back by yourself to get her."

"All right." Before he slipped away, Noah positioned Ann in the concealed viewing point he had used the previous day. He approached the animals slowly, so they didn't become agitated and alert Raymond.

Ann watched Raymond at the table while Lola washed dishes. Secured to the stove leg, Lola dragged the ankle chain and retrieved two empty milk glasses. She slipped a knife into her dress pocket. After all the dishes were clean and put away, Raymond checked them. "Where's the knife, Lola?"

"I washed them and put them in the box."

Raymond felt her pockets. He took the knife from her pocket and slapped her hard. "Don't do that again!"

"Hitting me isn't going to make me love you."

"You made me do it." Raymond unlocked the chain and jerked her to the bedroom. "The preacher's going to be here tomorrow to marry us. After we're married, I'm going to be in this bed with you."

"I'll kill myself first."

"I'm afraid not, Lola. You'll like it. You'll find out tomorrow."

Ann wanted to fire a bullet and save them from the trouble of secretly stealing Lola. When Noah got back, she told him what had happened. She asked, "May I shoot him?"

"We're not murderers. God has given us a lot of grace. Let's give grace too."

130

"I didn't mean it. If I had, he would already be dead. Did the animals drink the sedative?"

"Yes. I waited to be sure they were sedated because I didn't give them very much. I want them to be awake in the morning. Let's get some sleep."

Noah had already found a fallen tree, with a large branch lying flat against the ground. He put the tarp and blankets in the narrow space between them. Ann's back was safely against the tree trunk, and Noah could easily raise his head to look out. They snuggled together. Noah prayed, "God, please protect us and Lola tonight and also tomorrow when we rescue her. We pray that this is the right thing to do. If it's not, stop us without anybody being hurt. We love You, and we thank You that You are always with us. God, I thank You for bringing me to Harmony and for Roy attempting to bust my head open because it brought this wonderful woman into my life. She is such a blessing to me, and I love her so much. I can never thank You enough for giving her to me as my wife. I pray in the name of our Savior, Jesus."

"Amen. Noah, my husband, I love you too, very much." They held each other in the protection of the tree and slept.

The dawning of the next day awakened the people and the animals. Raymond milked the goat and the cow to get milk for Lola. Meanwhile, again chained to the stove, Lola cooked bacon and eggs. Raymond put the buckets of milk on the table and then set out dishes for the two of them. He filled two glasses with cow's milk then sat down. "Make cheese today."

"What if I don't?" Lola turned to the table with the pan of eggs.

Raymond saw the look in her blackened and swollen eyes. "Leave the pan over there. Come get the plates."

Noah remembered what Ann had said. *I guess Raymond found more reasons to punch Lola. I ought to shoot him for beating on a woman like that.*

Lola walked to the table with murder written in her expression. She grabbed the plates and filled them with eggs and bacon. She walked back to the table and slammed the plate down

132

in front of Raymond. Noah heard the sound of breaking china.

Raymond stood up, grabbed Lola by the throat, and punched her in the side of her head. Blood spattered the wall. He pulled back his fist and then buried it in her stomach. She doubled over in pain. Raymond picked up the other plate of food then pushed the broken dish across the table to Lola's place. It left a trail of grease and egg yolk. "Sit and eat. You need to be strong for our wedding night."

Noah silently commanded, *drink the milk.* Lola sat down and picked bacon from the broken china. Raymond ate every bite of food from the unbroken plate then got more from the stove. He hadn't touched the milk. Again, Noah thought, *drink the milk.*

Raymond sopped up the yolks. "Eat your eggs."

Lola tried to separate a bite of eggs from the dish. Both glasses of milk sat untouched.

Noah prayed, *God, cause them to drink the milk.*

"Then I'll have it." Raymond shoved bread

into the yolk-covered mess, crammed it into this mouth, and swallowed. It stuck in his throat.

"I hope you choke to death," Lola told him.

Raymond gulped milk to force down the food.

*Thank you, God! Now Lola.*

Lola's lack of cooperation and appreciation for him angered Raymond. He had built a house and barn for her. He had milked the cow to get her milk to drink, and she was going to drink it. He picked up the other glass of milk, pulled Lola's head back by her hair, and poured it into her mouth. She spit it into his face. He knocked her to the ground then sat on her stomach and pinched her nose shut. He poured milk from the bucket into her mouth. She coughed and choked until the bucket was empty. Most of the milk had spread across the floor when he got off her. "Clean up this mess before the preacher gets here." He slammed the door hard when he went out.

Noah heard Raymond splitting logs. He hated that Lola had been force-fed the milk, but thought, *I hope she swallowed enough.*

The sound of chopping slowed and then stopped. Raymond opened the door. "I'm tired. I'm going to-" He fell to the floor. Lola's jaw dropped open. She looked at him for a second then walked across the room and prodded him with her foot. He didn't respond. Immediately, she searched for the key to her chain. She got it out of his pocket and into the lock before her sedated body fell across Raymond.

Noah walked to the barn. He pumped water into the trough for the animals and filled his canteens. The horses to take, Honey Dew, Lola's tan-colored, medium-sized mare and Mateo, Sebastian's large, jet-black stallion stood in the paddock. He didn't know which saddles or bridles, so he took those that looked the best and put them on the corral fence. Next, Noah looked for the saddlebags that he had seen on the horses when Raymond had shot Sebastian. He found them empty. The woman's clothes and all other female items went into one bag. He had no idea which clothes were Sebastian's, so he put half the male clothing in the other sack.

Next, he looked for the shotgun he had seen on Sebastian's horse when he had been shot. He didn't find it in the house, so he went to the barn. He stood in the middle of the barn and asked of nobody, "Where would I put a shotgun?" After an extensive search that left him empty-handed, Noah led Mateo and Honey Dew to the house.

He wrapped the rest of the bread and bacon in a clean dishcloth and then rolled up the feather mattress, blankets, and pillows on Lola's bed. Outside, Noah hitched both saddlebags on Honey Dew and then laid the bedding over them.

It wasn't easy to get the unconscious woman onto the horse with one leg on each side, mainly because she was severely injured, and he didn't want to hurt her more. Hoping to make her more comfortable, Noah leaned Lola over the rolled-up bedding at the horse's rump. He told Lola, "I'm sorry to tie you up again."

He mounted Mateo and then saw the shotgun with a rifle. *Of all the stupid places, why put them out here where somebody can use them against you?* As he got them off the porch roof, Noah changed his mind. *Actually, since it's more likely that Lola would use them against him, maybe not.*

He went back into the house, slid the shotgun into its saddle holster, and got the shells. He slung the holster strap around Mateo's saddle horn and tied the ammo box beside the gun. *If I hide the rifle, that'll slow him down even more. He'll have to locate it before he can look for Lola. He'll find it eventually and not be defenseless.*

Even though Raymond deserved it, Noah didn't want to sentence the man to death by leaving him without a gun. Except for the bedding, and possibly some clothes, the man hadn't lost anything that had belonged to him. He also had his life. He didn't have the things he had no right to have taken.

# THIRTEEN

Noah rejoined his wife, "Success!"

"I can see that. Did you have any problem?"

"Other than keeping myself from shooting the man? No." Noah jumped down. He got out the bacon and bread, which they ate as they drank the water from Raymond's well. Since it was soft, Noah wanted to use their pack to further pad Lola. "Ann, my lovely wife, I want to put this under Lola. Help me."

Ann lifted Lola's body and saw her face. "I'm going back there to shoot him."

"That's what I meant about it being hard not to, and I had to watch some of it."

"Poor woman."

Noah positioned the soft pack where Lola's upper body would lay over it. Ann gently laid her forward. They retied the rope holding her. Ann moved Lola's hair out of her face. "We're going to take care of you. My husband, Dr. Luke Smith, is a very good doctor."

Dr. Luke Smith, the alias Noah had used in Little Rock, already sat on Mateo. "I'm glad you think so." He pulled Ann up behind him. "Are you all right riding back there?" he asked.

"I'm fine. I'll hold on tight."

"Perfect. I love your arms around me."

They rode north not on the road but close. Just before nightfall, they joined their family.

Noah lowered Ann to the ground. They stepped back into their alternate identities of Abraham and Lily. "Theo and James, help me get Lola into the wagon with Sebastian."

Eli started to untie the rope. He saw her face. "Raymond did this and thought she would love him when she got to know him?"

Sally went over and looked. "I'll make willow tea and cedar poultice."

Sebastian overheard Eli. "What's happened to her?" They carried her to the wagon. Roscoe climbed in and got the plants they needed before Noah and Eli passed Lola inside. Roscoe and Sebastian took Lola and laid her on the feather mattress. Stephanie handed Sebastian a bowl of warm water and a cloth. He lovingly wiped the blood from Lola's face. "I'm so sorry that I didn't protect you. Please, forgive me."

By the fire, Ann and Noah drank hot sassafras tea and ate morel mushrooms that Roscoe had sautéed with beef chunks.

Inside the dark wagon, the shadows of the flames flickered on the canvas. Lola woke. "I'm in Hell."

"No, my love," Sebastian softly replied.

"Sebastian, I didn't know there would be flames in Heaven."

"You're not in Heaven. You're alive. My friends rescued you."

"I'm alive? But you're dead."

"If Abraham hadn't saved me, I'd be gone."

"I must be alive. I hurt."

"Theo made something to help. I'll call him."

Lola requested, "Kiss me first." Sebastian's lips gently touched hers. She pulled her head away. "I'm sorry. I hurt too much."

Sebastian stroked Lola's hair. "It's all right."

"I wanted to be dead because I thought you were. I tried to make Raymond kill me."

"It looks like you came close to success. I could strangle him for doing this to you. I'm so sorry that I didn't protect you. Please forgive me."

"There's nothing to forgive. Raymond shot you out of the blue. How could you have prevented this?"

"I meant, I wish this hadn't happened to you. Let me ask Theo to get what he made for you."

"All right, I'm in a lot of pain."

Sebastian called out, "Theo, Lola's awake."

Roscoe walked to the wagon. "Hello, Lola. One of these women will put this poultice on you. Then we can give you a painkiller, but it won't take away all the pain. So if you want, we can put you to sleep again after you eat and drink plenty of water."

"First, I need to use the privy."

"I'll help you get out." Roscoe held out his hand.

Stephanie pointed. "Can you walk by yourself?"

"I think so." Lola hobbled away but soon returned.

"Where are you hurt?" Ann asked.

"Everywhere, I think. I want to talk with Sebastian. Give me the painkiller. I'll eat while we ride."

"We're staying here tonight," Noah informed her.

"We need to go. Raymond is insane. He'll shoot everybody."

"Like you, he's only just waking up, and we're hours ahead."

"Don't give him time to catch up." Lola begged, "Please."

Eli stated his point-of-view, "We shouldn't go into the swamp in the dark. If we hadn't seen that alligator, he would have eaten us."

"We have to go!" Lola cried out hysterically. "Sebastian, come here! I watched you die then barely survived Raymond's irrational and deadly temper! He'll find us! We can't take the chance! We have to leave! Right now!"

Ann offered a compromise, "We could at least cross the river."

"I guess we can do that," Noah agreed. "Let's get ready." Sebastian got up to help. Noah ordered him, "Stay in the wagon."

"Come on, Lola." Sally walked to the wagon with the medications. "Bring the food. You can eat while I take care of you."

Lola followed with mushrooms and beef, and a cup of sassafras tea. Sebastian took the food and then helped Lola climb in. "Abraham, I have to go out, so Nancy can help Lola."

With the antiseptic wash, Sally cleaned Lola's ankle that had no skin left due to the metal fetter. She wrapped it with the soothing and disinfecting cedar then did the same for Lola's stomach, arm, and ear. "I can wrap one around your eyes, or you can put it there when you're ready to sleep."

"I'll put it there later."

Sally called out from inside the wagon,

"We're ready," and then added, "Sebastian, you can come back."

He immediately complied. He wanted to be next to the woman who had miraculously been returned to him. As her family passed them in, Sally put their provisions into their designated places and then got out of the wagon. "Ready."

Roscoe commanded his long-haired donkey, "Shaggy, forward ho."

Lola felt much calmer when they arrived at the river and raised the flag up the pole to signal that somebody wanted a ride. Eli offered his knowledge from their previous journey when they had gone the other way, looking for Noah. "Theo, you negotiate. It'll take two trips. It should be around five dollars for each trip."

Noah watched through his spyglass. "I'll drive one wagon. Theo, you drive the other. The rest of you, stay in the wagons."

Eli, Stephanie, and Ann got into the wagon with the goats. Sally rejoined Lola and Sebastian.

When the ferryman arrived, Roscoe told him, "We need transportation across the river for eight people, two wagons, seven goats, sixteen mules, ten donkeys, and four horses."

After much haggling, since it was night and the ferryman would have to cross the river four times, Roscoe agreed to pay eleven dollars to get to the other side.

Raymond regained consciousness as they crossed. *Why am I on the floor?* He saw the empty ankle collar on the floor beside him. "Cursed woman!" He got up. Ammo lay scattered across the table. He looked at the stove. "And she took all the bread and bacon!"

He strode into the bedroom, where the empty dresser drawers and the bed devoid of the mattress, blankets, and pillow mocked him. He screamed profanities and flipped the bed against the wall. He dashed to the other room and rifled through the clothes left behind. He pulled out the drawer and smashed it on the ground. "She took all the good clothes! Sebastian must be alive and helping her! This time, I'm gonna make sure he's in the ground!"

He jerked open the door and reached above the porch roof. The weapons weren't there. He spat out more curses then noticed the corral. There stood his horse, his cow, and his goat. He walked over. *That's strange. They've been fed and watered. She didn't take everything or kill me either? She must love me, and now Sebastian has forced her to go with him. She must've hidden my rifle, so I can find it and save her!* Raymond went looking for his weapon.

Except for the two horses Noah had brought from Raymond's farm, their animals had rested the entire day. Therefore, once on the north side of the Arkansas River, they decided to keep moving. When they arrived at the old Cherokee boundary, Noah halted them. "We shouldn't go into the swamp until morning."

Sally brought up something to consider, "Although, nobody would believe we went in there in the dark."

"Do you think we'd be safe?" Ann asked.

Sebastian stated what he thought, "I've heard that people live in the swamp, and they'll eat you if they find you in there at night."

"Don't be silly, Sebastian. There aren't any cannibals in Arkansas," Lola refuted his belief.

"I'm just saying what I've heard," Sebastian told them, "and the air smells putrid."

Lola wasn't giving up. "Even if there were cannibals, with this much moonlight, we'd see them, and I don't care how bad the swamp smells."

"You'll get more or less used to the stink." Surprisingly, Stephanie added, "Not only do we have the power of God, but we have the power of the animals."

Ann looked at Noah. "Which is more dangerous: possible death tonight by who knows what in the swamp or possible death tomorrow morning by Raymond?"

Lola pleaded, "Raymond will kill us for sure. You can get us through the swamp."

"We are capable," Eli reminded them.

Noah capitulated, "If we use all the lanterns."

Even though Stephanie hadn't wholly accepted Noah's culture, she felt those ways would help them in the swamp. "Put on your medicine bags." She dug out her bone and eagle talon necklace.

While they got their medicine bags, Noah drew on his Mystery man training. "Let's put on the animal hides."

Sally looped her bag around her neck. "We'll either draw the animal spirits for protection or at least, scare everything away."

# FOURTEEN

The three sisters exchanged their dresses for cotton pants and shirts under buckskins, along with their leather gloves and hard boots. Ann felt hot. *It's better to have maximum protection.* Sally drew out the necklace she had made at Fletcher Creek. Ann saw it. "Nancy, I didn't know you finished your necklace."

Sally held up her creation. At the center was the shrew skull. On both sides were an eagle talon, coyote claw, alligator tooth, bear molar, and an elk molar. Each was separated by large bone beads with a longer hollow duck bone between them.

"Very nice." Noah tied it at the back of Sally's neck.

"Look at mine." Stephanie passed hers around. On both sides of a duck skull, she had a duck bone strung through its hollow center, and then an eagle talon, followed by an animal bone with a hole bored through one end and then hung perpendicular in the necklace, all separated by bone beads. From there, she had alternated between the perpendicular animal bones and the duck bones to the end. Like Sally's, it had enough string at the ends to tie it.

"Also very nice." Eli tied it around his wife's neck.

Like her sisters, Ann had strung animal parts. Two coyote claws curved toward each other around a large wooden bead with bone beads on either side then alternating coyote canine teeth, beads, and claws to the end.

Noah remembered Ann drenched in blood but victorious after their battle with the coyotes whose teeth and claws hung on the sinew string. "It's beautiful, just like you."

Sally requested help, "I can't get on my

coyote skin." Stephanie held the coyote skin to Sally's back. Ann tied a piece of rope around the hide and Sally's waist. Roscoe pulled the coyote head up. The ears rose up, and the nose jetted forward as if they were her own. Noah tied a soft buckskin strap over the coyote's head and under Sally's chin to hold it in place. Sally held out her arms while Roscoe and Eli tied its upper legs to her wrists at the paws. Roscoe, Ann, and Stephanie also dressed in coyote hides.

"Where did you buy all these skins?" Lola inquired.

Sally replied, "We didn't. We made them."

"We killed twelve coyotes in one fight," Stephanie informed Lola, "My husband killed two while he had broken ribs and a broken ankle. He was glorious!"

"The animals killed a few of them too," Roscoe boasted about his intelligent mules.

"All true." Noah thought about his wife wearing the skin, claws, and teeth of the coyote that had tried to rip out her throat. *The coyote is the trickster. He's cunning and stealthy, changeable just like Ann. She's mild, unaggressive, and loving, but she also has power. The coyote brought the original seeds of life. I hope one day Ann will bring forth a new life. Coyote is also the bringer of the ends of things and the beginnings of things. He's the maker of new directions. It's fitting. I hope we have Coyote power tonight.*

Noah put on the bear fur that fit him perfectly in symbolism. The bear represented courage, physical strength, and leadership. It also fit his physical body. When he had the bear head pulled over his own head, the bear's body ended at his bottom. He looked out from below the bear's lower jaw. They tied its front legs, so the clawed paws covered the backs of his hands. The hind feet lay on the tops of Noah's boots. The belly skin came all the way around his body. To hold the fur closed, he strapped on a two-pistol gun belt and his own belt, with a loaded twenty-round Lefaucheux revolver stuck behind it. Noah hung on a rifle and added his bow and quiver, all of which he wore on the outside of the bearskin.

Eli wore the skin of the alligator that had

tried to chase him down the previous fall when he had passed through the very swamp they were about to enter. He embodied the spirit of the alligator, which was emotional understanding, cleansing, and spiritual healing. Due to the limitations of what Eli had been able to do while recovering from broken ribs and a fractured ankle, he had worked on the alligator hide. He had enlarged the hole Stephanie had shot through the alligator's head. He could put his head through and let the alligator's head drape down his chest, or he could slide it back and place its skull on top of his head, with its long snout pointing forward.

Tonight, he had it on top of his head. He had already sewn a hood inside that covered the hole at the back of his neck, came up over his forehead, protected his skin from the animal's skull, and helped hold the massive snout in place. He had also sewn straps inside the alligator's legs that tied at his thighs and loops at the front legs that he could hold with his hand, slip over his wrist, or let go. The skin wrapped all the way around his body and tied inside with more straps.

With the head attached to the hood, the skin moved with him as if an alligator had stood up on its hind feet beside Stephanie. He dripped candle wax on the seat of the first wagon. In the wax, they stuck the human skull they had found in the upper springs of Fletcher Creek.

Noah handed Eli a pistol, one of the Lefaucheux revolvers, and a rifle. "James, after we get someplace safe, help me make this bear fur like your alligator."

"I'd be glad to."

As they got out the weapons, Sebastian saw something. "May I see your sword, James?" Eli handed it over for inspection. In the bright light of the full moon, Sebastian recognized the style and artisanship. "My Grandfather told me stories of the Spaniards who explored here in the 1500's. Their swords were excellent. Like this one, they had the mark of the dog. Where did you get this?"

Eli disclosed little about the location. "We found it in a pool on the mountains. That's his skull we stuck to the seat."

Sebastian told the others how he believed the

154

beautiful sword had gotten into the water, "One of those Spaniards must have fallen in and drowned."

Roscoe buckled on a set of guns. "Or he fell into the pool already dead."

Noah offered another alternative, "Or he was killed and then thrown into the pool to hide him."

"He's like the Indian in the cave. The past keeps its secrets. We'll never know." Eli held out his hand.

"Tonight, may I carry what you've brought from the past into the present?"

Eli kept his hand extended. "It's very important to me. I don't want it to get broken."

Roscoe jumped into the discussion, "You could have a sword fight with it, and it would destroy the other person's sword."

Sebastian explained, "I heard those stories because one of those men was my ancestor. I was told, 'One day, he disappeared.' Maybe this was him."

Eli lowered his hand. "You can carry it, but be careful. I don't want it damaged."

Sebastian strapped the sword around his waist. His family's past came home to him.

Roscoe instructed them, "Get the lanterns, fill them with bear oil, trim the wicks, and set them high. Even with a full moon, we should make the biggest, brightest field of light we can. We need to see anything that might attack and have time to take countermeasures."

They kept the goats in the wagon. They wrapped the other animals in the blankets they had made that spring to protect them during the blizzard. The new animals wore recently-made sets. They put the animals not pulling a wagon or carrying a rider between the wagons in three strings. Sally dug out the candlestick holders they had saved when their farm had burned down. Lola told her, "Those aren't going to help much."

Sally handed four candles and a bottle of matches to Lola. "Don't get out of the wagon. We can't protect injured people and the animals."

"We can help." Sebastian took the two candle holders. "We can drive the wagons."

156

"I'll ask." Sally gathered the family. "They want to drive the wagons."

Noah went to the back of the wagon. "Can you shoot that shotgun or a rifle?"

"We're both excellent shots," Sebastian replied.

Roscoe leaned on the rear boards. "That would be helpful. We'd have two more people in the middle around the animals."

"Lola should put on buckskin clothes and gloves. She can wear the goose wing collar I made." Ann climbed into the wagon. "We can put the elk skin on Sebastian."

"I'm putting the elk hide on Lola. It will protect her better. I'll wear the goose collar." Sebastian secured the skin around the waist of the woman he loved, while the others tied its head and legs. They covered her with bravery, agility, and independence.

Sebastian put on the white, snow goose collar symbolizing kindness, loyalty, clear communications, staunch defense, and compassionate keeping of the community.

Noah stuck eagle feathers into the goose

collar to add the power of the divine spirit, creation, and freedom. In his medicine bag under the bear fur, he kept the rest of his eagle feathers to bring the power of the divine to himself. He also carried the energies of the other items in his bag. "Everybody, come here." When they were all together, he prayed to the only true power, "God, we put our lives into Your hands. You created, and You direct the earth, sky, sun, moon, planets, and all the stars that You made at the dawn of creation. You control the plants, animals, birds, reptiles, snakes, insects, and everything else. Bring to us any that will help us, and keep away those that would harm us. If there are any humans, don't let there be a confrontation. We don't want to be hurt, and we don't want to hurt anybody. Cause whatever happens to bring You glory."

They all said, "Amen."

"Get into position." Noah took a lantern and rode Eyanosa to his place at the rear.

Eli held a lantern and sat on Ace at the front. Sebastian sat in the driver's box of the first wagon with the sword strapped on. His shotgun and shells lay on the seat beside the skull.

Positioned at the sides of the herd corralled between the wagons, Roscoe rode on King and Stephanie rode Redeemed. Each held a lantern, had two pistols in their gun belts around their waists and a rifle slung at their front.

Holding a candle in the candleholder from their farm, Sally waited on Roscoe's donkey, Smiley, in position behind them but in front of the rear wagon. Ann duplicated Sally's post but at the left on Noah's mare. They both had several extra candles in their medicine bags, a rifle, and two pistols held by the ropes at their waists. Noah had insisted that Ann also take a Lefaucheux revolver.

Lola drove the second wagon with a rifle and ammo. The four lanterns they owned blazed. Before they started in, Noah stated his concern, "We're too spread out. Even with the light from the moon and the lanterns, I wish we had more light. We should have bought lanterns in Perryville."

"Too late now. Let's move out." Eli stepped

onto the wooden causeway through the Cypress Swamp. They started the two-hour, four-mile trip encased in a sphere of light that extended a short way into the surrounding darkness.

To the wild citizens of the swamp, the sound of animal hooves hollered, "Here comes a tasty meal!" The wagon rolled onto the wooden boards and sent the call farther into the depths of the watery kingdom. The people on the walkway felt they could be heard all the way back to Raymond's farm. Eyanosa stepped onto the boards. They were fully committed to the task ahead.

# FIFTEEN

Green and orange glowing orbs surrounded them and moved toward them under, on, and above the surface of the water, as well as through the air.

"They know we're here," Sally alerted the others.

Stephanie sang, "Amazing Grace, how sweet the sound that saved a wretch like me." The others joined and found the courage to face their fear.

Most of the denizens of the swamp saw the parade of walking animals and stayed back. They knew to avoid alligators, coyotes, and bears. The insects, however, had no such understanding or fear. Even though the people had rubbed themselves down with crushed Allspice leaves, the insects robbed the members of the caravan of their blood. Also attempting to feast, ticks and spiders fell on them from above. Mosquitos and biting flies circled and homed in on exposed human and animal faces.

Ann brushed a spider from her arm, waved her hands, and swatted tiny attackers. She saw Sally also attempting to save herself from the onslaught. "If the only attacks are from these irritating bugs, I'll be happy." Ann resumed singing.

They hadn't gone far when Eli and an alligator, laying on the boardwalk, spotted their rival for the territory they both wanted to claim. Eli called out, "Halt!" which was repeated back through the line to Noah.

In reply, Noah hollered, "Hold your positions!" He didn't know what was going on, but he knew they needed to stay in place to protect the group.

Eli and Sebastian both aimed their guns. The

alligator hissed. Sounding ferocious, Eli roared his warning to vacate the area. The real alligator wasn't intimidated. It only knew to attack. It darted at its competition. Both men fired. Alligator blood and flesh flew out of the charging menace. The fight was over before it had begun.

To notify everybody that the issue was resolved, Eli hollered, "Clear!" He left his post and advanced toward the carcass. "Sebastian and Theo, come here." The two men arrived. "We should be sure." Eli severed the spinal cord and arteries at the base of the skull. "I want this carcass. Sebastian, will you ride with this monster under your feet?"

"Of course."

"Help me get it onto the wagon."

Before Eli got his hands on the thousand-pound alligator, Stephanie yelled, "Don't even think about it! Abraham, we're swapping places. James needs you."

As soon as she was at the rear, Noah rode forward. All he knew was that two gunshots had been fired. He was very relieved when he saw that it had only been a confrontation with an animal, and of course, that the animal had lost.

Eli knew his wife was right. Even though he didn't feel he was still injured, it hadn't been long enough for his ribs to have knit completely. "Help me get this onto the wagon, or Marie will kill me herself."

Roscoe tried to raise the heavy load. "Couldn't you have killed a smaller one?"

Lola jumped down from the wagon and went to Ann. "Lily, I think they could use you." Lola took up the position between the swamp and the animals.

Ann rode to the front. "Let's tie it around its rear legs, and use the horse to pull it up tail end first."

Before they got the alligator onto the wagon seat floor, more than frogs observed them. People awakened by gunshots had come to find out what had happened. In a boat, a man asked his companion. "Shouldn't we oughta shoot 'em fore they see us?"

The leader of the two-man swamp

reconnoitering detail replied, "They sure 'nough killed one a our gators, but I wanna watch. I didn't 'spect to find no walkin' gator or bear."

"Or a coyote on a horse. I swan, I can see clean through the one standin' on that wagon!"

"And look at them clothes. All shiny like metal."

When the alligator lay on the floorboards, Noah returned to his place at the rear, "Ready."

Back in their assigned positions, each of the others repeated, "Ready."

Eli heard 'ready' seven times. "Forward ho."

They walked for an hour, scattering hundreds of turtles and frogs back into the safety of the swamp. Red bites from the swamp creatures, that'd had no problem being successful in their attacks, covered the faces of the people outside of and in the boat.

Roscoe called, "Halt!"

Those walking on the boardwalk, and those riding in the boat thought, *why stop here?*

"That's black cohosh and spikenard. There's probably ginger and ginseng too."

Ann looked. Lantern light and moonlight illuminated the nearby plants. "They're not reachable from the causeway, and I want to get through this swamp. Let's move on."

Roscoe remained where he stood. "Those are extremely beneficial plants and very hard to find."

Noah offered a possible solution, "That looks like one of those floating islands. I could shoot a rope into it. Maybe, we can pull it over."

"I want those plants. Let's try."

Ann looked at the two men planning and gave up. "I'll get the rope."

"You think they spotted us?" the swamp man asked his partner.

"Course not, you idiot. They're not hiding, but I'll be danged if I know wut they lookin' at."

Noah tied a rope to a heavy arrow and then pointed it at the floating clump of swamp plants. Not knowing what the bear was aiming at, the two men on the receiving side ducked into the boat for protection. The arrow caught the vegetation. They pulled it close.

166

Roscoe showed those with him what he wanted. "Take the roots and rhizomes of every black cohosh, blue cohosh, spikenard, snakeroot, bloodroot, ginger, and ginseng plant in the mat. If you see any seeds, get them too. They look like these." He laid out examples on the boardwalk. He also took the few small pawpaw trees and planted them in one of the tubs.

They chopped, sawed, and picked apart the plants as they dissected the vegetative mat. Everything they wanted, they put in ten-gallon tubs. They threw the rest onto other mats of floating plant life. The younger swamp man huffed, "They stealin' our plants. We can't let em." They paddled toward the causeway. A barely visible man rose and drew his ghostly sword. The swamp men stopped.

The travelers through the swampy kingdom loaded their plants and then continued on their way, still followed by the swamp natives. "I bet they got plenty a food." The older one rowed closer. The transparent man again drew his sword, but they continued forward.

Noah saw movement, and then he heard a sound. Not turning to look, he called out, "Halt!" He vacated his position and rode to Eli. "Don't look, and don't act differently. I heard something in the swamp."

Eli whispered, "The swamp is full of things."

"This was different. It's a person or people."

"What should we do?"

Ann walked to the front to find out what was going on, "Husband?"

"I heard people on the right. Go back to your places, but walk on the inside of the animals, by their heads. Protect yourself from the swamp on the right. Lay your rifles across your mule's back, pointed into that side of the swamp. James, walk on the left of Ace and move to the left of the lead mules. I'll do the same with Eyanosa, and I'll stay on the left side of the rear wagon." He got off Eyanosa and walked on the safe side of the wagons with Ann. When they went past Sebastian, without turning his head to look at him, Noah said, "Get between the two lead mules at their heads and walk to guide them forward."

Ann assured him, "I'll tell Lola." She told Roscoe what to do. Then, from her new position, she whispered instructions to Lola. Lola climbed out of the seat with her loaded rifle and got between the mules pulling the rear wagon. As he walked to his place, Noah updated Stephanie and Sally.

The men in the swamp saw them shift positions. "They couldn't a seen us. Nobody ever sees us. It's nothin'." The men in the boat swatted away biting deerflies then rowed toward the group on the causeway. Large men with drawn swords materialized between them and the caravan.

"Where'd them men come from?" the younger man asked.

"Musta been in the wagons."

"I didn't see em get out an' them animal skin people ain't even seein' them soldiers." They paddled away from the group too large to attack. When the swamp men backed away, the new regiment vanished.

Eli and the others walked in the new positions of protection. Once they knew what to listen for, over and over, they heard a boat approach and then move away.

The swamp men rowed away for the fifth time. The younger of the two spoke, "How them always know when we comin'? Ya think them men in the wagons won't come out if we ain't in the boat?"

"Let's try." They knew which plants grew on land and which grew on floating vegetation. They jumped from the boat and then waited to take out the bear from behind.

"You're better an me. You take the shot."

"Give me the blow dart." They followed until they had a clear shot at the bear's neck. The man took a deep breath, put the tube to his mouth, and then blew as hard as he could. The dart, covered with a poison frog extract, flew into the neck of the bear. They waited for the bear to drop. It kept walking.

"Maybe they ain't real," said the man whose dart should have killed its target, even if it had been a bear and not a human. "I'm dreamin'." He punched his friend.

"Ouch! Ya didn't have ta hit me that hard."

"Guess we ain't dreamin'. I shoulda shot em in the face."

"We need ta get up ahead an' hide real close. It'll be hard ta get a shot, an' there be only two a us. 'Member, breathe in 'fore ya put the tube ta ya lips."

The light of the moon made the men jumping from clump to clump visible. Eli saw them get into position close to the boardwalk. He didn't want to kill a man, but they were about to leave him no choice. He thought there were two, but he didn't know for sure. He prepared for more. He had twenty bullets in the revolver. He popped more from his ammo belt into his hand, in case he had to reload fast. *Keep going,* he told himself. It had been over two hours since they had entered the swamp. Eli knew they were almost across.

Out of nowhere, the giant men again walked with the caravan. The wispy-see-through man in strange clothes stood on the wagon with his feet inside the alligator. The older man said to the younger man beside him. "Em big men back. It ain't worth it."

"There'll be easier ones." They deserted their pursuit. The eight people on the causeway saw the men leave. Ann felt tempted to wave but decided that might change their decision. She didn't acknowledge that she'd known they were there. The men of the swamp watched the group of walking animals, the giant men with swords, and the vapory man step off the wooden planks of their domain and continue away.

## SIXTEEN

With his recovered gun in hand, Raymond led his cow and goat to Perryville. He didn't know how long he would be gone and his good friend could use the milk. In Perryville, Raymond went straight to Adeline's. He put the animals in the barn and then knocked on the door under the stairs. "It's me."

Adeline opened the small window in the barred door. "Ray, what are you doing here? I thought you'd be married to Lola by now."

"Sebastian stole her. I need to rescue her. I'm giving you my cow and goat 'til we get back."

*Why is he so possessed? She doesn't even want*

*him. Why can't he see it?* "Come in and get some sleep before you leave."

*It's only fair that somebody loves me a little.* "All right, but I'm leaving first thing."

Adeline opened her door. "I'll pack you some food in the morning."

Ray asked, "Did you see either of them or anybody suspicious?"

"No, but one family did come through yesterday."

"Which way did they go?" Ray lay beside Adeline.

"They came from Little Rock and headed toward the river. It was just an old man and his family."

Before his mind focused on other things, Raymond thought, *they'd have come past the body. Maybe he wasn't dead.*

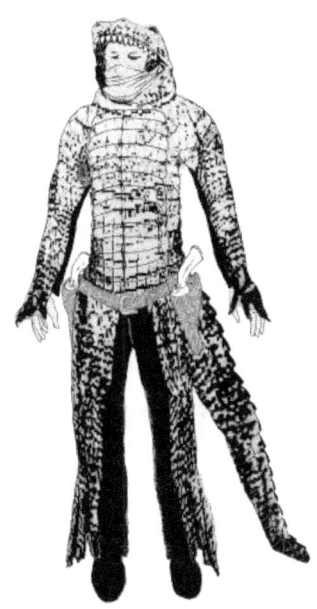

# SEVENTEEN

Halfway through the night, that old man and his family arrived at Kuhn Bayou. "We're stopping here," Noah announced.

Lola wanted to continue, of course. "We need to keep going."

"Abraham said, 'no.'" Sally jumped off the wagon.

"Why?" Lola asked.

Stephanie said, "Because we want to." Saying that Noah and Ann had gotten married there, or that she and Eli had stayed there for a few days after they had married, would give away who they were. If anybody ever asked

175

Lola or Sebastian who they had traveled with, they wouldn't have any useful information.

There wasn't any smoke coming from the chimney of the cabin in the woods. Eli knocked anyway. He hoped the owner, Harry Pitts, wasn't home.

Nobody answered the door. Noah relit the lanterns. "I'm glad we went through the swamp and got here tonight. If we had come tomorrow, we would have kept going." He opened the door and held the lantern inside. The only tracks in the dust were those of mice.

Ann followed her husband into the log cabin. "Abraham, there's something stuck in the back of your neck." Ann reached for the object.

"Don't touch it!" Noah barked.

Everybody eyeballed the object. "It's a dart," Eli reported.

"Help me get the fur off without letting it touch me or anybody else." Noah carefully shed the fur.

The dart had penetrated the hide. Blessedly, the tightness had created a space around his neck that had saved his life. To empty a glass jar, they moved matches from one container into the others. Noah picked out the dart with two chips of novaculite that he and Eli had made as they had practiced knapping. He dropped the dart and stone chips into the glass jar and corked them safely away.

Ann looked at the fur but didn't touch it. "Whatever is on that dart is still on the fur."

"I see that. It must be poison. Until we can find out how to remove it, I'll roll that part and the jar inside and tie it up."

Once the dart and fur were contained, Eli said, "Everybody except injured people, help get wood." They went to the shed behind the cabin. Eli whispered, "Harry hasn't been here since Marie and I left last fall."

Sally held out her arms. "I don't blame Minnie for leaving with Zachariah when she found out Harry hadn't really married her."

Ann added, "I'm glad they found each other."

Stephanie carried wood to the house. "Since we have an oven, let's bake bread. I want some of that great dill bread Nancy makes. Will you men put up the animals?"

The animals needed to graze, and the shed was too small for all of them, anyway. The men led them to the field where they had camped the previous September when they had waited for Harry Pitts to arrive with the key to unlock the bridge's gate.

The women left the dough to rise during the night. They planned to cook the bread in the morning. One fire burned in the kitchen stove and another in the front room's fireplace. They all slept on the floor with the goose down pillows they had made at Fletcher Creek, the feather mattresses they had brought from Bacon's Trading Post, or the mattress and pillows Noah had brought from Raymond's farm.

Later that night, one of the new members of the herd attempted to take control. Mateo was a strong stallion, surrounded by females. As soon as he had rested, he decided to assert himself. Eyanosa wasn't about to give up his harem without a fight. Mateo advanced. Eyanosa attempted to back him down. He reared, pummeled his challenger with his front hooves, and neighed ferociously. Mateo circled in from the side and bit Eyanosa's neck. The two snorted, reared, bucked, neighed, kicked, and attempted to rip flesh from each other.

The people inside heard the commotion. Lola screamed, "He's here! We're dead!"

Everybody in the cabin went for his or her gun.

"Raymond must be trying to stampede our animals." Noah ran to the field, where Eyanosa and Mateo battled for control of the herd. It wasn't a mild-mannered confrontation like it had been when they had merged Roscoe's animals with the injured mules Sally and Noah had acquired in Little Rock.

Lola shrieked, "They're killing each other! Stop them!"

*That woman has got to stop hollering.* Noah explained, "They won't kill each other. They need to figure out which of them is the leader."

The battle went on. Mateo drew Eyanosa's blood. Eyanosa kicked Mateo to his knees. Roscoe pointed out, "Soon, neither will be able to walk."

Mateo came up and charged. He tried to batter his rival just as Eyanosa had pummeled him. It was evident neither was backing down.

Noah ran to get the long whip. He dashed back to the fierce battle. Both horses bled from multiple bites and kick-wounds. Without touching either of them, he cracked the whip at the feet of and beside the heads of both horses. He hollered, "Back!" Noah jumped up and down and side to side to get them to focus on him. He continued to yell and crack the whip.

Noah led Eyanosa to food and water. Noah loved him and was telling him to back down. Eyanosa stopped attacking but continued to defend himself.

Mateo saw Eyanosa submit and realized he was after the wrong leader. He started toward Noah. Noah stood his ground and delivered a sharp, stinging blow between Mateo's ears. That got the horse's attention. Mateo stopped. With his ears still down, he stared at Noah. Noah didn't flinch. Mateo started toward him and received a smack across the chest. Mateo stopped again. Still in his puffed-up stance with

180

his ears pinned back, he snorted and pawed the ground.

Noah whistled Eyanosa over, reached into his pocket with his left hand and brought out an apple, which he gave to Eyanosa and then patted his neck. He pulled another apple from his pocket and held it out to Mateo. Mateo looked at Eyanosa. He looked at Noah. Noah whistled and held the apple toward Mateo, who kept his ears in an aggressive position but cautiously approached. He stopped just out of reach of the person who could inflict pain from a distance. The man didn't seem intent on attacking, and he offered a tasty opportunity to submit. Mateo reached for the apple. Noah let him take the treat with his mouth. Mateo went into a neutral posture as he munched the apple.

Noah had gotten both of them to submit and had established himself as the leader of the herd. He separated Mateo and Honey Dew from the others and took them to the shed by the cabin. He left the rest of the herd in the field under the control of Eyanosa.

# EIGHTEEN

Raymond woke early. He once again helped himself to Adeline's hospitality before he told her, "I need to get going."

Adeline dressed. "You should marry me."

"We've been through this before. You won't give up this place."

"If you'd live with me here, we'd be happy. I couldn't live on a farm. I'll go fix you a traveling bag. Come to the kitchen when you're ready to go."

Ray ate a breakfast prepared with love then took the bag of food Adeline offered and went looking for the woman who hated and feared

182

him. Ray thought it was likely that the people who had gone north would have tried to save an injured man, and the timing was right for them to have found Sebastian. Even though they had left before Lola got away, they were the only people who had come through. He didn't want to wear out his horse, but he had a lot of ground to cover. At a canter, he proceeded north to the ferry.

# NINETEEN

A hundred miles away, Judge Daniel Hall thought about the woman who had become an Indian's lover. She hadn't had even one single shred of remorse. *She's a beautiful woman. All kinds of white men would be glad to marry her. I'd have considered bedding her. &^% her, telling me she's going to have — how did she say it — "all kinds of relations" with that heathen and that she'd be right before God and I'm not. I'm not letting her get away with it!*

The thought of Ann engaging in relations with Noah Swift Hawk caused nightmares that plagued him at night and gnawed at him

184

during the day. He sat at his judge's bench and fumed. He grabbed the envelope that had arrived that morning. *This is what she ought to get.* He jabbed into it with his sharp letter opener, ripped it open, and pulled out its insides.

1, May 1840

Honorable Judge Hall,

It has come to our attention that discipline at the hard labor camp in Missouri has grown lax. As a result, unrest and chaos have led to a request for more guards. I find myself indisposed and unable to travel. As you are the closest court official, you are ordered to inspect the facilities at The Quarry. Make corrections where needed, arrange for the transport of troublemakers to the eighth district penitentiary in Arkansas, and take whatever other steps you deem necessary. Report your findings and corrective actions to this office as soon as feasible.

Sincerely,

*Micah Clemont*

His Honorable Justice
United States Supreme Court
Alexandria, Virginia

# TWENTY

In the cabin at Kuhn Bayou, the sun peeked through the clouds that threatened to unleash a storm. "Do you think he's looking for me?" Lola sat by the fire in the front room.

Eli replied, "I'm sure he is, but I think he's headed toward Little Rock."

Noah stirred the fire. "If he found his rifle, he might be, but I hid it well. Still, we should leave by mid-day."

"I'll take a shift watching," Sebastian told them.

Noah said, "We don't need to. He wouldn't have woken up until the same time as Lola.

187

Even if he left immediately and rode full speed, he'd only have just crossed the Arkansas. We have time, and the animals should eat as long as possible."

Sebastian declared, "Good because I'm not leaving until I've eaten several slices of that heavenly-smelling bread."

Eli rose. "Then I'll skin the gator and get the best pieces of meat. It'll be a lot easier to do it here."

Noah had slept in his boots. He stood up too. "And we aren't leaving until I get some mussels from the river."

"I'll come with you." Since water would ruin them, Ann went to the back room and changed out of her buckskins.

Noah reminisced as they walked to the river. "The mussels won't be as good as when Minnie cooked them in wine."

Ann agreed, "That was a wonderful day and eating them as your wife made them so much better. They were some pumpkins."

Noah and Ann stood in the bayou up to their knees while those in the cabin sorted and repackaged swamp plants to reclaim their washtubs.

Eli cut the scutes from the alligator's back then slit the leg skin on the tops and around the feet. He cut the skin from its jawline, peeled its head, and then detached the hide down to the front legs. Eli warned the others, "Prepare yourselves." He swung the ax one time and lopped off the alligator's skinless head.

Sally complimented her brother-in-law. "James, you're so strong. I don't know of anybody else who can do that."

Eli scooped out the brain and plopped it into a tin pot. He wanted clean alligator jaws. Therefore, to boil away the flesh, he put the head in the most enormous pot they had. Even then, the snout stuck out the top while the head boiled.

Noah and Ann came back with enough mussels for everybody to have all they wanted. They dumped them into fresh water in a ten-gallon tub and left them to breathe out the sand.

Noah offered to help, "I can cut off the meat if you want me to, James."

"Do whatever suits your fancy. I want to get this skin clean. I'm being very careful, so I don't nick it."

Noah asked, "Did you get the jaw meat?"

"It's cooking in the pot."

Sally helped Stephanie remove the mussel beards. "Lily, read another of Hank's letters."

Ann had sorted them by date. She brought out the next. "It's another one almost worn away from reading. Look at the teardrop stains." She held it out to the others before reading.

"December 29, 1837

Hank,

I'm not going to make it. I don't want to be a man who can only sit around while others take care of him. I wish I had seen you again. I know I was hard on you but you can be so much better than me and I wanted you to try. As far as I can see you never have. I remember when your mother put you in my arms and said I had a son. That was a very happy day for me. I guess I could have been a better father. I always did love you. I wanted you to be strong and not

190

soft like a girl so I was hard on you. I'm sorry I didn't tell you that you did good but only told you to do better. Your mother tells me that you thought you could never be good enough for me and that I don't love you. I wish she had told me sooner but I guess I still wouldn't have been different. It's only when a man knows he's dying he sees how he should have done things. I'll probably be gone before you get here, if you do come. As long as it's been since your mother asked you to come I guess you won't. Probably you don't love me and don't care that I'm dying but I would have liked to have told you in person how much I love you and thought you were a good helper and was proud to have you as my son. Christmas is about Jesus being born and how much his father loved him. This year I thought about you. I finally understand how a father loves his first son and how hard it is to lose him. I guess you'll be glad I'm gone. I wish I hadn't made you hate me.
YOUR FATHER LOVES AND IS PROUD OF YOU.

Pa"

Stephanie remarked, "That changes what I think about him."

"Me too, especially since I've read all the letters." Ann laid down the paper.

Eli reiterated what he had said before. "My children will know I love them, just like I've always known that Pop loves me."

"Fathers are so important to what a person becomes." Ann added, "We're fortunate women to have husbands who know that."

Sebastian's father had never told him he loved him, but he hadn't been mean, and Sebastian had always believed that his father loved him. Still, he felt robbed by his father's distance. He turned to Lola, "If you still want to marry me, I promise our children will know I love them."

"Of course, I still want to marry you, and I promise our children and you will know I love you."

Ann put forward an idea. "All these letters are addressed to Dover. We could go home that way."

Since they were still getting the mussels ready to cook, butchering the alligator, and waiting for the second batch of bread to bake, Sebastian said, "Read another letter."

Ann read.

"December 31, 1837

Dear Hank,

Your pa tried to hold on hoping you'd come home but he passed yesterday. I'm going to miss him so bad. He wasn't perfect but he sure tried hard and provided everything we needed. I don't know how we're going to make it without him. He wrote you a letter. I added it in with this letter. I wish you had come home.

Ma"

Ann knew she couldn't leave it that way. The women cried as she opened the next letter.

"February 22, 1838

Hank,

We need you to come home. Ma isn't trying since Pa died. It sure would cheer her if you'd come home. When she got your letter, she was so happy. She reads it every day. I wish it had gotten here before Pa passed. He died very sad over you. That letter would have let him go to his grave in peace. You're a good man to have written it. Roy is doing all right but he's sad and worried like me. Richard's been coming to court me. I know you never cared for him but he's going to be a judge and I don't want to continue to live like we have. I love you Hank. Come home and visit us for a while then you can go back to your life at Dover.

Love from your sister,

Edith"

Ann asked, "Is it all right to read one more?"

"It is with me," Roscoe replied.

"July 5, 1838

Dear Son,

It was so nice to have you home for a while. I hope you liked all the bread and jam I made for you. We wouldn't have been able to get the fields planted this spring if you hadn't come home. We've been having problems with those Indians again. They're always fishing at the river on our land. I've tried to reason with them and tell them this is my land and they should stay off it. Mostly, it's the same one who always told you and your Pa that the land doesn't belong to any man and that he'd been fishing right there long before we ever came here. He told me I was living where I didn't have a right to live but he would let us stay only he was going to keep fishing there. We might move. It's too hard to fight them without your father. If Edith marries Richard, we might go live with them. I hope everything is going well over there in Dover.

Love, Ma"

Noah felt he had to speak up. "He was right. The land doesn't belong to any man, even though we stake our claims. Many Indians are starving because they've lost their hunting grounds. But I'm sorry that woman was having a hard time."

Stephanie spoke up, "Hank went and planted fields? Isn't that strange?"

Eli imparted his confusion in reconciling what he knew about Hank Butterfield and the man in the letters. "But he was an outlaw who robbed people. He attacked that man, you know who, only because he had on Indian clothing. In Maumelle, Abraham saw his box of stolen goods with the music box his gang stole from that house they burned down."

Sally hoped it wouldn't upset her sister to hear more, but asked, "Do you want to hear another?"

Stephanie agreed. "Maybe it will help make things clearer."

Ann read the next letter.

"August 5, 1838

Dear Hank,

Richard asked me to marry him. He said Ma and Roy could live with us. You should see the fields green with the plants you put into the ground. I hope you'll help us get the crops in this fall then we'll sell the farm. Please come to the wedding on the first of September. We all love you and hope to see you.

Edith."

Ann already knew what was in all the letters and told them, "It's hard to reconcile how a man can behave like two extremely different people. The next two letters were in the same envelope and dated the same day."

"Well, don't just sit there. Read them," Lola commanded.

"November 19, 1838

Hank,

Wasn't the wedding grand? You looked so handsome and I saw Clarabelle looking at you. You should come home and marry her. You must admit she's an attractive woman and a wonderful cook. A man couldn't ask for more. It's only been six weeks but your brother is making things very hard. He won't do anything Richard tells him to do. Talk to him when he brings you this letter and tell him he must do what Richards tells him. I also want to tell you that you're going to be an uncle.

With love and affection,

Edith."

Sally questioned in disbelief, "Somebody wanted to marry him?"

Ann replied, "Oh, yes. I'll get to that one, but first, the letter that came with this one."

198

"Dear Son,                    November 19, 1838

Thank you for coming to the wedding. Richard is a good man. He's been working hard to get all the Indians out of our new state of Arkansas. I don't know if Edith wants you to know but the baby is due in April. We sold the farm and the crops. We didn't get much. I think it's because Mr. Handsome knows how much of a bind we were in. At least it's gone and I don't have to worry about running a farm alone. Richard and Edith are going to take care of Roy and me. Roy is almost grown and won't be with us long and that's good. He's being very difficult. Ever since I told him I was going to sell the farm, he's been angry. He says I sold his birthright. I tried to explain that I have no choice. Try to reason with him for me. Even though you've only been gone for a few months, I miss you already. Clarabelle asks about you every time I see her. She asked for your address. I gave it to her. I hope you don't mind. She'd make you a good wife and you could come home to live.

Love, Ma"

"Read the next one, Lily." Noah passed her the pile of letters.

Ann informed them, "It's the last one."

"November 22, 1838

Hank,

I hope you don't mind that I've written to you. I so much enjoyed seeing you at Edith's wedding. How are you doing over there in Dover? I sure would like to see you more often. Maybe I could visit with Edith when she goes to see you. I think about you and how fine a man you are helping your mother at the farm after your father died. I'm so sorry about him passing. I'm sure you miss him. Things are well with me, but I'm lonely here. Ever since we were children, I always thought you and I would get married one day. If you ever have that in your mind, let me know.

Hopefully yours,

Clarabelle"

Lola said, "I wonder what happened?" Sally broke out in tears and fled to the kitchen. "What?" Lola didn't understand.

Noah couldn't tell her everything. "He died."

Lola replied, "That's so sad. He probably would have married her."

Ann had read the letters days before and had already thought about them quite a bit. "That's the end result of hatred, prejudice, not understanding other people, and the lack of desire to live in peace. It robs you of what could have been and at the end it brings death and sadness."

Lola added, "And it robs other people too. Clarabelle will never marry him now."

Roscoe pointed out the other side of that coin, "Or, it may have saved her from a horrible life, married to the bandit he was."

Noah thought about something he had read in a book he had gotten from Murray Strong's library. "I read about a person acting like different people and each one not knowing about the other."

"Do you think the Hank in those letters didn't know about Hank, the outlaw who wanted to shoot that Indian?" Sally asked from the kitchen.

"I don't know, but maybe," Noah replied.

"I wonder what God does in that situation?" Stephanie wondered, "Does the evil side take the whole man to Hell, or does the good man take them into Heaven? Or does God split him up and send each part where it deserves to go?"

"I don't think we can know until we're in Heaven and can ask Him." Noah went over and looked at the mollusks in the tub. "I think these are ready."

Ann reported how the letters had affected her. "Those letters certainly give a person something to think about. I haven't stopped pondering."

Sally called out from the kitchen, "We need to go to Dover and find his house."

Noah sliced off the two lengthy tenderloins from the alligator's back then the big slabs of muscle from both sides of its tail. Eli scraped the last trace of flesh from its hide and then covered the skin with salt. He placed the four feet, with claws still intact, on the skin. He salted them down too, folded the sides of the large hide over them, and then rolled it up.

Roscoe went into the kitchen to cook the pearly mussels in goat's milk. He and Sally put together a delicious meal that they ate as they sat on the floor. Ann picked up another shell. She slid the mussel out. Something clinked against her tin plate.

"What was that, Lily?" Stephanie asked.

"I don't know." Ann stuck her fork into the mussel and removed it from the plate. Under its body was a half-inch ball. Ann put it into her cup of water then took a closer look at the object, shimmering with a pink luster. "It's a pearl!" She handed the cup to her sister.

Stephanie exclaimed, "It's beautiful!"

After everybody had examined the pink pearl, Ann wrapped it in a piece of cloth, put it in an empty buckskin pouch, and then slid it into her medicine bag.

Sebastian pulled over another uneaten batch. "We should check for more."

They opened all the remaining mussels, checked all the discarded shells and the sand in the pail they had used to wash the mussels. They even strained the milk broth but didn't find any more pearls.

"Should we get more?" Stephanie asked.

Noah said, "We'd kill them to get them open. I don't want to do that just to look for pearls."

Lola reminded them, "And we should get going anyway."

Sally said, "I wonder if the people who used to live here ever found any."

Stephanie had met the two who had owned the cabin. She thought about what she knew of Minnie Pitt's life. "I doubt it."

Sebastian suggested, "Let's harvest another large batch. It'll only take a few minutes to steam them open. We can get them out of the shells while we ride."

Noah thought of something. "We could put the mussel meat into brine and eat them in the future. We should do the same with the alligator meat in the pot." He walked over to

204

the cooking head. "Anybody want an eye?" Everybody declined. He slurped one into his mouth and popped it with his teeth. He followed it with the other. "I'll pack this meat."

They finished their meal then spent a few hours stripping mussels from the places they thought were most likely to have caused the mollusks to form a pearl, especially the fine red sand. Rain sprinkled them. "All four tubs are heaping. We have enough." Noah waded out of the bayou.

"And we don't want to be in the water if lightning comes." Ann also made her way to the edge of the river. The rest of them followed.

"It will take all eight of us to carry these four containers." Stephanie asked Sebastian and Lola, "Can you two carry one?"

Lola replied, "I'll try."

After a few very painful steps, Sebastian saw that Lola's bruised and beaten body wasn't able to complete the task. "Put it down, Lola. We'll come back for this one." *I hope I don't have to carry this. I do have a hole in my chest.*

The other six got the tubs into the cabin and

started the process of steaming them. They threw the alligator bones and the coals from the front fire into the bayou then thoroughly removed the evidence of their visit during the long process of cooking the many muscles they had pried from the underwater rocks. It was late in the day when all the mussels had been steamed open. None of them wanted to lose any more time or allow Raymond to close the gap between them any further. They packed up the pots then carried the stove's hot coals in the metal washtubs and dumped them into Kuhn Bayou.

"If he's coming this way, I hope the cabin will be cold when he gets here." Noah pulled the door shut.

Roscoe had money. He didn't need a pearl, and he didn't want to spend more time with smelly mollusks. "I'll drive a wagon."

Ann already had the pink pearl. "I'll drive the other."

"I'll help with the mussels," Lola offered.

Sebastian also wanted to look, in case there were more pearls. "Me too."

Stephanie said, "I should help as well."

Sally climbed in. "I want to find at least one."

Eli didn't want to be left out. "There's room for me to help shuck."

Noah didn't feel he needed to keep the proceeding fair as he had with the men of Fletcher Creek. He decided to leave the others to their search and sat beside his wife. The pearl seekers sat in the back of the wagon with the four ten-gallon washtubs of hot steamed mussels. They rode away in a light rain.

Lola suggested, "Whoever finds a pearl is the owner. Agreed?"

Eli proposed, "Some people may shuck faster. Let's divide them equally between us first. If somebody finds one in their portion, it's theirs."

"That's fair." Stephanie agreed with her husband.

Sebastian concurred, "I think so too."

They counted out equal piles. Each took a gallon-sized, small-mouthed glass jar with a little of the brine they had made at the cabin then started the search. After they opened and examined a shell, they removed the meat with the sharp tip of a knife, dropped it into their brine jar and then tossed the shells together into the empty washtubs.

Only a few minutes into the process, Stephanie exclaimed, "I feel something!" She pushed the hard object into her other hand.

"You found one." Eli examined the small creamy oval.

Lola felt desperate to find at least one. "You hardly started. I hope we'll find a lot."

When they shelled the last mussel, they had found only the one pearl but had five gallons of mussels in brine and were almost at the road to Dover.

## TWENTY ONE

While the ferryman carried Raymond across the Arkansas, Lola left the cabin at Kuhn Bayou. To prepare for what he saw brewing in the west, without help, the man winched his boat up the ramp and out of the water. Raymond had already hurried on.

Lola and Sebastian approached Dover as Sargent trotted onto the boards barely above the water that skimmed under the swamp causeway. The falling rain drowned out the sound of his hoof beats and the splash when the horse, in a slow ballet, slipped on the wet boards and gracefully slid into the swamp.

Raymond scrambled out. He helped his horse get its front legs on the boardwalk. Sargent's rear hooves couldn't push against the gooey swamp bottom. Raymond pulled Sargent by the front legs until most of his body was on the boardwalk then jumped back into the water and tried to raise one of Sargent's rear legs. That didn't work. He got behind the horse and pushed, but to no avail.

The water slid apart behind yellow eyes headed their way. Raymond pulled his rifle from the holster strapped to the horse. He fired. The eyes sank from view. *I hope that means it's not still coming. Something's gonna sink its teeth in me before I get this* \*^%%& *horse out.* He pushed as hard as he could. "Get your &&^%$$# rear end up! You #$#$%%&^* horse!"

Splinters pushed into Sargent's knee as it got back on the boardwalk. The horse drew his last leg up and was out. Raymond hauled himself onto the planks. Underneath his poncho, his clothes dripped swamp water. *We'll both be safer.* Even though slower, Raymond walked in front of Sargent as the cold rain pelted them.

The creek that gathered the rain fed the swamp. The water rose above the wooden planks. A cottonmouth snake swam past Raymond's boot. *Maybe I should ride again. No. If we go in, we may not get out, and I'm sure my ammunition is too wet.*

Raymond trudged on. He was cold. The raindrops hammered the water and filled his mind with misery and unhappiness. He figured he had another hour in the swamp, and the water had already climbed halfway to the tops of his boots. *What am I doing here when I could be in my dry, warm home or with Adeline?*

A freshwater eel swam past his feet. Raymond had on leather boots, but Sargent's legs were exposed to everything. Raymond stopped. He pulled his spare clothes from his bag, wrapped them around the horse's legs up to its knees, and then tied them on. *I hope the cloth is thick enough to keep away teeth and fangs.*

The water slowly rose. They trekked as fast as Raymond thought they could safely walk. He told Sargent, "I think I see the end of this Godforsaken swamp."

The water had reached the top of his boots when he saw a set of eyes. *@\*&$%\*^! There's no way my gun's gonna fire. That gator can swim right up to me. &^%^$$\*%$%! There's another one! Ride or be alligator food!* He jumped on Sargent and urged him to run. The alligators closed. Raymond hollered, "Faster, horse!"

Raymond wasn't sure of the exact location of the causeway. He pointed Sargent toward what looked like an opening in the trees ahead. He wasn't a praying man. He begged God anyway. "God, if you're there, get us out of here. I'll do anything."

They were close to the end of the causeway when the alligators arrived at Sargent's legs. Raymond looked over his shoulder. Jaws that seemed large enough to swallow them whole opened to latch on. He yelled at the being he thought had let him down. "God, why didn't you save us?!"

Sargent's feet hit the muddy ground, submerged under the high water. He got more traction and surged forward as the alligator's jaws snapped with bone breaking force on empty air. Leaving the jaws of destruction in the swamp, they charged out of the water. They didn't stop running in case the alligators decided to chase them onto land.

When Raymond felt safe, he signaled the horse to stop and rest. "Thank you, God," he prayed gratefully. Then he wondered, *why did God save me? I tried to kill a man, and I'm still planning to kill him.* He continued to reflect. *I beat Lola pretty bad too. I don't deserve to be saved.* Then, he rationalized why his actions weren't his responsibility. *She's the one who made me so mad. She made me hit her, and Sebastian stole her twice.*

# TWENTY TWO

Noah stopped at the fork in the road. Due to the protection of the wagon cover they had purchased in Little Rock, everything inside was dry. Noah didn't want the water sheeting off his poncho to get in the wagon. He rearranged the material to funnel the rain away from the opening. "Open up." He talked to those inside through a slight opening. "Should we go to Dover?"

"I need to understand about Hank, so I'd like to," Sally replied.

"Do they have a preacher?" Sebastian asked.

Roscoe arrived from the other wagon. "Maybe."

214

Lola said, "I'd like to find out."

Noah adjusted his poncho again. "Also, we need to get someplace where we can preserve the alligator meat. We can't do it out here in the rain."

Sally remembered the alligator meal she had made with Melvin, the soldier she loved but had left behind in Little Rock. "I'd like to make jambalaya."

"If we find his house, we may be able to use it for all these things," Ann added, "Let's go to Dover."

*I don't want to be crammed together.* Eli said, "Let's go all the way tonight. Theo, slip out of your poncho and into the wagon. I'll take over."

"I'm doing fine," Roscoe replied.

"You've been in the rain for hours. It's my turn." Eli opened the wagon cover.

"All right, James." Roscoe loosened the string around his face. Noah held the poncho as Roscoe slipped into the wagon.

"Turn it around." Eli stepped out into the wet poncho.

When she had thought about the jambalaya,

Sally started thinking about her first love. Her heart ached. She didn't want to talk to anybody. "I'll take over for you, Lily." She plopped her fur hat on her head.

Ann felt frozen. "The poncho is waterproof, but you need to stay warm. Wear wool pants and a wool shirt under it, Nancy." Ann handed Sally her mukluks and doeskin gloves with india rubber inserts. "You next," Ann ordered her husband.

Noah didn't want to put anybody else in the rain, but he had also been in the cold for hours, so he entered the wagon.

Eli rolled up his brother-in-law's wet poncho. "Two of us are enough. I'll bring up the rear. That way, I can protect everybody better."

"Forward, ho." Sally directed Eyanosa onto the road to Dover.

Heavy clouds blew in and blocked the sunlight while Sally and Eli piloted the wagons. The sun was up, but they could barely see. Much later, Sally hollered, "Halt!" She hoped Eli would hear her over the torrent of rain. He didn't hear, but it didn't matter. He saw, did the

216

same, and then walked to the front to find out why.

Sally brought up her concern. "I'm afraid we'll get stuck. I can't see the water pooling in low areas until we're in it. The grass right here isn't underwater. If we rope off this knoll, the animals can eat."

Noah heard the comment, "Can we get the wagons and animals off the road?"

Eli reported, "I can't see past the front of the wagon. I'll have to go look. Hand me a rope." So he would be able to find his way back, Eli tied himself to the wagon. They anxiously waited for several minutes.

"I see him," Sally informed those in the wagon.

"We can circle the wagons in the field, but the ground is so waterlogged, even though it doesn't look like it, we may get stuck. It might be better to stay on the road. We can tie a rope from the wagon to the edge of the trees then across the trees and back to the other wagon to keep the animals in the field."

"What do you think?" Noah asked the people sitting around him.

"We should get off the road. If Raymond comes, he might not see us," Lola stated her desire.

Sally agreed, "Since it doesn't look like we'd get stuck, that's fine with me."

Roscoe always thought about what was best for the animals. "If we can keep the animals safe with grass to eat and get off the road without getting bogged in, that would be best."

Noah agreed, "We'll throw out the alligator meat if we have to. I'd rather be safe. Back the wagons into the field."

"I hope Eyanosa and Mateo don't fight." Ann held out Noah's poncho.

Noah went back into the rain. He gave both Eyanosa and Mateo an apple. "Don't fight." He helped Eli and Sally secure the animals in the rope corral on the knoll. They hauled the tubs of shells out of the wagon and dumped them on the ground then carried the empty containers to the corral to fill with rainwater for the animals to drink. Eli and Sally left their wet ponchos in Noah's hands as they climbed into the wagon.

Lola stated the obvious when they piled in. "It's crowded in here."

218

"I'll keep watch tonight." Noah climbed into the animal wagon. He peered out but saw only a wall of rain.

Inside the other wagon, they stacked everything they could at the ends and then covered the remaining floor space with tarps, mattresses, blankets, and pillows. They tried to sleep, but the night was an eternity of elbows, knees, and feet in the wrong places.

## TWENTY THREE

Raymond rode across the Kuhn Bayou Bridge, built so high that it always provided safe passage. He needed to get out of the deluge and warm up. He knocked several times before he tried the knob. It turned. He opened the door saying, "Anybody here?" Nobody answered. He searched the cabin. *There's almost nothing here. It must be abandoned.*

He looked out the kitchen window. "That's good. There's a shelter. I'd rather not have Sargent in the cabin." He went back into the rain falling so densely that he couldn't see beyond his horse. With the rain beating against his face, Raymond put Sargent in the shelter, and then made his way back to the cabin.

The people who had deserted the cabin had left wood and kindling inside. He squatted and started a fire without putting his hand on the warm stones of the fireplace. Much later, when he did lean against the chimney to throw in another log, the fire had burned long enough that it didn't matter. He sat safe, dry, and finally warm inside the cabin. He ate food packed with love by Adeline. He pulled out the remaining set of blankets from his farm and stretched them out in front of the fire to dry.

He contemplated the two women. *Why don't I take up with Adeline? Lola doesn't deserve to have me.* As he fell asleep, he thought, *no woman's gonna make a fool of me.*

## TWENTY FOUR

In the morning, at the wagon, it still rained a gully washer. They ate cold dill bread with congealed greasy smoked bear sausages, fresh apples, and cheese. The two stallions didn't appear to have fought in the night. Noah assumed they had resolved the dominance issue. They harnessed a new set of animals to the wagons and corralled the rest between them.

To make their stop less visible, Roscoe scattered the piles of shells. *How did they miss that?* He leaned over and picked up a small orb pelted clean by the rain. *Guess they weren't looking for black.* He slipped the pearl into his pocket, dispersed the remaining shells, and then sat in the driver's seat. "Ready."

Eli started forward. The knoll had shed the rain and kept the ground from becoming too waterlogged. Even so, the wagons squished tracks into the wet dirt when they pulled out of the field. The rear wheels slung mud onto the animals corralled behind. Just as fast, the rain washed them clean. Noah slept while they plodded through the depressing weather.

Lola expressed her fear, "I hope all this rain hasn't blocked our way."

Sally replied, "I guess we'll find out."

"If high water stops us, there's nothing to do but wait. Remember what happened before?" Stephanie didn't add more. She didn't want to give away their identities by telling the story of Smitty, Ben, and Roy washing away in the flooded Cadron Creek.

Much later, Eli heard roaring. He was sure of the cause even before Gum Log Creek came into view. He told the dry people inside the wagon, "We have our answer."

"What answer?" Lola inquired.

"Whether or not the rain has blocked our way?" He slowed to a stop. "The road is too narrow to turn around, and the wagons can't back that far. We're stuck."

From between the puckering strings, Ann looked at the water screaming past. "We'll have to wait, even after the rain stops."

"Oh, no!" Lola filled with fear. "He'll catch us!"

Sebastian tried to calm her. "We don't know he's coming this way."

Eli added, "There are a lot of other ways he could go. The chance he picked this specific one is small."

As she had since the first night, Lola demanded, "We have to move on. We've got to cross."

Ann stated, "Not this time."

"He's going to kill us!" Lola warned them.

Sebastian commanded her, "Calm down. We can't cross. You have to deal with this."

"Don't tell me to calm down!" Lola snapped.

Sebastian put on a poncho. "I'll go look at

the creek." He got out of the wagon. "Abraham, will you come?" Out of hearing, Sebastian told him, "She's in a lot of distress. I don't know what to do for her. She was never like this before."

"She went through a horrifying experience. She can't just deal with it."

"Could you sedate her again?"

"We have some. Can you get her to drink it?"

"Probably not."

In the wagon, Sally remembered how she hadn't been able to make herself not be afraid. She believed Lola had suffered too much already. "Lola, something happened to me that scared me badly. I even passed out, thinking I was going into that same kind of situation again. I can't overcome it. I asked to be sedated because I knew we had no choice. I trusted my family to get me through it in an unconscious state. I can do the same for you."

"I won't be able to run if I'm asleep."

"You can't outrun a bullet anyway, but you don't have to irrationally agonize, either."

"I'm not irrational. Being knocked out won't keep him from coming."

Sally knew when a person couldn't overcome. She decided to explain why she understood. "I lost my lantern in a pitch-black cave while alone on a ledge above an abyss. A year later, I needed to go into a cave. Even knowing that people's lives depended on it, I couldn't do it. Instead, I passed out."

"You understand. Sebastian doesn't."

"Even my family, who think they understand, don't really know the power it holds over you."

"I'll trust you. I'm putting my life into your hands because I believe you understand. Give me the sedative."

Sebastian slipped out of his wet covering back into the wagon. "I'm sorry, Lola. I want to help you."

"I know you do. I still think it's a horrible mistake to stay here without even trying to cross or go around or something, but I'm going to drink this." She took the cup from Sally. "Otherwise, I won't be able to keep myself from

226

jumping into the creek and trying to swim across." Lola drank the concoction straight down.

Sebastian sat beside her and put his arm around her. "I promise; I won't let anything happen to you." Lola leaned her head against Sebastian and tried not to think until she fell asleep.

They rigged up a shelter between the wagons to keep the animals out of the rain that had pelted them for over twenty-four hours and then spent the rest of the day in the wagon, believing that nobody would travel in the terrible weather.

## TWENTY FIVE

Raymond glared at the torrential rain on the other side of the window. "I'm not letting Lola get away with tricking me." He opened the door and stepped outside. The biting raindrops stung his face as he pushed against the strong wind all the way to Sargent. The horse refused to walk. "All right, Sargent, you're right. We'll stay until the rain stops." He left Sargent in the shelter and went back to the cabin.

# TWENTY SIX

Beside the flooded creek, Noah dragged out his paper, pencils, and erasers. "It's very unsafe not to be able to turn a wagon around."

He, Roscoe, and Eli had intimate knowledge of the construction of the wagons from installing brakes a few months earlier. They illustrated as they discussed how to solve the problem. Everybody participated in the discussion except Lola, who blessedly slept. By nightfall, they had a plan they thought would work. "When we're in a place where we can do the work, we'll modify the wagons." Noah folded the papers. *Ann and I have to get as far from Judge Hall as possible. Eli's not going without his father, and Stephanie's not going without Eli. The girls will be so unhappy without each other. I really hope Tom will give up his store.*

They spent another squished-together night trying not to be annoyed or to annoy the others around them. Eli and Stephanie decided to take watch duty for the entire night to give the rest of them more room to sleep and to provide the two of them more sleeping space the following day.

During the night, Sally's bony elbow woke Ann. She heard the beautiful sound of silence. *It's stopped raining. Thank you, God.* After the sun came up, she got dry wood from the tarp they had suspended inside the goat wagon and started a fire. The dampness had seeped into all the bread. Ann hated to lose it. She remembered the first breakfast Melvin had prepared for them when she had been a prisoner the previous fall. She milked the goats, set the milk by the fire, and then got the rest of the ingredients ready to cook the bread that would not be savory any other way. She started the bacon frying and the coffee brewing.

The aroma opened Noah's eyes. He pulled on his boots. "Good morning, wife." He kissed Ann's cheek. "That coffee smells wonderful."

Ann poured two cups. "Husband," she smiled and handed him one.

Noah took a sip. "It's nice to have something hot."

It wasn't but a few minutes before everybody sat at the fire, including Lola. She tried to determine the proximity of Raymond. "How long have we been here?"

"One and a half days," Ann handed Lola an empty coffee cup.

Trying to help her not be afraid, Sebastian emphasized his point. "If he was coming this way, he would be here already!"

Eli repeated what he had said before, "I've never thought he was coming this way. He would have gone to Little Rock. That's where you were trying to go in the beginning."

Lola focused on getting the people in control to move on. "Can we cross yet?"

Noah explained the situation again, "It'll be days before the water is low enough to cross."

"Can't we travel up the creek and go around the headwaters?"

Stephanie stated what Lola could see for herself. "We can't get the wagons through the trees, and we can't turn around. We're staying right here because we can't do anything else."

"I can't. He's coming!" Lola again filled with clear and mounting agitation.

Sally reminded her, "We can give you the sedative again. You can eat and such before you fall asleep."

"Not this time. Sebastian, we need to go."

"Eat breakfast and have some coffee before you go." Noah poured the last of the coffee into Lola's cup then sat beside her.

"Can we leave right after?" Lola asked Sebastian.

Sebastian, already seated beside Lola, assured her, "We surely will."

Ann brought Lola a plate of French toast. "Isn't it nice to be out of the rain, drinking hot coffee?"

"Yes. That's nice." Lola ate, drank her coffee, fidgeted, and checked her surroundings. She started to lean. Noah reached over and caught her as Sally took the plate and cup from her hands.

"Much obliged." Sebastian breathed a sigh of relief. "I hate that I lied to her."

Noah replied, "Eventually, she'll understand that it was kind to sedate her again."

Ann took the dishes. "The best thing would be a miracle, so we can cross before she wakes. Let's pray for that."

Sally prayed, "God, don't make Lola go through this terror any longer. Help us cross the creek before she's awake. Let her know that Sebastian did exactly what he told her he would do. He didn't let anything bad happen to her, and he took her across the water after we ate, regardless of how long after we eat that happens to be. We ask for help, in the name of Jesus."

Sebastian prayed too, "God, don't let me have lied to the woman I love. As Nancy asked, get us across the creek before Lola wakes. Please."

All said, "Amen."

Eli stood up. "We can walk along the creek both ways. Let's see if we can find anything helpful."

"Good idea." Sebastian carried Lola to the wagon. Noah got inside and took her from him. He laid her on the mattress.

Roscoe pointed out, "You can search farther if you ride."

Sebastian turned to Eli. "You go upstream. I'll go downstream."

"When the sun is directly overhead, come back." Eli saddled up. They went off in their assigned directions. Everybody else stayed at the wagons, in case Raymond or anybody else arrived.

## TWENTY SEVEN

A hundred miles away in Little Rock, Daniel Hall kissed his wife. "I don't have a choice. I'll be back as soon as I get the hard labor camp under control. You know it will take a determined man like me to get it done." *And I bet I'll find a man willing to kill to earn his freedom.*

Much closer to his quarry, Raymond let the fire in the cabin's front room burn out. The stove's fire still burned. He fried smoked ham and made coffee. All his clothes were dry, packed, and ready to go. He had staked Sargent on a long tether in the grassy field to eat before they left.

Raymond didn't wait for the stove fire to go out. Instead, he closed the dampers to suffocate it. He gobbled the ham, cleaned his pots and dishes, and then packed them. He carried his saddlebag to Sargent, mounted up, and then sat on his horse and thought about his choices. *Should I keep looking for Lola and Sebastian or go home?* He told himself, *the swamp's going to be even more treacherous than before. I'm not going back through that.* That left him one choice. *I'll look for Lola.*

Sargent cantered west until they came to the road to Dover. Raymond stopped. *They'll suppose I'll assume they're going west as fast as possible, and therefore won't think they'd go north. So they'd go north.* He turned onto the road towards Dover.

# TWENTY EIGHT

Sebastian rode east beside Gum Log Creek. He found one tree fallen across the creek that a person possibly could walk upon, but that wouldn't get the wagons across. When the sun was straight up, he turned back.

Eli rode west until he came to a tree that had stood beside the creek for hundreds of years. For the last several years, water had eroded the soil from the tree's roots. The eight-foot-wide tree had miraculously remained standing with barely a grip on the bank. He had an idea. It would only be a short time before the tree fell, so they wouldn't be altering what would happen soon anyway, and it might work. He

237

returned to the wagons. "I think we can empty the creek for a few minutes. There's a gigantic tree that's about to fall. It's practically down already. I think we can push it over. I'm sure it will sink into the creek bottom and be above the water. The water will stop flowing for a minute before it rises over the tree. If we're ready, as soon as the water is gone, you can race across."

"We'll get everything ready before us men go to the tree. You women, get across as fast as you can when the water is gone. We'll walk across on the tree then go northeast until we get back to the road. If we can't get the tree to fall, we'll come back here." Noah gulped the last swallows in his cup.

Sally wanted to try, for Lola's sake, "All right."

They packed everything and walked the goats into their wagon. They put the strongest mules in the harnesses and then tied all the other animals to the back of the rear wagon. Sebastian returned. "I didn't find anything." He failed to mention the tree that could allow access to the far side.

238

Eli tied the little donkeys at the end of the line. "Sebastian, put Mateo in the harness. Come with us."

The men walked west. Stephanie and Sally sat in the seat of the front wagon. Ann was set to drive the other. They waited and watched upstream with their spyglasses. The men seemed to be taking forever. Maybe it was because she had listened to Lola's paranoia. In her gut, Ann felt Raymond was on the way.

"I see what you mean, James." Roscoe looked at the tree.

Noah added, "How did it survive the recent wind and the current water flow?"

Sebastian commented, "Maybe this won't be as easy as you think. As you said, it did survive the wind."

"How are we going to push it, or are you planning to cut it down?" Roscoe asked.

Eli had brought the big two-person saw. However, he planned to use it to make a safe walkway across the creek. "We'll cut down those two tall trees. They'll fall across the creek; then we'll push them together. Abraham, you're

239

the best climber. Would you go up and tie the ropes?"

Noah started up the tree. "God, don't let it fall with me on it." He tied the four ropes very high. As he went back down, Noah fed the lines around branches in a way that he hoped would cause the tree to fall in a direction that would allow them to get out of the way.

Eli and Roscoe already had one of the smaller trees down. Noah rejoined the others when the second tree fell across the creek. They rolled them together. So the trees couldn't move and plunge them into the water while they crossed, they drove pieces of a broken branch into the ground on either side.

On the far side of the creek, they got into position. Eli instructed them, "The branches will be deadly if you don't get past their reach. As soon as it starts to fall, drop the rope and run straight out as fast as you can. Ready? Pull!"

Sebastian strained as hard as he could. He thought his stitches were going to pop. He heard a loud slurping then felt the loss of tension on the rope. "Run!"

To the crashing of breaking wood, the men sprinted away. The humongous tree flattened the forest as it toppled. Tons of wood slammed into the earth. The shockwave knocked the men off their feet. Water and mud spewed yards into the forest when the tree buried deep into the creek bed. Water escaped through the void where the root ball had ripped a hole, but the path out didn't grow fast enough. The water rose behind the tree.

Ann, Stephanie, and Sally felt the quake at the wagons. Stephanie called out, "Get ready!"

Raymond felt the ground move. "What was that?" he said aloud, as unknown to him, the creek emptied.

Noah got back to his feet, "Everybody safe?"

The men reported back that they were. Eli pulled a rope. "Try to get the ropes or as much of them as you can." He walked to the creek and kicked in the log bridge they had made to get across.

Stephanie commanded, "Forward run!" She flicked the reins. The mules were up to a gallop before they hit the almost-dry creek bed. Ann zoomed into the creek at what she thought was the top speed of the miniature donkeys. The animals tied to the back sprinted as they were pulled along. Stephanie and Sally came out the far side and continued to race forward.

Ann looked upstream. The returning water approached rapidly. *We have to go faster.* "Run!" She snapped the leather leads.

Little Jack and Little Jenny could barely run as fast as the rope pulled them. Then, the returning water slammed them. It was too much. They went down. The power of the animals ahead dragged them. Ann had no idea what had happened, but she heard the donkeys braying frantically. As soon as she knew she had cleared the creek, she stopped and ran to the rear.

Sally watched out the back of her wagon. She saw the wagon stop. "Halt!"

Stephanie pulled back. "Whoa." The two women jumped down. Sally reported as they raced, "She ran to the back." They found Ann kneeling beside Little Jack and Little Jenny, lying on the ground.

"What happened?" Stephanie asked.

"They must have been pulled on the ground."

Sally knelt beside Ann and checked the donkeys. "I don't feel any broken bones, but they are scraped up. Maybe they're in shock. We need to comfort them." She sat beside Little Jack, put his head in her lap, and then stroked his face and neck. Ann did the same for Little Jenny. Stephanie sat between them and ran her hands down their backs. Raymond neared as the sisters talked to the donkeys softly and attempted to help them understand that they were all right.

Their men came toward them. They had expected to meet the wagons further up the road. Since they hadn't seen any tracks in the soft dirt, they hurried back toward the creek. They saw the wagons stopped just beyond the water and ran as fast as they had to avoid the falling tree. The women were not at the first wagon. They ran to the second. They weren't there either. Afraid of what they would find, they sped past and then saw the three women, sitting on the ground with the two little donkeys.

"What happened?" Roscoe asked.

Ann again stated what she assumed had happened. Eli pointed out a pertinent fact. "It couldn't have been far. You're barely past the creek."

"I think they're mostly scared," Sally replied.

Roscoe looked. "They're only scratched."

Ann had an overwhelming feeling that they were in danger. "Let's try to get them on their feet. We should get away from the creek."

Raymond arrived at the long, densely wooded curve leading to Gum Log Creek. Roscoe gently pulled Little Jack's halter to let him know to stand. The donkey complied. When Little Jenny saw Little Jack get up, she did too. Noah climbed into the wagon and hunted for Roscoe's buffalo hide. Eli went over to untie the ropes.

"We need to get out of view, right now." Ann's scalp tingled a warning.

Stephanie climbed into the seat of the rear wagon. "Leave them tied. I can get this wagon around the front one and then we'll have them in the middle again." Eli and Sebastion jumped in the back. Ann ran ahead and got on the front wagon with Sally. They rolled forward on the right edge of the road. Stephanie flipped the reins and directed the mules to the left. There wasn't an inch between the wheel's hubs when she passed. Roscoe walked beside his donkeys as they rolled out of view on the same massive curve in the road that Raymond traveled.

Sitting beside Ann, Sally felt very relieved. *We're on the Dover side of the creek. When Lola wakes, Sebastian will have taken her to safety, just as he promised.* The wagons continued to Dover.

Noah, however, remained at the creek. With the buffalo hide they had brought from Pine Bluff, he smoothed away the marks in the soft ground. *From the other side, unless well-trained, no one will see the tracks. I don't think Raymond is, and anybody Judge Hall may have sent is probably too far away to get here before the tracks are gone. I hope we've tricked Raymond and whoever Judge Hall has sent looking for me and Ann.*

## TWENTY NINE

Raymond had followed the tracks from the clearing littered with pearly mussel shells. *Must be them. Adeline said they had lots of animals.* Proud of himself that he had reasoned correctly, he tied Sargent to a tree. *They're trapped at the creek. I'll sneak up and catch her.*

He quietly slipped through the forest. At the creek, he found no wagons. Raymond examined the sharp-edged tracks in the road. *They went into the creek. They sure are stupid. There's no way they could have gotten a wagon across.* He stood up and peered through his looking glass. *They went in, but they didn't come out. As horribly as Lola*

246

acted, *it's right that God drowned her. All I was trying to do was make a nice home for her.*

Raymond headed downstream. *After I find Lola's body, maybe I'll try to convince Adeline to live at the farm, or I could sell the farm and buy Adeline's place. I'm the man. We need to live at my place. Then she could run the inn for me. Besides, she's the sweet one.*

No evidence of a wagon's passage appeared in the creek below the crossing. "They must be small wagons to have been washed such a long way." He continued to search for Lola's and Sebastian's remains. As darkness fell, he came to the lone tree across the torrent of water. He nudged it with his foot. *Seems stable.* He stepped on and then paused. "Wait a cotton-picking-minute! If a wagon came this way, it would've hit this log." He walked upstream a short way and looked at the log through his glass. "Not a mark on it! Where did they go?" *She's still out there.*

With his arms out for balance, Raymond started across the wet tree. Several careful but wobbly steps in, the log rolled. He lunged toward the bank but only ripped a bush from the waterlogged dirt. Sweeping past the bank, he saw an overhanging branch ahead. He set his mind to the task and grabbed.

Having missed his quarry only by yards, Lola's pursuer climbed out the same side from which he had started across. Noah and Ann's hunter was hundreds of miles away but equally unsuccessful. The judge, however, had never considered giving up as an option. Vexed that he had found no offender debased enough to take on his agenda, he didn't speak of his desire to eliminate Noah and Ann. Instead, he rounded up the few men who had incited the others into a minor rebellion at the hard labor camp where men quarried Mozarkite. Judge Hall felt sure that he would find a murderer willing to take on his agenda in the eighth district prison. He commandeered a detachment of soldiers from the local arsenal to escort The Quarry troublemakers and himself to his objective.

# THIRTY

Sebastian knew Lola would soon wake. He drove the wagon with the pucker strings untied and open. Lola opened her eyes in the dark. The last thing she remembered was eating breakfast. *Why is it dark? Why am I lying down?* She felt the wagon moving. *We must have gotten across the creek. Sebastian did it. He promised me, and he made it happen. There can't possibly be a better man.* "Sebastian."

"I'm here. Are you able to come out?"

Lola gingerly made her way to the wagon seat. "Where are we?"

"Right outside of Dover. "

"How did we cross the creek?"

"You wouldn't believe what we did!"

"Stop for a minute. Then you can tell me."

Sebastian called out, "Halt!" Lola painfully got her sore and stiff body off the wagon. "Don't go far," he told her. She was back in a few minutes. "Ready," he called out.

When seven people said, "Ready," they started up again. Sebastian told Lola how they had stopped the creek, and then the wagons had charged across, but they had dragged the little donkeys.

"You did all of that for me?"

"All of us did it for all of us, but I made a promise to you, and I wanted to keep it, so we tried to find a way across, and we did. It wasn't anything I would've ever thought up, but it was incredible. When that tree hit the ground, it knocked me down. There isn't another giant tree there to stop up the creek. If Raymond did come this way, he won't be able to cross for days."

"Did you tell them to sedate me again?"

"I had no idea Abraham was doing that."

250

"I'll have to thank him. I don't mean to be this way. I'm scared out of my mind. I can't go through what happened again."

"I know, my love. We all understand. Nobody is upset with you. These people know how to deal with everything. They knew they needed to help you, and they did."

"It did help me, and now we're safe."

"Tomorrow, we'll find a preacher and get married. Do you still want to go to your grandparents? We might be able to find a steamboat going east."

"We don't have money anymore. We can't expect these people to keep helping us. That's why I wanted so much to find a pearl."

"Me too, but Lily and Marie, who already have everything, were the only people to find one."

"What will we do?" Lola asked.

"I don't know. With Raymond after us, we can't go back to our families in Perryville."

"I'm so afraid. I don't know what we'll do."

"Somehow things will work out."

Ahead, Roscoe conveyed his thoughts, "We

shouldn't go into town. We don't know where to go, we can't discover anything at night, and we can't just stop in the street. We should set up camp in the first place with enough grass."

# THIRTY ONE

Dover was much like any other small town with a store, a saloon, and several homes. It was different in that it also had a county court and records building. Eli followed his usual effective technique. He went to the store to buy a few items and gather intelligence.

The fortyish female storekeeper was more than happy to spread the gossip. "We don't have a preacher here in Dover, but the clerk can do it. He married Gertrude and Harry Pitts over at the courthouse. I'll tell you, that Gertie was madder than a hellcat when she found out Harry had married two other women."

"What did she do?" Eli asked as if it was just a curiosity and not that he was a friend of one of those other women.

"The sheriff of Harmony came here last fall with one of em. I think her name was Minnie. Anyway, come to find out, Harry hadn't even married that one. He just made her believe he did and took her money. That woman's taken up with some young buck and doesn't care beans 'bout old Harry anymore. She told Gertie where she could find Harry. Gertie flew outta here to confront him. Robert tried to stop her, but she was determined. She said she was gonna find the lying, cheating, horrible excuse for a man and ruin his life. She hasn't come back."

Eli made small talk and beat around the bush until he also found out that neither Hank Butterfield, Roy Butterfield, nor any of their friends had been seen in Dover for more than a year. "That ain't unusual, though." The shopkeeper told Eli, "Even when they are here, we don't see much of 'em. Their place is way up on the north road. It isn't in town. I don't

254

wanna claim 'em anyway. I never cared for a single one of 'em."

Eli paid for the molasses, rice, and makeup requested by Sally then rode back to their camp with the knowledge they needed. First, he reported to Sebastian and Lola, "If a civil ceremony is acceptable, you can get married." He then told everybody, "I have a good idea where the Butterfield house is located. It's empty right now." Eli did not pass on any information about the scandal that involved their friends: Smitty, Zachariah, and Minnie.

"James, let's sneak over and investigate the house." Noah picked up his saddle. "Theo and Sebastian, come with us?"

"Maybe I shouldn't leave Lola."

Ann already had a reason for them to leave. "You men go on. We need to plan for the wedding celebration without you listening in."

Sebastian looked uncertain, but Ann shooed them away. "Go on. Get outta here."

The men rode off. Lola turned to Ann. "We probably won't get married anytime soon."

Stephanie asked, "Why not?"

*I don't want to ask for money. A preacher probably would've married us without a fee. I'm sure there's a charge to perform a civil marriage.* "The timing isn't right."

Even though Lola hadn't said anything, Ann remembered the problem she'd had with the fee for her own marriage. "I want to give you a wedding present. I want to pay whatever fees there are for you to get married."

"You don't have to do that."

"I know, but I left you alone with Raymond, knowing he might do all kinds of horrible things to you. I owe you."

"I don't know for sure if Sebastian is ready. If he is, I'll take you up on that offer."

Ann's friend, the sheriff of Harmony, had secured and hidden the record of her marriage to protect her and Noah from the lashings Judge Hall had originally ordered. Judge Hall had believed he had proof that she and Noah had violated the prohibition against interracial marriage. Since the record had not been filed, Judge Hall had changed the sentence to hard labor rebuilding the ferry and dock of the Military Road crossing at Cadron Creek.

256

Judge Hall had also decreed and recorded the annulment of their marriage. That annulment still sat heavy on Ann's mind. Even though they had served the hard labor sentence, Ann and Noah knew Judge Hall wouldn't rest until he had eliminated them. They refused to give up their marriage anyway. "Wonderful. Have a civil marriage and file the papers immediately. Have no doubt that it's real. Then, if the men think it will be safe, we'll celebrate at the house."

Stephanie asked, "What kinds of things do you like?" The four women set to planning.

On the other side of town, Eli stopped in the road. "I think that's the house. The woman in the store said the house had black shutters and a black door, and that it's up in the woods just outside of town."

They hid in the trees and studied the house. Eli looked in a window with his looking tube. "It's the Butterfield house. I see Roy and Hank in a picture."

Noah considered the picture. He had never seen Hank. When Hank had been screaming insults behind him, Noah had not turned around. Then, Roy had knocked him out with a rifle butt. When Noah was conscious again, Hank was already in the ground. "That's Roy. The others in the picture must be Hank, Edith, and their parents."

After they had scrutinized the house for half an hour, Sebastian huffed, "Goodness gracious, nobody's in there playing possum. It's empty. Let's go over."

"Not yet," Noah replied. They circled the house. Noah looked toward the house and away from the house in all directions. "The house is situated for getting in and out without being seen."

Sebastian pressured again, "Then let's go. There's no sense in waiting a month of Sundays! We can sneak over if you want to."

"Be patient," Noah rode away.

"Don't you think he's as slow as molasses?" Sebastian turned to Eli.

Eli replied with his honest opinion, "I do not think we should go over. When Abraham says it's time to go, you can be sure it's safe and that we'll go over by the best route."

258

Sebastian exclaimed, "That's ridiculous! We're wasting time. What does he think, he's an Indian or something?"

Roscoe advised Sebastian, "If it wasn't for his patience, you'd be dead. Grow some patience of your own."

Noah went back to Roscoe, Eli, and Sebastian. "Let's go."

"What?" Sebastian didn't understand.

As they followed Noah into the woods, he explained. "I'm looking for the path he used to get wagons in here."

"The road," Sebastian replied sarcastically.

Noah chose to ignore the snide remark. "Sometimes he would have, but I can tell he also brought wagons in through these woods, and I want to bring our wagons over secretly."

Sebastian grew curious. "What makes you think he brought wagons through the woods?"

"Because of what I know about the family, the objects I see in his house, the space behind the house, and the cut branches on the trees." Noah pointed at branches that had been cut many years before.

When he saw the trees indeed were missing limbs, Sebastian replied, "All right, I believe you." As they wound through the forest, Noah pointed out the places altered by humans. Sebastian was impressed. *I'd never have noticed those tiny changes. Now that Abraham pointed them out, I see them.*

Eli didn't see everything Noah saw, but he had learned how to look and saw many of the signs before Noah spoke of them.

Noah stopped in the hidden wagon trail. "Right here, you can go north or south." They took the left path and came out south of their camp on the road they had traveled the previous night. They rode up the road and rejoined the women.

Noah jumped off Eyanosa and hugged his wife. "Get ready, my love." The women packed while the men got animals into the harnesses. When they headed south, Ann, Sally, and Stephanie thought nothing of it.

"Dover is the other way." Lola stood in place.

Sebastian informed her, "This is the way to

go. He could find the way in a blindfold. Trust him."

When alone, Lola changed the subject, "Lily wants to pay the fees to get married."

"Why?"

"She says she owes me because she could have saved me before Raymond beat me."

"I want to get married right now, but do you want to get married with a black eye?"

"Nancy says she can hide it."

"Let's make sure. I don't want to be thrown in jail because somebody thinks I hit you."

"I'm so happy. We're finally going to be married!"

The wagons stopped at the back of the house. Noah was sure nobody had seen them arrive. He walked straight up to the house and took a key out of a cubbyhole.

Sebastian asked, "How did you know the key was there or even that the house was locked?"

As he unlocked the rear door, Noah explained, "It had to be locked because there are stolen items inside, and I know Hank had planned to be gone for a while. I knew it was here because nobody ever hides a key far from the door it unlocks. This is a good place to put a key to keep it out of the weather, and there is a space in the plants right beneath it."

"Oh!" Sebastian followed Noah into the house. "How do you think of these things?"

Noah put the key into his pocket. "Training and common sense." To be sure all was well, Noah checked every room before he went back to the wagon.

Eli already had the tub of alligator meat at the back. He and Noah raised it out without saying a word. They had grown to know each other, just like Ann, Stephanie, and Sally knew each other.

"When can we go to town?" Lola asked.

"As soon as we chop enough wood. We aren't going to touch a single stick of the wood already here. We don't want to give away that anybody was here," Noah replied.

Eli offered, "Go on. I can do it."

Roscoe held up a palm toward Eli. "Wait a few more weeks. Go find branches. I'll chop them."

Sally worked on concealing Lola's injuries. Sebastian told her, "They'll know something is wrong if she wears that much makeup."

"First of all, nobody in Dover has any idea how much makeup Lola wears at any other time. Secondly, they may not think a woman should wear makeup, but they have no right to tell you what kind of woman you want to marry. And thirdly, Lola either wears this much makeup or wears black eyes."

"You're right." Without saying another word, Sebastian watched until Sally finished. "You're very beautiful, my love!"

Noah asked, "Lily, do you need anything?"

"I told Lola I want to give her the wedding gift of paying for them to get married. She didn't ask for money, but I know they can't possibly have any."

"Wonderful idea! I'll do it."

Ann held Noah tight. "Much obliged. I love you, my husband."

"Are you sure you or your sisters don't need me to do anything?"

"I don't think so. Will it be all right to have a celebration here?"

"It should be."

"We'll get ready. How long will you be gone?"

"Give us four hours." To confuse anybody tracking either group, Noah went up the other secret route through the woods, so they would enter town from the north.

The front entry door into the Butterfield House opened into the living room, which filled the front half of the space between two sets of bedrooms. The back door was in the kitchen, which occupied the left third of the back area between the sleeping quarters. In it, was a cooking stove and cabinets with countertops. The remaining two-thirds of the rear space was a dining room with a table large enough for a dozen people, with an equal number of chairs. Sally commented, "This is a huge house for a single man, or even two when Roy was here."

Stephanie replied, "Charlie, Pete, Ben, Al, and Gus must have lived here too. Let's go over the place with a fine-toothed comb. Maybe we can find something that will help us understand the Butterfields."

264

Sally, Roscoe, and Ann searched the opposite end of the house from Eli and Stephanie. The bedrooms had eight-foot-high ceilings unlike the center of the house where the rooms opened all the way to the roof sixteen feet above. Sally stepped into a bedroom closet. "It's curious the way they built these. They're so deep."

Roscoe agreed, "Leaves a lot of wasted space between the rooms."

Ann knocked on the wall then ran her hand along the corners. She examined the clothes rod held in place with a long peg through a deep bracket. "Or maybe not." She took the few sets of clothes off the rod. "Put these on the bed."

Sally had no idea what Ann planned, but she wanted to be part of the action. "Don't do anything until I'm back." She laid the clothes on the bed and dashed back to the closet.

"Ready?" Ann asked.

"Yep," Sally replied.

Ann pulled out the peg, removed the clothes rod, and leaned it in the far corner. She slid the dowel back in and used it to rotate the bracket like a doorknob. The wall swung away on hidden hinges. "Don't go in! I'll get lanterns!" Sally ran out of the room.

"James! Marie! I need you! Help me get lanterns and matches."

"Lanterns?" asked Eli. "It's the middle of the day!"

"Come on. You'll see." Sally dug four lanterns and a bottle of matches out of the wagon.

Eli stepped into a four-foot-wide, eight-foot-long space between the bedrooms running from one closet to the other. "The house is arranged the same on the other side."

Stephanie perused the items on the narrow shelf that rose to the ceiling. The aroma of the red cedar lining was almost too intense. She opened a box, "Lefaucheux revolvers!"

Eli examined a small crate beside them. "And bullets. There're only three boxes here. The man in Little Rock told us they bought six crates of rounds. Edwin has one revolver and one crate of bullets. A thousand of them are gone."

Sally stood beside him. "That sounds about

right. They shot at least a thousand rounds into our house."

"I think so too," Ann agreed. "I guess this is how 'evil Hank' kept 'good Hank' from knowing anything."

Roscoe called out, "Plus, I've found seven rifles, lead balls, powder, flints, and—"

Just then, Ann made a startling discovery. "Dynamite!" She continued to read the writing on other crates. "A whole lot of dynamite. Why would they need this much dynamite? Or any at all?"

"I don't know, but we better be very careful with these lanterns." Eli retreated with the lantern he held close to the crate to confirm the writing.

"What are these?" Sally unrolled a heavy cloth with several tools in long, slender pockets.

Roscoe took them. "These are lock picks."

Eli looked over his shoulder on his way out. "Let's move everything into the wagon."

Sally quoted her other brother-in-law, "Abraham always says, 'Do what you can with what you have at the moment because you don't know if you'll be able to return later.' There's another latch at this end. I'll go open the wall, so we can take things out both ends."

Eli and Roscoe took the last box of dynamite to the wagon. Ann, Stephanie, and Sally went to see if the other end of the house also had a hidden room. Stephanie stepped into the second secret room. "I guess they were the same man in some ways."

The shelves held pictures of Hank's family, a pair of lady's gloves, and the smoking pipe that Hank's father held in one of the photos. At the far end of the room, a small schoolroom-style desk sat with its top open. Inside were a stack of blank papers, papers already written upon, quills, and bottles of ink.

A lantern hung from the ceiling above the desk. Beside it on the shelf was another lantern, several bottles of lantern oil, a package of wicks, and a large box of matches.

"Should we take this too?" Stephanie asked, "I feel like we're violating Hank's inner being."

Sally suggested, "We should send these to his family."

Ann put the wicks in her pocket. "However, we can use more lanterns, as well as the oil and wicks. I'd like to keep this little table and the chair. We should take everything and decide what to do with it later. Besides, I want to read what he wrote."

"I agree." Eli untied the hanging lantern.

Stephanie stepped out of the room. "I want to search for other secrets."

"I'll go with you." Sally followed.

Roscoe put the giant box of matches in his pocket and left with all the bottles of oil. Ann put the pictures and memorabilia inside the writing desk. Eli set the lanterns on the bedroom floor, along with the desk and the small, intricately carved chair. He closed the door.

"You find anything else?" Eli stepped back into the house after loading the furniture.

"Not yet," Sally replied.

Roscoe advised them, "Even though Hank will never be back to use anything in this house, we should only take things that were hidden. Eventually, somebody will come here. They won't know anybody was here if everything in plain view is still here."

Stephanie said, "Who would know what was here?"

Roscoe clarified, "I mean, we shouldn't take everything. It'll add too much weight."

"I agree," Eli joined the search.

# THIRTY TWO

Noah, Sebastian, and Lola passed under the hickories and oaks behind the Butterfield house. The temperature was lovely. The woods smelled like moist earth. The red-breasted and blue grosbeaks sang. The mockingbirds mimicked the songs of the shiny blue indigo buntings, as well as the red, green, and blue painted buntings that flitted through the woods.

Lola felt the birds sang of her happiness. She would have whistled the same songs if she had known the melodies. Traveling slowly to locate the forest alterations that marked the wagon

271

path north, they still arrived at the road in half the time that Noah had estimated. They looked for something to designate the exit from the road. After they had identified a gnarly tree as the marker, they proceeded to Dover.

Thirty minutes later, the three of them walked into the county clerk's office. Sebastian told the sandy-haired man in the small, moldy office, "We want to get married."

"Fill in this form. There's a desk in the hall. If you want me to marry you, check here. If you're getting married by a preacher, check here. The preacher has to turn in this paper within thirty days." The clerk wiped his nose as he left to retrieve a paper.

Sebastian took the form. He and Lola went to the desk to fill in the blanks.

*I wonder if Smitty filed my marriage papers. He knows how much this marriage means to me.* Noah asked, "Do you have anything filed in this office for Ann Williams?"

The clerk clearly remembered the whole incident involving filing the paper for Ann Williams. The woman with the sheriff who had

272

submitted Ann's document had asked to see a marriage record. That was when Gertie had learned that another woman believed she had married the same man as she had.

"There is a record. Unless I have a court order, I can only give a copy to the people involved."

"Can you tell me what type of record?"

"A land sale."

"Much obliged. How would a person prove who they are to get a copy?"

"Mostly, I know all the people with papers in this cabinet. I don't know Ann Williams. She could get Sheriff Wyman to come here."

Sebastian and Lola came back into the room with the marriage application. Sebastian handed the paper to the clerk who looked it over. "When do you want me to marry you?"

"Now, if we can," Lola replied.

"In Arkansas, there's no waiting period to issue the license or time to wait after issuing it to perform the marriage, but we do need two witnesses." The clerk looked at Noah. "Sir, would you serve as a witness?"

*I should have thought about that. Eli and Stephanie had to have two witnesses. I'd invalidate their marriage by signing under a false name.* "I'm sorry. I can't." He casually walked out of the building but rode away in a heavy sweat. Sebastian and Lola were shocked.

"I'll get some people. The fee is one dollar." The clerk left the flabbergasted couple without a penny to their names.

Sebastian turned to Lola, "Wait here." He stood beside their two horses. *What would Abraham do?* It occurred to him. *Follow the trail.* He followed the tracks of Eyanosa to the store. He went inside. "Abraham, what's wrong?" he asked.

"I don't want to talk about it. Lily told me to pay the fees. I'm sorry I forgot." He handed Sebastian five dollars in coins.

"I appreciate the money, but I don't want to upset you."

"You didn't do anything wrong. Go get married. I'll be waiting on the north road."

"We'll see you there."

Sebastian returned to the courthouse. The

clerk, the clerk's wife, and his brother were already there. Sebastian handed the man a Spanish Piece of Eight.

"Do you have rings?"

"No," Sebastian told him.

"Not a problem. Stand over here." The clerk's witnesses had done this before and were already in position.

"We are gathered together in the presence of these witnesses to join Sebastian and Lola in matrimony, which is an honorable estate, not to be entered into unadvisedly or lightly, but reverently and discreetly. If anyone can show just cause that this man and this woman may not lawfully join together, let them speak now or hereafter remain silent."

Nobody spoke an objection, so he continued, "Sebastian De La Cruz and Lola Davis, I require and charge you both that if either of you knows any reason why you may not lawfully be joined together in matrimony, do now confess. If any persons are joined together otherwise than as prescribed by law, their marriage is not lawful."

Neither of them had any reason to not

marry, so they didn't speak. The clerk continued, "Sebastian De La Cruz, will you take this woman, Lola Davis, to be your wedded wife, to live together in the estate of matrimony? Will you love, honor, and keep her, in sickness and in health, and forsaking all others, keep yourself only unto her, as long as you both shall live?"

Sebastian responded, "I will."

"Lola Davis, will you take this man, Sebastian De La Cruz, to be your wedded husband, to live together in the estate of matrimony? Will you love, honor, and keep him; in sickness and in health, and forsaking all others, keep yourself only unto him, so long as you both shall live?

"I will."

"Sebastian De La Cruz, take Lola Davis by the hand and repeat after me."

John Clark said the required words which Sebastian respoke. "I, Sebastian De La Cruz, take thee, Lola Davis, to be my wedded wife, to have and to hold from this day forward, for better, for worse, for richer, for poorer, in

276

sickness and in health, to love and to cherish until death do us part."

Lola repeated after John. "I, Lola Davis, take thee, Sebastian De La Cruz, to be my wedded husband, to have and to hold from this day forward, for better, for worse, for richer, for poorer, in sickness and in health, to love and to cherish until death do us part."

"For as much as Sebastian De La Cruz and Lola Davis have consented together in wedlock and have witnessed the same before this company, and thereto have given and pledged their troth, each to the other, and have declared the same by joining hands. Now, by the authority vested in me by the State of Arkansas, I pronounce you to be husband and wife and extend to you my personal wishes for a happy married life, and my gratitude for granting me the honor and privilege of extending the marriage rites to you on this wonderful day. Ladies and gentlemen," he paused, "I present to you, Mr.& Mrs. Sebastian De La Cruz."

John handed Lola three sheets of paper. "Read these over. The last two are duplicates."

To any minister of the Gospel or Justice of the Peace legally authorized to marry,

I, John Clark, — Clerk of the County Court of Pope — do hereby certify that bond and security have been taken in my office to issue a license for a marriage shortly intended between Sebastian De La Cruz and Lola Davis. These are therefore to license and permit you to join together the aforesaid Sebastian De La Cruz and Lola Davis in the holy State of Matrimony, according to the rites and ceremonies of your church to which you belong.

Given under my hand,

May 28th, 1840.

*John Clark*

John Clark

I do hereby certify that the within named couple, Sebastian De La Cruz and Lola Davis, were lawfully married by me on the 28th day of May in the year of our Lord, 1840.

Witness: *Madeline Clark*

Witness: *Robert Clark*

Marriage Filed 28, 5, 1840

*John Clark*

John Clark

They handed the papers back. John stated the next fee, "It'll be one dollar to file the marriage with the county of Pope, and fifty cents for the services of each witness."

Sebastian plopped two Liberty Dollars into John's hand. "This is for you." A bit piece joined the silver dollars.

"Much obliged." John put the twenty-five-cent piece in his pocket and the dollars in the cash box. He removed four bit-pieces, handed two to each witness, and then gave the duplicate document to Lola.

The newly-wedded couple walked out of the county building hand in hand, mounted their horses, and rode north with their marriage certificate.

Noah waited at the hidden entrance to the Butterfield House. "Greetings, Mr. & Mrs. De La Cruz."

"Greeting to you as well." Lola didn't question him about deserting them because Sebastian had already told her not to ask.

"Let's go find out what good things have been prepared." Noah rode into the woods.

Lola pointed out, "We're going to be early."

Noah assured her, "It will be all right."

When they were close, Noah halted. He could see his family through the window. Everything looked normal. He told Sebastian and Lola, "Wait in the woods. If I don't salute you, ride away, go on your way, and don't come back."

"We aren't going to desert you if there's trouble."

"All right, this is how we'll do this. If I salute, everything is safe. If I stand at the kitchen window with my back toward it, we're safe, but it's not safe for you, so leave. If you don't see either of these, we're in trouble. Get the sheriff or somebody."

"We'll be watching," Sebastian replied.

Noah rode to the kitchen door at the back of the house and knocked three times with a long pause between each knock. Eli knew that meant Noah was back and everything was safe outside. He went to the door and opened it using their secret procedure. He wrapped his fingers around the edge, so they were visible outdoors, signaling that everything was safe inside. Noah turned to the woods and saluted.

Sebastian and Lola rode out of the woods. Eli told them, "Put up the horses and then come in." He left the door open and walked into the living room. "They're here."

"Good. I was getting hungry," Roscoe replied.

Sebastian, Lola, and Noah strolled into the living room filled with wildflowers. Sally asked, "Are you married?"

Lola looked adoringly at Sebastian. "We are Mr. and Mrs. De La Cruz."

"Congratulations!" they all exclaimed.

"Let's eat. I'm starving." Roscoe led them into the dining room. Along with Roscoe's always requested light and delicious cake, the table held alligator jambalaya and an assortment of other good things to eat.

Sebastian pulled out the chair for Lola, "My lovely wife." She daintily sat. Pleasant laughter and happiness filled the house as they ate and talked.

Ann took Noah to the kitchen and told him

about the secret rooms. He sneaked outside and peeked in the wagon. *We'll have to rearrange.* He went back to Ann. "We don't have to hide this from Sebastian and Lola."

Ann didn't want to speak for the others. "Maybe you should ask the others first. I'm not the only one involved." Noah privately got the opinions of the others. Sally told him, "I'd rather wait until tomorrow. I want this day to be all about Lola and Sebastian." Noah agreed. The rest of the day, they celebrated and stuffed themselves with food.

# THIRTY THREE

Ann made sure Lola and Sebastian slept at the other end of the house. After everybody had retired, she raised the clothes rod, disengaged it from the bracket, and opened the wall.

Sally heard the sound, opened the door on her side, and stepped into Hank's writing room with a lantern. "I wonder why he hung the lantern."

Ann thought about the attic that had been in her home before the Butterfield Gang had burned it down. "It's strange. There's no access to the space above these rooms. There's a lot of wasted space up there."

Noah thought about it. He pulled the string from which the lantern had hung.

*Sprong.* A latch disengaged.

"The end of this shelf could be a ladder." Noah climbed up then raised a section of the ceiling boards between the door and the shelves. He placed it on the side, reached down for a lantern then climbed up and through the scuttle hole.

The only window was in the peak of the roof centered in the outer wall. Thick tapestries hung over every inch of the walls. Four layers of rugs covered the floor, including a cut out attached to the back of the small door. The sixteen-foot-wide by thirty-two-foot-long area spanned the house above the two bedrooms. It had a large bed, a chest of drawers, a floor mirror, and shelves filled with books. Two chairs sat at a large table with writing materials and two lanterns. An overstuffed sofa, wood stove, clawfoot tub, washbasin in its stand, and a chamber pot in a chair also occupied the room.

Sally said, "They must have put this furniture in here when they built the house."

"He would only have a room like this to hide somebody." Ann frowned.

Noah stroked his chin. "I wonder if he has another on the other end."

Ann replied, "Probably. There was a hidden room on the lower floor, but I didn't see a string."

Sally looked at the books. "This looks like one of your blank binders." She took it off the shelf, flipped it open, and read, "This morning, mean Hank brought my food. I hope he doesn't stay very many days this time. I know he'll be back to force himself on me. I don't want to be with him. He's mean and rough. He hurts me. I hate him."

Sally turned several pages then read another entry. "Mean Hank was still here this morning. If I had a knife, I'd stab him. I wish I could get away."

A few pages farther, Sally read, "My favorite Hank brought me supper. I'm glad he's the one here tonight. I'm so happy to be with my husband again. I know he's passionately in love with me. He read a poem he wrote for me. I

286

asked him to let me go. He said he couldn't. If he didn't turn mean, I could still love him. I think he's possessed."

Noah said, "So, he was like different people."

Sally unfolded a paper. "Here's the poem.

"Life was a misery.
Anger filled my history.
Come marry me were the words in the letter.
Nothing could have been better.
Now she fills my life with joy.
I hope someday she will give me a boy.
Honey waits on her lips.
I drink her love in gulps not sips.
In her arms, bliss overtakes me.
Love is the vision I see.
Ecstasy now exists in the nights.
I wake to the most beautiful of sights.
The woman who brings me delight.
She makes my desire ignite.
For her, I would even give my life.
This is to tell you: I love you, my wife."

Ann sighed, "I always thought it was strange that he drew his gun. Surely he would have known he would be shot, and he lay there dead with a smile on his face. I think he did give his life. At least, the good part of him did. It's too bad he had his other side. He could have been loved. I wonder what happened to the woman."

Sally went to the last page. "A new Hank came today. He acted like a boy, he said he knew about the others, but they always held him in. He said he had always wanted me, but he cried for me every time one of them forced himself on me. He told me that he wants me to stay because he needs me, but the others weren't going to let him be with me, so I should get ready to go.

"I asked what had changed. He said he was part of the man who married me, but he doesn't have any control. When they first married me, he thought they were the only ones.

"That was when we lived in the bedroom downstairs. I didn't know about this secret room. When Gus and the rest of the gang came, I met Hank, the outlaw. The man I married

288

hasn't been here for months. Last night was frigid. The outlaw came up to get warm. I snuggled close and put my arms around him because I was freezing. Hank, the boy, told me, 'We felt loved.' He said he had returned with the man I married.

"I remember how sweetly we made love that night. In the morning, the open letter from his father was on the desk below. My husband and the boy read it for the first time. The others haven't come back. The boy said he and my husband are afraid they will.

"As we talked, I realized he was the boy I had known when we were children. I told him: if he wanted me, I would lay with him, and we did. I thought I could make him strong enough to keep the others away. We spent the day reminiscing about life when we were growing up. I love him so much.

"Suddenly, his expression changed. He told me that he loved me much more desperately even than the man I had married. I asked when he was going to let me go. He said he wasn't going to allow that because he needed me too much. He cried and said it hurt him terribly every time I said I wanted to leave. The man I married would never have wept. I don't think I've met this one before. He left, and I'm still here.

"I should have left as soon as my childhood friend said he would let me go, but I loved him, and I wanted him to know."

Since it was the last thing the woman had written, Sally concluded, "I guess she escaped."

Ann told them what she thought had happened, "Everything is clean and put away. I think he released her."

Noah didn't state his opinion. *More likely she's dead. I doubt the boy could have kept the others at bay. The other manifestations of Hank wouldn't have stayed out of it or allowed her to leave, but I've read that letter. It might have incapacitated them.* He walked to the scuttle hole. "Bring the book."

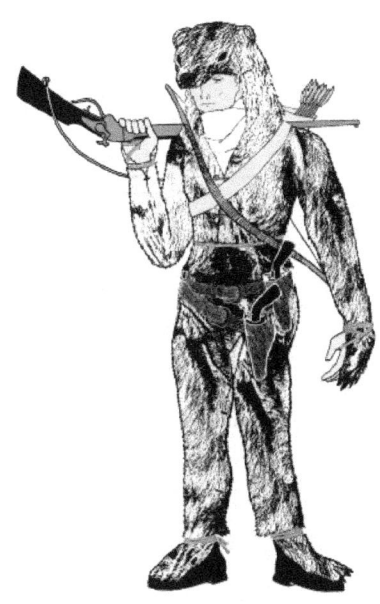

## THIRTY FOUR

After they ate freshly baked biscuits and fried eggs, Eli said, "We found secret rooms. Want to see?"

Lola looked in, "A closet isn't a secret room." Eli removed the rod and opened the door. "Now that's a secret room!" Lola exclaimed.

Eli went inside with Lola and Sebastian while the others remained outside. Stephanie stood in the doorway. "We found family pictures, lady's gloves, a pipe, a writing desk, a small chair, lanterns, oil, wicks, and matches. We put it all in the wagon. There's another room on the other side."

"Is it like this one?" Sebastian asked.

Ann said, "Pretty much, but we found guns, ammunition, and dynamite."

They were about to leave when Noah stopped them. "We discovered something else last night."

"You did?" Eli asked.

Noah reached in and pulled the dangling string. The latch above popped. When they were all in the large room, Sally told them about the diary. She had stayed up the previous night and read the entire journal. "They had her. I guess I should say, 'He had her.' After reading the diary, I think of Hank as 'them'. Anyway, she lived here four months."

Lola knew how horrible that would have been. Even though it had only been a few days, it had also happened to her. "I don't know how she survived."

"You can read this." Sally handed Lola the diary.

Stephanie strolled among the furniture, "Although, this is a nice room."

From reading the journal, Sally knew it

wasn't comfortable. "It's freezing in the winter."

"What about the other end of the house?" Sebastian inquired.

Noah walked toward the way out. "We'll find out together."

As they left the room where the nameless woman had been confined, Sally told Ann, "I want to see that letter from Clarabelle."

"You can see them all. Why?"

"I think he married Clarabelle. When she tried to leave, he locked her in this room."

"So, you want to compare the handwriting?" Ann asked.

"Exactly."

At the other end of the house, they opened the secret room and searched for a way into the area above. Noah and Eli searched above the shelves that could have made a ladder. They didn't find any evidence of a door.

Sebastian noticed that the inch-wide trim failed to extend all the way to the closet. "There's a hole in this. I need something small."

Eli felt the hole. "This must be what that

thingamajigger is for. I'll be right back." Eli returned and handed Sebastian an L-shaped piece of metal. "Since you found it, you open it."

Sebastian inserted the small end into the hole and pulled the six-inch end of the tool. The trim slid out of a slot and swung into the room. He did the same with the trim on the other side then examined the long exposed edge. Halfway along, he once again felt a small niche. He inserted the L key and tried to draw it down with no success. He yanked toward the closet. Nothing happened. He attempted away from it. It slid barely an inch.

"It must have been in a groove," Roscoe commented.

Sebastian pulled down. A crack opened. "Somebody, get your hand around the edge and jerk it down."

Eli stepped on the bottom shelf and pulled. The door swung down, crashed into the opposite wall, and then hung flush on hinges. "This opening is much larger than the other one."

Even though the shelf could support a person, it wasn't in a position to get into the hole. However, it did look like a person could get his hand around the edge. Eli stepped up, held on, leaned out, and felt inside the opening. "I feel something." He tugged it.

"Looks like a ladder." Sebastian reached up to help. "It's heavy."

Noah and Roscoe crowded with him under the opening. When they had the contraption all the way out, they pulled down a set of stairs.

"You first," Roscoe told Sebastian.

Sebastian took Lola's hand. "You second." His eyes rose above the ceiling. He remained silent, entered the room, and then looked down at Lola with his finger over his lips.

They entered the space that matched its counterpart in size, but not function. The shelves, walls, floor, and ceiling were made of cedar boards like the small room below. At the far end, six cedar sawhorses each held a saddle with a bridle lying over it. Many closed trunks sat around under a thick layer of dust. Equally dusty wrapped-up and tied paper packages and boxes of all sizes filled the shelves. A mink coat and several oiled leather slickers hung on clothes trees. Sets of women's and men's shoes and boots sat in neat rows on the shelves.

Roscoe hung his lantern on one of the hooks suspended from the ceiling. "I know it's hot and stuffy up here, but let's go through everything."

Eli opened the shutters of the one tiny window in the peak of the room, "Even with the calming aroma of cedar, I'm mad. It's very distressful that the Butterfield Gang took all this from innocent people."

Lola opened a trunk. "How many people do you think they robbed?"

Stephanie commented without thinking, "This must be why they were so mad at us."

"Why were they mad at you?" Lola asked.

Stephanie realized she had made a mistake. *How am I going to get out of this?*

Noah stepped in, "I helped some people Roy Butterfield had attacked, robbed, and shot."

Sally dragged her finger through the dust on a shelf of bulging drawstring bags. "There's no way to know who owned any of this. We won't be able to give it back."

296

"There's way more than we can fit in our two wagons." Stephanie tried on a pair of shoes.

Sally thought about the woman who had been a captive of Hank Butterfield. "We should write a letter to Hank's mother and sister and tell them that Roy is dead. This house is theirs, unless we can find the woman who married Hank."

"Can we take any of this?" Sebastian asked.

Stephanie had been reading the case law book given to Noah by the brother of one of Roy's victims. As usual, she remembered what she had learned. "We can take what we want. It's stolen, and therefore no more one person's than anybody else's." Stephanie picked up a different pair of shoes.

Noah tried on an oiled leather slicker. "I don't understand why Roy was murdering and robbing people when he had all of this, and he looked half-starved."

"He must not have known this is here." Sally held a bright red silk evening gown against her body. "I'm going to try this on."

Lola thought about Raymond. "Or he liked

murdering, stealing, and watching people suffer."

"Probably both," Noah took off the coat, "This one fits. I'm keeping it."

"I want saddles and bridles that will fit our favorite mules." Eli picked up a saddle to try on Ace. "I'll be back and get another for Redeemed."

"So many trunks." Ann opened another. "I found more letters."

Stephanie spoke up, "I don't want you to read any of them. It's too upsetting. They make me care about the people. I'd rather not know." She remembered something else from the law book. "Anything that has identification, like that trunk with those letters, we have to put aside untouched. It can't legally be taken. Someday, whoever gets this house should return those things to the owner." Stephanie tried on a third pair of shoes that matched the fancy dress she had bought from a friend at Fletcher Creek.

Ann opened a parasol. "If we can find enough, everybody should take one of these."

She was careful not to reveal that they would soon be crossing the prairie under the scorching sun.

Eli plopped a wide-brimmed felt hat on his head, "Or one of these."

"Or both. Don't I look lovely?" Roscoe twirled a red parasol above his head.

Sally came up the stairs wearing the red dress, "You're a silly man!"

Roscoe helped her up the last stair. "You definitely should keep that lovely dress." He handed her the red parasol. "This one matches the dress of the gorgeous young lady. I'll find a different one."

Each of them gathered large piles of clothes for both working and dressing up, along with fancy shoes, walking shoes, and high boots. Lola also took the mink coat. Noah put a chain watch in his trouser pocket. "I'll get the clothes and boots Roy was wearing when Esther shot him. We should leave them here."

"Good plan. I don't like having them," Stephanie replied.

Lola casually suggested, "We could put

together all the money and jewelry that has no known owner and divide the money equally among us. We can draw straws to set up the order of rotation and take turns picking pieces of jewelry."

"Seems fair to me," Ann pulled a bag out of a hidden compartment. "Before we divide the money, everybody should select something to carry what they're taking. I want this beautiful sea chest and this bag." She emptied the contents in the communal pile.

Questions about the way God operates rolled in Roscoe's mind. "Do you think God put all this here because he wants us to have it? It got here because of Hank and his gang robbing people. Surely God wouldn't have made Hank rob people."

Sally stated her opinion, "God didn't make Hank rob people. He's just taking away what Hank got the wrong way and giving it to people doing things His way."

Noah looked through the many pieces in the jewelry pile around which they sat. He took a wide gold armlet. *The wagons we've been using* belong to Roscoe. We can't carry all of this and keep space open for animals. "I saw a sign about wagons for sale. I want to buy one."

"I'd like a wagon too." Sebastian drew a gold wedding ring and slid it on Lola's finger. Lola did the same for him followed by Eli, Stephanie, and Ann, who also selected wedding rings for their spouse.

Noah's turn came again. "I'm picking a ring for Lily, but I'd also like to take this bracelet that matches the one I already have and skip my next turn. Would anybody mind?"

Nobody objected. After divvying out the jewelry and money, Roscoe put his portion of money into the hands of Sebastian. "This is a wedding present."

After they packed everything they wanted and had removed eight full trunks, there wasn't a visible dent in the booty.

They closed the stolen loot room and went back to the other side to look at the books. Noah found the same Edgar Allen Poe book he had purchased for his friend Edwin. He took *The Narrative of Arthur Gordo Pym of Nantucket.* Lola picked *Paul Clifford* by Edward Bulwer, and *The Water-Witch* by James Cooper. Sebastian selected James Kirke Paulding's *The Lion of the West*. Eli decided on *Twice-Told Tales* by Nathaniel Hawthorne. Stephanie took another Poe book *The Fall of the House of Usher*, and *The Legend of Sleepy Hollow* by Washington Irving. Ann saw the name George Byron and decided she wanted *Don Juan* then also selected *The Spy* by James Cooper. Sally picked *Peveril of the Peaks* and *The Talisman* by Walter Scott. Roscoe saw *The Prairie* by James Cooper. "Maybe we should take this one too." He laid it on top of *Old Ironsides* by Oliver Wendell Holmes.

They carried the new books to the wagon then took all the fiction books they had already read into the house and put them on the shelves. Stephanie picked up a bottle of scented water. She handed bottles to Ann, Sally, and Lola. "I think this is fair, considering how many books we've left."

Noah picked up another bottle and walked toward the scuttle hole. "We need to get going. I want to get the wagons and be home before dark. We'll rearrange everything tomorrow."

Roscoe pointed out, "You don't want to be rushed when selecting something as important as a wagon."

"True." Eli closed up the second secret room. "We'll go early tomorrow."

They didn't think they would have to leave suddenly, but the men crammed everything into the wagons in case they did. Meanwhile, the women filled the downstairs bathtubs and heated water on the stove. They all went to bed, smelling like roses, lilacs, or lavender, instead of sweaty people who had worked all day in the treasure room.

Early in the morning, the men went to Dover. The women removed everything from the wagons. Ann picked up Roscoe's satchel of utensils. *This is way too heavy. I don't want to pick this up every time we need something. I'll get out the utensils we use and pack the rest.* Ann opened the satchel, removed several cooking tools, and discovered a sack at the bottom. She opened it then covertly looked around. Nobody was paying any attention. *Now I know why Roscoe insisted on staying with the wagon in Little Rock.*

*He obviously doesn't want anybody to know he has this. I'll keep his secret.* She closed the bag holding what looked like thousands of dollars, put it back under the utensils, got out of the wagon, and then hid the satchel under the stack Stephanie had created for items they wouldn't access until after they arrived at their final destination.

The men came back with a prairie schooner and a smaller farm wagon. Neither wagon had brakes or a cover, nor were they coated in pitch. The two big mules Noah had purchased in Dover pulled the prairie schooner. Two medium-sized mules that Eli had just acquired drew the farm wagon.

"This is all we could get." Roscoe informed the women, "We think we can make them work."

Eli explained, "The goats will go in my farm wagon when we have to carry them. The mules I bought can pull them. After we clean the current animal wagon, we'll have Roscoe's conestoga wagons and Noah's prairie schooner for everything else."

304

Sebastian added, "Abraham said he'd carry our trunks to Fort Smith. I'm going to give him our horses when we get there. That way, Lola and I can take a steamer and go east like we originally planned."

"Perfect." Ann told them, "I want to wash our bedding and clothes, especially the clothing from upstairs. We can use the dirty, soapy water to clean the wagons."

Sally washed floorboards. "This goat urine isn't coming out."

*I don't want to sleep next to soaked-in feces and urine.* Stephanie spoke up. "Let's cover the floor with the tarp that got ruined in the blizzard."

"The good part won't be long enough." Ann continued to scrub clothes on the washboard.

Stephanie didn't give up, "It's ruined anyway. We could cut it and turn the bad part around. It'll go up the side."

Lola suggested, "Or we could put a rug from upstairs in there. Maybe, we should put the tarp and a rug. It would help insulate it and what about Roscoe's other wagon?"

"I'll go ask." Ann went over and explained their plan.

Since the tarps were his, Roscoe's answered, "I don't have a problem with you cutting up the ruined tarp, and you can use one more if you don't cut it up. We'd still have enough to snap together into a tent."

"We can use blankets from the stolen trunks." Sally happily climbed out of the smelly wagon.

Stephanie ascended the stairs behind her sister. "Together, we can solve any problem."

Lola joked with her, "Maybe we can't solve every problem of humanity."

While the clothes and wagons dried, they composed letters to Hanks' mother, sister, and wife in which they explained that the sheriff of Maumelle could verify Roy's death.

The third morning, they rode away on the northern trail through the woods.

# THIRTY FIVE

Three days of Eyanosa and Mateo nipping each other every time Noah wasn't looking wore on everybody's nerves. They were thrilled when they arrived at Harmony. Roscoe prepared to talk with Tom Yates while Eli hid outside of town.

The rest of them headed to the giant cave on the northern edge of what had once been the Williams Farm. "Do you want to go to the farm while we're here?" Noah asked.

Ann said, "I don't know if I can handle seeing the remains, but I don't think I can stay away either. What do you want to do?" She looked at her sisters.

Stephanie answered, "I want to see how Zachariah has things coming along."

Sally said, "I feel like Lily."

Noah still didn't know. "So, are we going?"

The girls looked at each other, before answering together, "We're going."

The girls grew tenser as they neared. Noah spoke up, "We don't have to go."

"Yes, we do," Stephanie told him.

Ann beheld the lush fields, previously charred black by the Butterfield Gang's fire. "I don't know why I thought the fields would still be littered with ashes."

Sally said, "I was afraid of that too. It's so beautiful." She looked at the fields, green with tall corn, and started to cry. That sent Ann's and Stephanie's tears flowing as well.

"What's happening?" Lola asked.

Noah said, "I think we can trust them."

"This was our farm. Last year, horrible, evil men burned everything to the ground," Ann explained.

"Our parents are buried here," Sally added.

"Those men almost killed us, but Abraham

saved us." Stephanie felt grateful for her brother-in-law. "During the fire, he got us into the well."

"Which also nearly killed us when the fire burned up the winch," Noah stated the consequence of that plan.

"We got out," Sally reminded him.

Ann proudly stated, "He even saved Theo."

"How did he save you?" Lola asked.

Roscoe put his arm across Noah's shoulders. "I had pneumonia. Abraham treated me."

"Then we all owe our lives to Abraham." Sebastian hadn't realized that he and Lola weren't the only people.

"Nobody owes me anything," Noah told them.

When almost to the place where the house had stood, Ann exclaimed, "Look!"

Stephanie saw what Ann had seen. "He's building it back!"

A low wall of stones stood on the footprint of the original house. Ann threw her splayed-out body face down in the cleared ground in the middle of the outline. Her sisters did the same.

Noah stayed back and let them have the time and space they needed.

"Our home's being resurrected." Ann sat up. "Come close to me." The sisters sat in a circle, held hands, and looked at each other. "I miss Mama and Papa."

Stephanie looked into her sisters' eyes. "Me too, but I just lost a huge sorrow that's been sitting on my heart."

Sally and Ann replied, "I did too!"

"Let's go to the creek." Sally stood up.

As they walked down the slope, Ann called out to the others, "Leave the wagons and join us!"

Noah was happy that they wanted to include him and started toward the girls. Sebastian and Lola stayed where they were. "Come on," he told them.

"We'll keep watch over the wagons. You go. This is about your family."

"Much obliged." Noah ran to catch up.

Ann put her arm around his waist. "Farm, Noah is my husband now. He would have loved you."

310

"I do love you, Farm!" Noah called out.

"You're so sweet." Ann hugged Noah's waist as they walked.

Sally sat on the creek bank. "Take off your shoes." She dipped her feet in the cool water. The others did the same. "Ann, do you remember last spring when we did this?"

"I will never forget spending that beautiful day with my wonderful sister, Sally, while my other wonderful sister, Stephanie, explored the cave with our future husbands."

"Eli kissed my ear and held me close when we rode to the cave. I knew then that I loved him."

"Even though he stole your peppermint when you were children?" Noah teased her.

"I'd give him thousands of peppermints to have him," Stephanie replied.

Noah became somber. "We men aren't as hard and practical as you might think we are. I'm not saying that you wouldn't, but make sure you tell him."

"I do, but I will, and I love you too. I'd give up a ton of peppermints to have you as my brother-in-law."

"I'm glad you told me. I want my sisters to be happy with me."

Ann whispered to Noah, "Your wife has given up everything to have you."

Sally flicked water with her toes. "Noah, I remember the deer you shot."

"That was very impressive shooting." Ann joined Sally's toe maneuvers.

After an hour reminiscing with their feet in the creek, Sally said, "Lola and Sebastian probably think we've died."

Noah assured her, "Take your time. It's all right. We may never be here again."

Stephanie sighed. "Look at the fields. With the bluestem grass and crops covering the rolling hills, it's beautiful again."

"The most beautiful place in the world," Ann asked her husband, "May I carry dirt in my medicine bag?"

"I'm sure that's acceptable."

"That way, I'll always have some of home." She scooped up a handful of dirt and rolled it up in the sleeve of her dress. After several more minutes, Ann stated, "We'd better move on."

312

Sally drew her feet out of the water then lay back in the grass. "First, we need to let our feet dry. Then, there's one more thing we need to do."

"Does the sky look bluer here?" Stephanie basked in the pleasure of being home.

Ann looked carefully. "I believe it does."

After they put on their shoes, they walked to the graves of their parents. Stephanie spoke to the gravestones. "I'm glad you're both with Eli's mother."

"And that you're all with God." Ann voiced her agreement.

Sally said, "I am too."

Noah echoed the sentiment. "I'm happy that I got to meet you." They all believed that Noah had talked with Chris, Emma, and Hattie when he had fallen into the river at Pine Bluff and then frozen and temporarily died.

After they had spoken to their dead parents, they walked to the place where the barn had stood. Noah spoke of the horse he had ridden from his home in Indian Territory. "Arabella, words can't express how horrible I feel that you're gone. I'm so very sorry for what happened. I miss you more than I can explain." Noah also apologized to the spirit of the horse, Dusty. "I'm so sorry I got you back from Roy, only for Gus to burn you alive."

Ann knelt and lovingly stroked the ground. "He was so happy when he came home and saw us."

Sally added, "Also, when he saw Samson."

"At least he was happy again for a while." Stephanie put her hand on Ann's shoulder.

Ann let her anger rise. "I know they're dead. I still want to wring the necks of those men."

Noah squatted beside Ann and gently put his hand on hers. "God made them pay for what they did. The only one we don't know about is Ben."

Ann rose to her feet. "He repented. I think God sent him home to live as a decent man."

"I hope so." Stephanie had led Ben to God on the way to Little Rock. He had seemed like a different man before he had washed away down Cadron Creek with Smitty and Roy. They knew Smitty and Roy had survived. They believed Ben had too.

Ann ambled to the well. The roof that had collapsed during the fire had been rebuilt. "Goodbye, well. Thank you for saving our lives." As she got tin cups from the wagon, she went back to being Lily. She told Sebastian and Lola, "Come have some of the best water you've ever tasted."

Lola thought, *it's just water, but it's their home.*

Sebastian walked to the well. *All of their bodies have been in it. I'm not sure I want to drink any.* He brought their two cups anyway.

*Lily's right, it's delightful.* "Do you have more in the bucket?" Lola held out her cup.

"I'll draw again." Sally lowered the bucket to the water. She heard the splash sooner than she had expected. "The water's up!" She poured everybody another cupful.

After her second cup of water, Ann said, "Goodbye, wonderful place. Be good to Zachariah and Minnie."

They went to Rock House Cave and drove all four wagons in side by side. Even with her fear of caves, Sally had no problem going into the large open recess in the mountain ridge.

## THIRTY SIX

Eli could hardly contain himself. He wanted to run to his father. He knew he couldn't and sent Roscoe in alone. Roscoe saw the sign, Yates Mercantile. Just as Eli had described it, the town was no more than a dirt road with two short rows of buildings and wooden boardwalks that ran from one end to the other.

The saloon stood across the street from the store. On the same side as the saloon, after a personal home, Roscoe saw the plaque that read, Dr. Gridley. Beyond the doctor, more buildings looked like homes. Then, at the end of the street, he saw an opening large enough for a wagon.

Roscoe opened the door of the store. A man turned when Roscoe stepped inside. *That can't be Tom Yates. Eli said his father looks like him.*

"How may I help you?" The storekeeper limped to the most recent stranger in town. Lately, outsiders had not been rare in Harmony. A federal marshal had been there looking for Noah Swift Hawk and Ann Williams. The shopkeeper couldn't imagine any of them breaking a federal law, but he had told the marshal the truth: the last time he had seen them, they were leaving with the town sheriff and men accused of burning down the Williams Farm.

After him, a young fellow had come looking for the Williams family. He had stayed until the soldiers arrived and arrested him for being AWOL. They had taken away a wretched man, not because he would spend time in jail, but because he hadn't found Sally. The AWOL soldier had left a message with the saloon keeper. He had insisted that it was a matter of life and death, and had asked Joe to tell everybody in town that soldiers would keep returning until they found Noah and Ann, and to warn the family to keep hiding and stay away from Harmony.

The slender man with a slightly wrinkled face, short grey hair, and hazel eyes, who had just entered the store, was the most recent newcomer. The storekeeper thought, *that man must have worked hard his whole life. He looks sixty, but he sure is in excellent condition.*

The stranger stated why he was there, "I'm looking for Tom Yates."

That wasn't close to what the storekeeper had expected. He had thought the man would ask about the Williams girls and the young men who had left with them. "Mr. Yates has gone east. I'm running the store."

"He's gone east?!" The unknown man looked flabbergasted and irritated. "For how long?"

"I don't know. He went to visit his folks."

"When was that?!"

"Early this spring."

Without another word, Roscoe walked out the door. *Why didn't God keep Tom here? Why is*

318

*He tearing apart this family?* He went to the livery, which was right where he had been told it would be. A well-muscled, blond-haired man worked the forge in the back of the livery.

"Greetings!" Roscoe called out.

The man was at a critical point in the work he was undertaking. He didn't stop. "What can I do for you?"

"Are you Smithfield Wyman?"

Pretty much nobody called him Smithfield. "Yes."

To be sure he was talking to the correct person, Roscoe asked, "What happened to the oldest sister on the way to press charges?"

Smitty put down his hammer. Nobody except himself, Zachariah, and Minnie knew anything about what had happened to Ann. "She was almost strangled with a chain by Gus."

"Had to be sure," the stranger replied.

"What do you know? Is everybody all right?" Smitty hoped his friends were well.

"They're all fine and all together."

"All five of them?"

"With me, we are six."

"I'm so glad!" Smitty exclaimed.

"What is the situation here?"

"People have come looking, but nobody's been here since April."

"Is it safe for them to come into town for a short while?"

"I think so," Smitty told him.

"Eli may be here in a few minutes, but maybe not. He wanted to see his father. The others won't come until tomorrow."

"Tom isn't here. When they didn't come home last winter, we thought they had died. Tom was heartbroken and left in early March."

"Do you think he's coming back?"

"He said he was. He has a lot of money and time invested in the store. Plus, he still hopes his son will come home."

"I'll tell Eli. He'll probably wait and come into town with the others."

"May I know your name, sir?"

"Roscoe Bacon."

"Pleased to meet you, Roscoe Bacon. Much obliged for the good news."

"Don't pass the news on to anyone."

Smitty agreed, "I won't."

Roscoe mounted up and rode back to his friend. He knew Eli was going to be extremely disappointed.

The second he saw Roscoe, Eli asked, "Is it safe for me to go? How's my father?"

"It's safe, but your father isn't there."

"Where is he?" Eli's heart filled with fear.

"He went east to see his parents."

"Did he leave me a message?"

"I don't think so. When you didn't get home last winter, everybody thought you had died."

"I understand. Let's go to the cave."

"Don't you want to go home?"

"It's Pop that made it home. Without him, home is with my wife and our family." *This is what I've been dreading. Stephanie won't be happy without her sisters, but I'm not leaving without Pop.* At Rock House Cave, Eli told the others, "I have to wait. Go on without me."

Noah offered the compromise he had known he might have to make since the previous winter when he had reunited with his family. "We'll wait for you in Indian Territory."

"We don't know how to find your home," Stephanie replied.

Noah already had a plan for that as well. "Until next spring, I'll come to Fort Gibson the first day of every month to look for you."

Sally said, "Let's at least go to town tomorrow and talk with everybody before we go."

"Nancy, don't you want to stay here?" Stephanie asked.

"I've been thinking about this. I love everybody so much, and I don't want to be without any of you. It's not about wanting to be with Ann more than you. Harmony is too close to home when I'm not able to be home."

Stephanie felt the same way. "I understand." Because of her secret, it hurt more to lose her sisters. *I'll be alone. I'm scared.* She prayed. *God, please bring Tom home right away.*

Ann and Sally stuck close to their sister for the rest of the day. Ann asked Noah, "Would you be upset if I don't sleep beside you tonight? I want to be close to Marie."

"Of course not."

322

Ann then asked, "James, would you mind if I sleep next to Marie? I'm going to miss her so much."

Eli knew it would be difficult for them. He felt guilty for making it happen. "I don't mind."

To the extent that they could sleep when all three girls were upset and sad, the sisters slept close together.

Even if only for a short while, they were going to part. Eli went to Noah in the morning. "I don't think I can go through with this. They're so unhappy."

"Hopefully, it won't be forever. Your father is just as important. Even though it will be very upsetting, we'll all be able to do it."

# THIRTY SEVEN

Smitty failed to keep his word. The town was currently safe, so he had spread the news. Everybody waited in the street. When they saw the wagons, they repeatedly yelled, "Welcome home!" until all four wagons and forty-one animals had filled the street from one end of town to the other. Eli felt overwhelmed. "I'm glad to be home."

Laura, the daughter of the town's doctor, hugged Eli. She didn't let go. "I've missed you, Eli."

Eli promptly informed her, "I'm married." He wasn't interested, but he was surprised.

Laura had always treated him as if he was miles beneath her station in life.

Laura said, "Did you marry that farm girl? What's her name, Stephanie? I see she's trying to act like a woman and finally wearing a dress."

Stephanie was ready to fight, except for her secret. She walked away but heard her husband speak. "I did. I got the best woman in the entire world to marry me."

Stephanie appreciated him standing up for her. *He's perfect.* She noticed Minnie. "You're having a baby! This is wonderful!" *I feel so much better.*

Eli joined his wife as Stephanie told Minnie, Zachariah, and the rest of his family, "We went to the farm. We saw you've planted all the fields and you're rebuilding the house."

Zachariah replied, "The whole family is moving to the farm after we finish the house."

"I'm glad. I feel that my home survived."

Earl hobbled over. "Welcome home, Eli. I have a message for you from your father." He handed Eli a letter. "Your father believed you would show up eventually."

Eli silently read the letter, folded it, and put it in his pocket.

Zachariah said, "Excuse me a minute." He hurried over to Noah and Ann who were getting the animals into the corral with Sally, Lola, Sebastian, and Roscoe. Zachariah called out, "Noah. Ann."

Lola asked, "Are those your names?"

They had hoped they would be able to maintain their aliases. Too many names were flying around. Given the current situation, there was no way to preserve them. "Yes," Ann replied.

"Hello, Zachariah." Noah exited the corral.

Sebastian put Mateo and Honey Dew in one of the stalls in Smitty's livery before he and Lola went with Dr. Gridley to have their injuries examined.

Zachariah took Noah and Ann aside. "I want to apologize to the two of you for the way I acted when we were going to Little Rock."

Noah told him, "You don't need to apologize. I understand. Ann is a very desirable woman."

"Still, I behaved poorly and selfishly, but I'm glad you married Ann. Now I have Minnie, and we couldn't be happier."

"I'm so glad." Noah had noticed Minnie was very pregnant.

Zachariah turned to Ann. "You are very beautiful and intelligent, but you're a wild woman. You'd have been too much for me. However, you're perfect for Noah. I'm sorry I tried to keep you two apart. I know that upset you a lot. Will you forgive me?"

"You're forgiven." Ann wasn't going to tell him he didn't need to apologize because she thought that he did. He had made her very miserable, but she was willing to forgive him since he had apologized.

Noah was very curious. "Tell us what happened in Dover. We were told that you, Minnie, and Smitty created a huge upset. We didn't pry for information because we didn't want to draw attention."

Zachariah related what had happened.

***

The Williams' sisters had sold their burned-up farm to Zachariah. To record the deed transfer, Zachariah and Minnie had followed the Sheriff of Harmony into the clerk's office in Dover. Smitty had asked, "Do you accept documents from either Harry Pitts or Harold LeBarron?"

The clerk had replied, "I know Harry Pitts, but I haven't seen him in a very long time. I assumed he was out of the business."

Smitty handed him the transfer of deed, along with the note Minnie had written and signed as Harry Pitts. The clerk looked it over. "I'll just be a minute." He left the room.

Zachariah had assumed the man was comparing the signature to a previous document. That was until a woman stormed in and demanded information. "Where is my husband?!"

Zachariah had asked, "Who's your husband?"

As if the words were poison, the red-faced woman spat out, "Harry Pitts."

"He had a third wife?" Almost not believing, Zachariah had told her what he knew. "I saw him in Little Rock as a barrister named Harold LeBarron. He has a wife and a baby."

The woman had called Harry every name your mama wouldn't want you to hear. Then, Minnie had lowered the boom. "And I thought he had married me. He used the money my father left me to build the toll bridge."

Shaking with rage, the woman ordered the clerk, who had returned not long after she had arrived. "Look it up, John!"

John went to the back to look for a record of a marriage between Minnie and Harry. He had to scream, "Gertie!" to get her attention over her tirade. When she turned, he said, "Only marriage filed for Harry is with you."

Gertie told Minnie, "I'm sorry he did this to you. When did he pretend to marry you?"

Minnie sympathized with her fellow victim. "April 2nd of 1836, but don't be sorry. You didn't do it. He did."

Gertie had explained what had happened in her marriage. "That's the year he told me if I didn't make him a baby, he was going to find somebody who could."

Minnie let the cat out of the bag, "That explains why I never got pregnant. He's the one who's sterile, and that baby in Little Rock probably isn't even his."

Gertie had raged around the clerk's office, knocking over chairs. "I'm going to Little Rock to ruin his pretty little life with his latest victim."

Minnie tried to calm her. "I've been thinking about this since Zachariah told me about Harry. You'd be ruining the life of that innocent baby. Just go on with your life and forget him. That's what I'm going to do."

Gertie's tears had flowed. "You're not married to him, I am. I'm not free to go on with my life. He's already cost me one man." She'd looked into John's eyes then flew across the room. "I'm going to Little Rock!" She stormed out of the building.

The clerk had blinked back his own tears. He held out the note supposedly from Harry. "Is this real?"

Minnie had always been the one to do the forms. Even though Harry had submitted them, she had signed his name every time. "It's as real as any other paper he filed with you."

Moisture threatened to leak from the clerk's eyes. "I'll record and file it." He'd hurried to the back room.

When the clerk finally returned, Zachariah asked, "Can you marry Minnie and me?"

John replied, "That's definitely something I can do."

***

Zachariah wrapped up the story. "He married us. As you can see, we proved it's not Minnie who can't have babies." Zachariah rubbed Minnie's belly. "Right, little guy?"

Minnie reminded him, "The little guy may be a girl."

"That's fine with me too." Zachariah looked as happy as a man could be.

Noah told them what he knew. "Gertie wasn't back in Dover when we were there."

Minnie repeated, "I told her to leave him alone and go on with her life."

Sally, who had also listened to the story, imparted her thoughts, "Trying to get even never works out well."

Noah, Ann, and Sally saw Smitty and his wife, Mara. They went over to speak with them. Mara asked, "Will all of you have dinner at my house?"

Ann replied, "We'd love to, but I don't know what anybody else has planned. I'll find out and let you know."

"I have some news," Mara whispered.

"What is it?" Sally asked.

Mara stepped out from behind Smitty. "After all these years of trying, we're going to have a baby."

"That's wonderful!" Ann and Sally both exclaimed.

Smitty explained, "Doc told me I was always too hot around the forge. After being away for months, everything was right when I first got home. Guess I'll have to stop working for a while to have another."

Noah said, "I never knew that would matter. I'm going to see if it says anything about that in any of my books."

"Maybe Doc Gridley will let you look at some of his books. I figure he must have read it in one of them."

Noah had lived with Doc and Nellie for a short time while recovering from the blow to his head. He had a special fondness for them. "I'm going over there now. I want to say hello to him and Nellie." Noah saw Nellie and walked over. "Give me a hug."

Nellie was happy to oblige. Noah was such a nice young man, and she had so enjoyed him when he had lived there. Nellie came right out and stated what she had concluded during the short time Noah had been home. "So, you married Ann."

"I did, and we're very happy."

Nellie informed him of her foreknowledge. "I knew you would. I'm happy for you both, and it looks to me like Eli and Stephanie are together."

Noah confirmed Nellie's suspicions. "You're a very observant woman, and also correct."

At the corral, Sally and Roscoe explained why six of the mules looked pieced together.

Ann went with Joe to look at his saloon's floor where she had led the attempt to save Noah when he had lain there bleeding. Joe pushed open the swinging doors. Ann stepped inside and saw that the bloodstain had become a permanent part of the saloon. "Why don't you sand it away?"

"I want it to be there. When I tell people about the shootout and attempted murder, I point at the bloodstains on the floor."

"Everybody here knows Hank was shot dead and we barely saved Noah. They all know the blood of those two men covered this floor."

"But other people don't."

"What other people?" Ann didn't think anybody who didn't live in town or around it ever came to Harmony.

"A federal marshal came here looking for you and Noah. Then, there was the soldier boy who was here looking for you. Next, other soldiers came to get him and wanted to know what we knew about the whereabouts of the rest of you. They hauled away the first soldier who came here."

334

"The first soldier who was looking for us, was his name Melvin?" Ann asked.

"Sure was. He seemed like a nice young fellow. He stayed here three weeks, hoping you'd get here. He asked me to hide him, but I didn't. I told him I had no place to hide anybody. When he begged to be able to write a letter, I realized he was here because he wanted to be with Sally."

Ann's chest constricted. "I'm so sorry we didn't get here in time." *I don't want Sally's heart to be broken again. It's my fault. I just had to stay for that dinner party with Martin and Dollie Harrow.*

"They let him write the letter before they took him back to Little Rock. I felt horrible that I hadn't helped the boy."

Ann blurted out, "I have to go!" pushed open the swinging doors, and ran out. *I have to find Noah.* He wasn't in the street. *He must've gone to visit Doc and Nellie.* She ran down the boardwalk and knocked on their door.

Laura opened the door. "Yes?"

"Is Noah here?" Ann asked.

Laura replied, "He is," then continued to stand in the doorway.

Ann eyebrows furrowed. "May I come in to speak with him?"

"Of course," Laura stepped back, so Ann could enter. "Why did you cut your hair?"

"It's more involved than this, but I did it because I miss my parents."

"A woman should have long hair and wear a dress. You don't seem to be able to get it right." Laura took Ann to the examination room where her father was looking at Noah's head. Lola and Sebastian were still there.

Ann ignored Laura's comment. She didn't care about her opinion. With apparent anguish, Ann said, "Noah, I have to tell you something."

Doc asked, "What's wrong?"

"Melvin came here looking for us, actually for Sally. He was going to run away from the army to be with her. They found him and took him back in chains. He left a letter for Sally. It's going to rip her heart out."

Noah tried to comfort his wife. "It's upsetting you, it's upsetting to me as well, and it's really going to upset Sally. But maybe it will be good because she'll know he chose her." Ann stood in the room not feeling comforted. "Come here." Noah held his arms open.

The doctor stated the truth. "There's nothing you can do for a person with a torn heart, except love them and be there for them."

Laura still stood in the doorway. "She should feel happy. She has somebody who loves and wants her."

Ann hoped so. "Maybe she'll look at it that way."

Laura suggested, "You should read the letter first. Then, maybe you'll know what to do?"

Noah flatly rejected that idea, "Absolutely not. It was written to Sally. We'll have to help her however we can."

"Let her find out on her own," advised Sebastian.

Ann replied, "I guess you're right. It's just that I wish she didn't keep getting hurt, especially because of why we missed him."

"We can't change anything." Noah held Ann.

Over at the corral, Horace asked Sally and Roscoe, "What did you do to make so many people come to town trying to find you?"

"Who came here?" Sally asked.

Horace's wife, Betsy, told Sally, "A marshal and some soldiers."

Sally assumed Judge Hall had sent all of them. "Didn't Smitty or Zachariah tell you everything?"

Smitty shifted from foot to foot. "I told them we weren't successful, that Gus had died on the way, and the other two had gotten free."

Zachariah held Minnie's hand. "I told them that we met Minnie on the way and the two of us realized we wanted to be together, so I left to marry her on the way home from Little Rock. The rest of you were working on a construction project for the state and would be home later."

It wasn't Sally's story to tell. She figured Zachariah and Smitty had thought the same. "I think Ann and Noah should tell the story."

Patty stood beside Zachariah. "We're curious about what happened. We were surprised when our son came home a married man and the owner of your farm. Where will you live now that you've sold your farm?"

Sally felt uncomfortable under the questioning. "Everything hasn't been decided. Excuse us, please. I want to find out what Doc thinks about Lola and Sebastian's injuries." She took Roscoe's hand and hurried to Doc's office. She opened the door and stepped inside. "It's Sally and Roscoe."

"We're in the exam room. Come on in," replied Doc Gridley.

As if it was a personal insult, Laura stated, "You cut your hair too!"

"How is everybody?" Sally entered the room, followed by Roscoe.

Doc stated his professional opinion. "Everybody should heal up fine. That man who shot Sebastian because Lola didn't choose him and then beat on Lola, he should be jailed."

"What about Noah's head?" Sally asked.

"His skull bone knit back together fine, and the skin is healed. Of course, he'll always have the scar. I even believe his brain didn't get completely scrambled."

"You're horrible, Doc," Noah chided him.

Sally sensed a lot of tension in the room. "Then, what's wrong?"

Ann decided to tell Sally because she was going to find out anyway. She held both of Sally's hands and looked into her eyes. "Melvin came here looking for you. He wanted to go with us, with you I should say, but they found him and took him back to Little Rock in chains for being AWOL. I'm really, really sorry."

Sally tried to absorb the news. "He's in jail because I asked him to come with me?"

"I'm sorry," Ann repeated.

Sally knew Ann was blaming herself. "This is not your fault. Don't tell yourself we could have been here sooner. Those people needed us. God sent us there to help them. He just made it happen through you."

Ann hugged her sister. "Still, I'm very sorry."

"I am too. I want to be alone for a while." Sally walked toward the door.

Ann told her sister, "Go see Joe. Melvin left you a letter. If I can help, I will."

340

"You can't." Sally left the room.

Ann turned to Noah with tears in her eyes. "She's losing him again. I'm so sorry."

"I know. Come on. Let's go talk." Noah took Ann by the hand.

Roscoe stood abandoned in Doc's office. "Hello. I'm Roscoe Bacon. I need to thank you for saving Noah and giving me a family." He held his hand out to shake Doctor Gridley's hand.

"Lawrence Gridley," he replied as they shook hands, "but folks call me Doc."

Sally went to the saloon. "Please rent me a room."

Joe said, "You can stay in a room for nothing." He handed her the letter. "This is for you."

Sally took the letter. "I'd like to rent it and have a hot bath. Do you have lilac-scented toilet water?"

"I'll get the bath set up with the scented water." He collected forty-two cents and handed her a key.

"Much obliged." In the room, she stared at

the unopened letter lying in front of her on the table. *I should rip it up and not even read it. He's going to beg me to come to him.* She continued to be unsure about reading the letter. It upset her that he had tried to find her and had paid the very price he had told her he would pay. Mostly, her heart was gushing emotional blood because she missed him terribly. *He's sitting in jail. I should at least read the letter.* She heard a knock.

"Water for the bath," Joe called out.

Sally unbolted the door. "I'll leave it open for you." She continued to stare at the letter that threatened to jump off the table and destroy her.

After multiple trips, the hot bath was ready. The letter remained unopened. Joe saw it. "He begged me to hide him, but I didn't know who he was. We all have regrets." He left the room.

Sally was tense in every muscle of her body. She undressed and tried to soothe her mind by enjoying the scented bath. It barely touched the edges of her frayed mind. *I don't know what I can do, or change. Melvin ignored the cost and made me his choice. I can't do the same. I'm cold-hearted.* When the water was too cold to be comfortable, she got out and lay on the bed. The day was hot, and the room was warm. Blessedly, she fell asleep.

## THIRTY EIGHT

Ann and Noah slipped into the wagon. "I know I need to stop thinking that everything I wish didn't happen is my fault. But this time, I know it is."

Noah said, "You're being too hard on yourself and Sally's right. God took us to Fletcher Creek to save twenty-two people. They didn't starve, they learned how to live in the woods, and now they'll all get an education as well."

"Plus, you helped Esther and Candace after Roy Butterfield shot them," Ann added to the list of good things that had happened because of the way they had fled Little Rock.

344

"Edwin and his family are much better off working for Murray, and I think Murray and Candace may get married. I saw the way he looked at her and how concerned he was about her."

"But Melvin is in jail because he fell in love with Sally when we rebuilt the ferry and because we didn't get here for months."

"I don't want him to be in jail either. We didn't make him come here. He chose that all on his own. I'll tell you one thing: God has used all this to show me what comes from being prideful. I need to be careful about that. I was starting to forget it again. This reminded me to be so very careful about the decisions I make."

Ann confessed, "Me too." She knew pride had also been and was still a snare for her. "But I have the best possible antidote for what ails me, and that is you, my husband."

"I'm glad you think so. I try to be what you need. You do the same for me, and you make me a better man." After cuddling for a few more minutes, Noah said, "We should tell Eli and Stephanie about Melvin."

"I agree."

So they didn't get sidetracked by more people, they sneaked around the outside of town. They arrived at the store's back door and walked in. The bell on the door jingled. Earl, his wife Clara, Eli, and Stephanie came into the store.

Ann said, "There's something we found out that you should know. Melvin was here. He went AWOL, I assume to go with us, so he could be with Sally. They caught him and took him back to Little Rock. He left a letter for Sally. She has it. She's taken a room at Joe's."

"Should I go talk with her?" Stephanie asked.

"She wants to be alone."

Eli pulled an envelope from his pocket. "And Pop left a letter for me too."

Earl related what he knew about the situation. "I knew the soldier was here looking for you. If I'd known he wasn't trying to capture you, I could have hidden him."

"Eli, what did your father tell you?" Noah asked.

346

"He said he was worried about me and missed me very much. He now knows how his folks have felt for the last two decades since he ran away with Ma. He said that he needed to make things right with them. He wished I had been here, so they could meet me, but he felt that he shouldn't wait. He'll come home when he can. The timing depends on what happens with his folks. He said he wants Earl to keep running the store until he returns because he has an agreement with him. Pop hopes I'll understand and not be upset."

Ann's shoulders slumped further with more emotional weight. "I'm sorry we made you miss meeting your grandparents."

Eli discerned that Ann felt responsible. "I never had any expectation that I would meet my grandparents, so don't be upset."

Stephanie clarified the situation, "It only means that Eli and I will have to stay here for a while."

Ann dejectedly stated, "I know," then asked Noah, "Can we stay until tomorrow or should we leave today?"

*It's going to be hard enough for them without making them separate immediately. Even though this is the most likely place to be caught, it's worth staying.* "We'll stay. I need to talk with Doc again. Do you want to wait with Stephanie?"

"Yes, I'll stay here."

Noah showed Doc the medical walking cane Stephanie had given him, as well as the other tools he had bought in Perryville. "Do you have any books you'd sell that would help me use these?"

Down the dirt road, Zachariah and Minnie stood in Smitty's doorway, speaking with him. After they saw Noah go back to Doc's, the three of them walked down the boardwalk. At the door, they heard, "I'll sell you some of them. A few I use all the time and want to keep, although they'd be the books most useful to you."

Smitty knocked on the door.

"Enter," Doc called out.

Zachariah asked, "Noah, may we speak with you privately?"

Noah knew Doc had padded certain walls

for the privacy of his patients. "May we use your exam room?"

The doctor made a sweeping gesture toward the room. He went to the parlor and joined his wife, daughter, Roscoe, Sebastian, and Lola.

Noah closed the door. "I'm listening."

Minnie explained what was on their minds. "We don't know what you do or don't want us to share."

"You mean, about my marriage with Ann?"

"Yes, and everything that happened as a result."

"Tell the truth. We've only been trying to make it harder to track us, not because we don't want anybody here to know we got married, or that the state of Arkansas says we can't be and aren't."

"What took you so long to get home?" Zachariah asked.

"It's safer for the people who helped us if I don't give you details, but the first delay was because there was too much snow to travel. Then, Eli was injured, and we had to let him recover. Next, we came across Sebastian who had been shot and was bleeding to death, so we helped him. Then, we rescued Lola. Most recently, high waters blocked us."

Since both Zachariah and Smitty would have known who he was, Noah asked, "Why didn't you help Melvin?"

Smitty said, "Why would we? He was one of the soldiers guarding you at Cadron Creek."

"Right, you wouldn't have known."

"What wouldn't we have known?" Zachariah asked.

"He's in love with Sally. She wanted him to come with us, but he said he couldn't because he'd be AWOL. We didn't know he'd change his mind."

Minnie replied, "I'm sorry. We thought we were helping you by not helping him."

"I understand." Noah didn't add that Sally was distraught. "Zachariah, I'll pay you to look over our wagons and fix them. One has a cracked axle held together with a metal strap. Two need pitch. I need you to fix them as fast as possible."

"I'll look them over right now." He and

Minnie left to work on the wagons. *The extra money will be a huge blessing. I'm making a home for Minnie, and I'm not taking a cent from her to do it, but I do need to pay Smitty some of the money I borrowed to buy the farm.*

Laura saw Zachariah and Minnie leave. "I don't see what he sees in her. She's so plain, but he acts like she's a plate of jewels."

"Personality has a lot to do with why a man selects a woman." Lola had also heard Laura's comments about Stephanie, Sally, and Ann. She hoped the girl would realize she should learn something about personality.

Nellie knew her daughter had incorrect notions about the value of people. She had no idea where they had come from. She told herself she would talk with Laura later. Doc went to his examining room and found the door open. Noah and Smitty still stood inside. "I'll put together those books for you, Noah. I'll write to my old teacher and get him to send me replacements. A dollar should cover these four books and shipping. I'll give you these other books."

Noah took a ten-dollar gold piece from his pocket and handed it to Doc.

"You don't need to give me this much."

"These books will teach me more than ten-dollars-worth of knowledge. I have a gift beyond measure with Ann as my wife, and both her sisters, Eli, and Roscoe as my family. That's all because you put my head back together. So please, take it."

"Since you insist," Doc Gridley put the coin in his pocket then stacked the books.

"Smitty, are you ready?" Noah asked.

"Let's go."

Noah picked up the books. "Doc, I'll talk with you again later." Noah and Smitty went to Smitty's house.

Noah and the rest of his family, along with Sebastian and Lola, had already decided what to do about the Butterfields and their home. When Noah put the books from Doc into his wagon, he got all the letters to Hank, everything that Hank had written, Clarabelle's journal, and the messages they had written to Hank's mother, sister, and wife. Noah handed Smitty the package, along with Roy's clothes. "We know Edith lives at Fort Smith. It seems that Hank was headed that way, so it's likely they're all there. Read everything then decide what you think is the right thing to do."

Smitty wanted to confirm Roy's status. "You're sure Roy is dead?"

"Completely sure, I saw his body, and he was wearing the boots with the shiv."

"And you swear you didn't kill him?"

"The sheriff in Maumelle can confirm that Roy was killed by the woman he shot when attempting to rob her."

"I'll go through this. If I think I should, I'll try to deliver everything to Clarabelle Butterfield. If I can't find her, I'll try Edith Atwood. Last, I'll try their mother."

"Much obliged."

Smitty put the package in his house and then walked with Noah to check on the wagon repairs. Horace, Clyde, and Zachariah were mounting a new axle on the wagon with the removable back and sideboards.

"How are the wagons coming along?" Noah asked.

"All the others are good. We've already got them coated with pitch and put a fresh layer on the other wagons too. We'll do this one after we get the axle on. We didn't have a spare already made. We're using the axle from Horace's. I'll make another to replace it. We should have this done by the end of the day."

"Perfect." Noah stayed and listened to Horace talk about the problems he'd had with his guts since he'd been shot. Clyde spoke about the shortage of work and money in the area. Zachariah told Noah all the details about his work on the farm.

# THIRTY NINE

After the pleasant conversation, Noah went to look at Joe's saloon floor. Noah talked with Joe, "My blood being permanently joined with Hank's is how it should be. Turns out that fight forever entangled our lives with the Butterfields. Tell me what happened with Melvin."

Joe spoke with Noah about Melvin trying to hide, how he got no help, and then was captured and taken away. As the two men talked, Sally woke. She opened her eyes and looked at the letter on the bed beside her. She unsealed it and read what Melvin had wanted to tell her.

Dear Sally,

I'm a fool. Nothing could ever be more important to me than you. Shortly after I spoke with you, I heard about Judge Hall coming across Ann and Noah. He had Captain Cornish looking for you for weeks. I realized I was giving my allegiance to the wrong people. These people are not honorable like you and your family. I don't want to spend my life with them. I want to spend it with you, not only as a wife but as a person. I thought you would come here to Harmony, and I could still find you. Maybe you'll get this letter. Even though I chose too late and lost you, I want you to know that I did choose you. Don't be upset that I'm in jail. Even the chance that I might find you was worth being found AWOL. I only wish I hadn't been caught and was with you. I'm not asking you to come and wait for me to get out of jail. Then you would also be stuck with people who are selfish, mean, and prejudiced. Go with your family and be happy. Because of the person you are, I know you'll find somebody who will love you beyond everything. Give your heart to him completely and have a glorious life but know that I love you. I love you. I love YOU.

Wishing I was yours,

Melvin.

Tears rolled down Sally's face. It wasn't fair that circumstances had taken him away from her again. She decided to answer and started down to the saloon, where Joe and Noah still sat at a table.

Noah saw her on the stairs. "Sally, is there anything I can do for you?"

She explained, "I'm going to write a letter to Melvin. I hope somebody might be able to get it to him."

Joe felt guilty. He promised, "I'll find a way to send it to him. I'll get you some paper and a pen."

Sally took the envelope, paper, quill, and ink bottle back to her room. She sat down at the table.

My dearest Melvin,

I got your letter. I want you to know how much it means to me that you chose to be with me and tried to come with us. Circumstances, caused by the same people you spoke about, prevented us from getting to Harmony until after it was too late. I deeply regret that. There is nothing I would have liked more than having you with me to share our love for a lifetime.

I want you to know, just as you want me to go on and find somebody else, that I wish for you to find someone to love you and for you to love her in return. I wish you a happy, meaningful, love filled life. Even if I love another in the future, I will never be able to give the place you hold in my heart to anybody but you. Eli tells me I can continue to love you desperately and still be able to love another person. That is what I wish for you too.

Wishing I had become your wife and with infinite never ending love,

Sally

She left the letter to dry.

# FORTY

Mara and Smitty walked into the saloon with four of Mara's delicious apple pies. Behind them, Minnie carried a dutch oven full of boiled new potatoes, swimming in butter. Sally stopped on the stairs. "What's happening?"

Joe explained, "We're all gonna eat here. Everybody's bringing something."

"I'll get my sisters." She walked across the dusty street to the store. Ann and Stephanie pulled their dishes out of the oven. Sally said, "I didn't know to fix something."

Ann put the chafing dish on a hot pad. "This is from all of us. We'll be over in a few minutes."

"I'll wait for you."

Everybody in town joined for the banquet, reminisced about the past, complained about the present, and planned and hoped for the future. They remained long after the meal. Horace was the first to leave with his family to get the children to bed. By midnight, all the townsfolk had gone home, including Eli, Stephanie, Ann, and Noah who went to Eli's house attached to the store, since Earl was still living in his own home. Everybody else had rooms at Joe's.

At breakfast in Eli's home, Sebastian announced his plan. "Lola and I are going to ask the Egglestons if we can buy their house when they move to the farm. I know I told you I would give you our horses, but Mateo isn't going to live peaceably with Eyanosa, and I want to keep ours. I'll pay you for bringing our trunks."

Noah replied, "You don't have to pay us anything. But you better find out if they will sell because we're leaving this morning."

"We'll come right back and let you know." Sebastian and Lola left.

Zachariah answered the knock. "Come in."

"We have a proposition for you." Sebastian entered the house.

Meanwhile, Ann, Sally, Roscoe, and Noah helped Eli and Stephanie remove from the wagon what belonged to them. Ann conveyed what they all felt. "I hate this, but they came here before, and they'll come again. We can't stay."

"I hate it too. Sally, are you sure you won't change your mind and stay?" Stephanie hoped that at least Sally would remain with her.

"I'm sure. But I hope you'll come soon because I'm going to miss you so much."

They soon had everything that was staying behind in the house. Sebastian returned with Lola. "We've bought the Eggleston's home."

"That's wonderful." Stephanie hugged Lola. She took Eli by the hand and stepped away. For a minute, Stephanie whispered to Eli.

They came back over. Eli said, "Stay here with us until the farmhouse is built."

Lola looked at Sebastian, who nodded his head. "We'd love to." The De La Cruz's trunks joined the other items inside Eli and Stephanie's home.

"There's too much space." Tears flowed down Ann's cheeks. She pleaded with Eli. "I can hardly stand it. Please beg Tom to come west."

Stephanie cried too. "I'm afraid I'll never see you again."

All with torn hearts, the group stood and held each other. Eli assured all of them, including himself, "I'll make sure Pop knows we want to go with you."

Noah continued to hug them. "Eli, take good care of Stephanie and yourself because I love you both."

Eli prayed, "God, please keep everybody safe and happy. Bring us together as soon as possible, along with my father. Even though we'll be apart, help us to feel the love that we know the others have for us. Let this separation work for the good and to bring glory to Your name. In Christ's name, we ask."

They all ended the prayer with, "Amen."

Noah exclaimed, "Wait! We need to do more work on the wagons!"

"What?" Ann didn't know what was on her husband's mind.

Noah called the town together. He told them his plan, "We need to put a coat of pitch on the inside of Roscoe's wagons. We also need a lot more on the prairie schooner and the animal wagon. We need to make sure that they won't leak. I want to hire Horace.

"We need Zachariah to make wagon bows for the new wagons and Smitty to make fittings to hold them. Clyde, we need to alter all the wagons. They need to be able to go both ways. We came up with a design. On top of that, the farm wagon and prairie schooner need brakes.

"We need to rent Smitty's corral and fields for grazing. We need to buy tarps, two wagon covers, linseed oil, axle grease, and a hundred eggs. I guess we had better pack the eggs in cornmeal. I don't want any to break, plus we need oranges or lemons or both."

"That's going to take days," Zachariah informed him. Earl echoed the statement.

"We have to wait however long it takes. It's too dangerous to travel without getting these wagons right. Who can I hire to move everything out and then back in when the wagons are ready? Who can I hire to get citrus fruit?" Noah knew these things would be beneficial for them. Most of all, he knew they needed to remain together longer. Maybe they would even be blessed, and Tom would get home before all the work had been completed. He also knew it would be a legitimate infusion of money into the town they loved.

Ann realized what Noah was doing. He looked at her. She mouthed, "I love you."

Noah smiled. Ann appreciated his choice. Even though it was very dangerous to remain, the girls needed more time to prepare their hearts to part.

Earl told Noah, "I can get plenty of eggs from farmers around here, but I'll have to go to Clarksville for citrus."

Eli also understood what Noah was doing. *God, keep the water high at Gum Log Creek. Keep Raymond away and whoever Judge Hall sends.*

## FORTY ONE

The following day, Daniel Hall handed Micah Clemont's letter to Warden Rufus Knapp of the Arkansas Eighth District Penitentiary. "By order of Supreme Justice Clemont, I'm releasing these men into your custody for the remainder of their sentences." He handed a second envelope to Warden Knapp. "These are the confinement orders sent from the warden at The Quarry in Missouri."

Warden Knapp read the documents. He told his man, "Show these soldiers where to take the prisoners." He explained, "Judge Hall, we already received notification to expect your arrival. The messenger has been waiting to take your report back to Alexandria. He's quite ready to be on his way. Do you require paper, a quill, and ink to write your report?"

"Since he's in such a hurry, I won't detain him while I inspect your prison. I'll write my report, and then he can be on his way. Tell him to prepare to leave immediately."

The report stated that three prisoners had been transferred to Arkansas and The Quarry was again running smoothly. The report and its carrier left the penitentiary after the mid-day meal.

Judge Hall wiped his mouth. "I'm ready to inspect your facilities. I must be sure these men will have no ability to depart these premises."

"I assure you, they'll remain in my custody."

"Did you not read His Honorable Justice Clemont's order that I take whatever steps I deem necessary?"

"I read it," Warden Knapp snapped.

*Unlike the labor camp, this place will be full of awful people. I should be able to find somebody willing to kill for his freedom.* "I insist that I be allowed to privately speak with the inmates until I am satisfied."

"That would be very dangerous."

"I can handle myself."

Warden Knapp issued orders to the guards. "Allow Judge Hall free access to the facilities and the prisoners." *Imbecile.*

## FORTY TWO

Seven days later, Earl limped into his house and kissed Clara. "I got a bushel of lemons, four hundred pounds of cornmeal, and four hundred pounds of bran. I bought so much, they gave me a barrel for nothing, but it isn't tight enough to hold water. Did the farmers bring in enough eggs?"

"More than a hundred. I bought them all."

Ann heard the store bell jingle. Earl rolled the empty barrel in as Roscoe and Ann walked into the store. Ann offered, "We'll help pack the eggs in the cornmeal."

"This isn't a watertight barrel. Will it work?" Earl asked.

"It'll work fine. I've packed them like that before," answered Roscoe.

Noah had the Butterfield money. He wanted to help the people of Harmony who had plowed fields and planted corn for the girls when they had desperately needed help the previous spring. He paid a day's wage, one dollar, to every person who had helped unpack and then repack. Noah also settled up with Clyde, Zachariah, Horace, Smitty, Joe, and Earl before he went to Eli's house.

After a family meal, Roscoe, the girls, Noah, and Eli sat in the front sitting room. Stephanie brought up the trade she hoped to accomplish. "Roscoe, I know it's not a fair trade, but Eli and I want to ask if you would trade Redeemed and Ace for the mules we bought in Dover. It's because we love them, and we want them to be ours."

"Redeemed and Ace are much bigger and stronger than either of the mules you bought in Dover, but Redeemed has never done one single thing for me, other than give me a hard time. I'll trade her gladly. Ace is special to me,

Eli. But you're more important to me than a mule. I'll trade him. Maybe that'll give you more incentive to join us after your father gets home."

Ann sipped black tea and thought about the night they had hunted the Butterfield Gang members, Ben Rowe, Roy Butterfield, and Gus Hutchinson right there in Harmony. She had spotted Roy while looking through the secret peepholes behind the pictures in the room she currently occupied. She thought about all the heartache and death caused by the Butterfield Gang. *We should have killed them that night.*

Stephanie brought her back to the present when she handed Sally a box. "I told Mama I was going to buy this for you one day. She told me we would when we had the money because she knew you would love it. This is from Eli, me, and Mama."

Sally knew what was inside. She picked up the silver brush and mirror that their mother had used to brush her hair every time they had gone to Yates Mercantile. "It's like you're giving me Mama. Being a gift from the two of you makes it even better."

370

"I know it's not equal in monetary value, but we believe it will mean something to you." Stephanie passed Ann her box.

"I've never had anything like how Sally has loved that brush set her entire life. What on Earth would you give me?" Ann opened the box. Inside was a huge jar of peppermint sticks.

"I know a peppermint thief is lurking, but I promise he won't grab any when you get out to the boardwalk." Eli joked about the time he had stolen Stephanie's peppermint stick when they were very young.

"This was always the treat Papa let us have. The peppermints you gave us when the farm burned up were a very special gift, and peppermint sticks were also a wonderful Christmas present when we were stranded in that snowstorm last winter. I'd say I'll treasure them always, but you know I'm going to eat them."

Stephanie told her sister, "That's what we had in mind."

Noah opened his box. He found an alligator skin cover that fit over the thick, cow leather sheath of the very long knife he had worn almost every day that Eli had known him. Eli enlightened him of his objective. "So you remember your brother and sister who took on two alligators, and won."

"I'd never forget you, but I love this. You'd better get your Pop and bring my wagon to Fort Gibson. Don't forget: I'll go there on the first of every month until next spring. I hope you're there long before then." Noah took off his knife and slid on the alligator skin cover.

"Roscoe, we want you to have this." Stephanie gave him his box. It contained a shallow wooden bowl. Eli had carved three men and three women on the inner surface. In the center at the bottom, he had added the symbol for a family.

"A family of six, and I'm included!" Roscoe hugged Stephanie then Eli. "It's beautiful!"

Sally wished she had thought about giving a gift to Stephanie. "I don't have anything for you."

"We didn't expect anything. We wanted to give something to you, so you won't stop waiting for us."

Ann told her sister, "We can't wait forever, but we'll wait until next spring." She turned to Eli. "What if Tom doesn't come home by spring? How long will you wait? Years?"

"I don't know, Ann. I should be allowed to give my father a reasonable amount of time."

"Let's enjoy the night." Noah stopped the argument.

Ann tried to soften her statement. "I know you'll come when you can. That is, if you can. It's just that I'm going to miss you both so much."

"I'll miss you too." Stephanie hugged her sister.

The townsfolk gathered early the next day. Lola hugged Noah. "I hate to lose you. You gave Sebastian and me our lives." Unlike Stephanie and Eli who would probably join the rest of their family later, Lola knew she and Sebastian would never again see them. Noah, Ann, Sally, and Roscoe shared hugs and assurances that they loved everybody in town, would miss them, and never forget them then drove Roscoe's two conestoga Wagons and the small farm wagon out of town.

# FORTY THREE

Noah, Ann, Sally, and Roscoe traveled south beside Spadra Creek. The shade of the shagbark hickories, the mild temperature, and the whistles of the bright orange and shiny black Baltimore orioles lessened their sadness. They made their way to the same place they had stopped the previous fall when transporting the last three of the Butterfield Gang.

Ann arranged logs to cook their evening meal. "Sally, remember the first time we were here? You said you didn't want to see any more new country. I told you exploring would be exciting."

374

"I remember."

"What do you think now?" Noah brought a bottle of matches.

"I wouldn't be the person I am today if I had never left the farm. I would be a timid little mouse afraid of everything and not a person who can take what life throws and throw it back. I like me."

"I like you too." Ann hugged her sister.

It was their first night without Stephanie and Eli. They felt the loss intimately. By previous agreement, since they knew it would only make them feel worse, none of them brought it up. *How can I trust a God who would rip this family apart?* Roscoe flapped his bedroll ferociously before he laid it on the ground.

Glad they didn't have to struggle to find a wide space between the trees, the following day they traveled on the road in dappled light surrounded by oaks, hickories, and elms.

After fourteen hours of daylight and no difficulties, they forded Horsehead Creek. They stopped just beyond the post office. They passed the evening peacefully, once again avoiding conversation about Eli and Stephanie. The night air was comfortable as they slept under the stars on their tarps and feather mattresses with the goose down pillows they had made at Fletcher Creek.

The end of the next day, they arrived at the town of Ozark. Still desiring to elude attention and any possible pursuers, they went into town only long enough to eat a meal at the saloon then continued west and stopped a short distance beyond.

# FORTY FOUR

On the other side of Arkansas, Judge Hall concluded his interviews at the Arkansas Penitentiary. *I've found my man. Tomorrow, I'll start the proceeding to have him transferred to The Quarry. I won't take him there, though. I'll keep him in Little Rock until I'm ready.*

# FORTY FIVE

Shortly after the sun came up, the sky filled with clouds. Noah, Roscoe, Ann, and Sally traveled through grassy valleys and pine forests. The first raindrops hit their faces while they forded White Oak Creek.

Noah called out, "As soon as we're across, get on your ponchos!"

"I'll get them." Ann climbed into the wagon.

Right before the thunderstorm let loose, they slipped on their India rubber ponchos and then walked under the pines as the lightning flashed. Ahead, Sally saw flat open land. "Last summer, Ann and I got caught outside in a thunderstorm. Lightning struck a little tree in

378

front of us and completely incinerated it. At the time, I thought it was exciting, but we can't lay low in that grass field ahead."

During the storm that Sally mentioned, Ann had worried about how she would protect Sally. She didn't feel any safer in the current storm. "Let's wait under the pines until after the lightning stops."

Thirty minutes later, water only dripped from the branches. Roscoe made a suggestion. "This is a good time to let the animals graze. They'll get plenty of water from the wet grass."

Noah thought back to when he had traveled east, hoping to find the farm originally owned by his life-long friend, James Williams. It had turned out to be the one owned by Ann, Stephanie, and Sally, nieces unknown to James Williams. "Mulberry Creek is just ahead. The two branches are split until right below Pleasant Hill. We don't have to worry about the creeks being too full from the storm, and there's no passage fee to cross the bridges. Those folks want travelers to spend their money whether the water is high or not."

"Are we going to avoid the town?" Ann asked.

Noah suggested, "We could, but the ground is so soggy. Let's spend the night inside."

They crossed the bridge. As the sun set, Roscoe stood at the inn's bar, "Three rooms."

Thinking the large group that had been at the inn would be buying supper, the innkeeper's wife had prepared them a meal while the thunder crashed and the rain poured. She had just taken the pies out of the oven when the thunderstorm ended. Much to her dismay the family had settled their account, hoping the water of Frog Bayou was not yet too high, and they could avoid paying to cross on the ferry. They had left the inn owners with a cooked but unpurchased meal. The couple running the inn hated it when that happened. The innkeeper's wife asked, "Will you want supper?"

"Yes. What'll it be?" Roscoe inquired.

"Venison stew, bread, cheese, and pie."

Noah's stomach growled. "We'd like to eat now."

"I'll bring it right out." Glad they would earn some money from the meal, the innkeeper's wife left her husband to check in their guests.

"I want a bath with lilac water. Do you have any?" Ann asked.

The innkeeper gave his guests the keys to their rooms. "I'll get it ready in the back room."

Ann said, "Don't you have tubs in the rooms?"

"No. You still want the bath?"

"Yes, right after we eat." Ann pointed at Noah. "We'll take turns with the same tub."

Sally decided to splurge. "How many tubs do you have? I want fresh water."

Roscoe also wanted to bathe. "I'll use the same tub of water after she's done. Knock on my door, and let me know when it's hot again."

Since they knew they would be stopping in towns from time to time, they had satchels already packed. Ann watched Roscoe carry his personals and the very heavy bag with all his cooking utensils and secret money.

The woman put the whole kettle of stew on the table, a large loaf of bread, four giant wedges of cheese, a full pitcher of apple cider, and an entire cherry pie. The generous fare surprised them. Noah sat at the table. "We've already paid, and nobody else is here. I'm eating a fourth of this."

As he set a large plate with ham chunks in hot scrambled eggs on the breakfast table, the innkeeper said, "I see you have goats."

His wife added apple muffins, honey, butter, English tea, sugar, and milk.

"We do," Roscoe replied.

The innkeeper probed, "Would you sell any?"

Roscoe thought about it. "How many do you want?"

"All of them."

"To eat or what?" Sally loved all the animals. Even though they weren't hers, she planned to refuse, depending on the answer.

"Not to eat. Our son can't drink cow's milk. If you'd let us have all of them, we'd have enough for Peter and some to serve our guests as well."

Roscoe set his bags beside his chair. "We'll talk about it."

382

"They do slow us down," Noah pointed out.

"I've had Billy, Fancy, and Bella a long time."

"They're yours, Roscoe." Ann held out her hand. "Please pass the muffins. It's the kids that slow us down the most."

"These people need goat's milk, but I want the milk too. Bella's the best producer. She'll make more if her kids are nursing. I'll sell him Fancy and her kids."

After the delicious breakfast, Noah, Sally, and Ann harnessed donkeys. Roscoe arrived at the wagons five dollars richer but three goats poorer. "I sold Fancy for three dollars since she's a milk producer right now. I sold each kid for a dollar."

"You got more than we paid to stay here." Noah started them out of town. "And we had plenty of food. Let's hurry. Maybe we'll be able to ford Frog Bayou."

Thunderstorms rolled over them. They continued under the elms, oaks, and pines while the lightning lit up the forest, and the storm drenched them. Noah and Ann walked beside the lead donkeys. Behind them, Roscoe and Sally directed the wagon with the four remaining goats inside. A second storm drove the group into the lead wagon. The goats remained in the other wagon while the rest of the animals weathered the storm. When it was safe to move on, they rode instead of walking in the mud.

"Stop!" Noah called out. The other two walked to the front wagon to find out why. "Pecan trees. Too bad it's not fall. I'd like to have gotten the nuts, but the leaves make a good treatment for ringworm. I want some."

They picked and threw leaves into the washtubs until they were full then left the trees behind.

# FORTY SIX

As they approached Frog Bayou, the ground again became soggy. Cypress trees joined the willow oaks and elms. Herons and egrets, fishing in the water took flight when the travelers approached. They clopped onto a causeway that prevented wagons from sinking into the marshy ground when standing water filled the low-lying areas as it currently did.

Noah led them along the long, low bridge spanning the wetlands east of Frog Bayou. "With this much water all the way out here, I'm sure we'll have to cross on the ferry."

They arrived at the Bayou. Roscoe raised the

flag to signal the ferryman. "By morning, we may not be able to cross even on a boat."

Soon, the boat arrived on their side. A thirty-year-old man with light-brown eyes, a full beard, and a tall, wide-brimmed hat that sat on top of his long, brown hair told them, "This ferry is owned by Vincent Young. He has authorized me to bring you across for two dollars each trip."

"Two dollars?!" Roscoe exclaimed, due to the low price.

"Don't argue. We don't have the time. It's going to take four trips with this small boat, and the water is rising."

"We agree!" Delighted, Roscoe handed the man two silver coins. He drove a wagon and one-fourth of the unharnessed animals onto the ferry. The second trip, the ferryman took the fare from Sally and then carried her, a wagon, and the second fourth of the animals. The third trip, they sent another fourth of the loose animals with Ann and the last wagon. The boat bounced and rolled across the water. The ferryman demanded, "Help me! Pull!" Ann put on her gloves, grabbed the rope, and helped. The ferryman lowered the gate when they arrived across the rough water. "The water's getting too dangerous. I can't make another trip."

Ann stood inches from the man and stared into his eyes. "Mr. Vincent Young, I assume. You are not getting off this boat until my husband does, but I'll help you pull the boat." They got all the animals off the rocking boat. *In case I have to force Vincent.* Ann went into the wagon and slid a Lefaucheux revolver into her dress pocket. She jumped out the back, onto the boat as Roscoe drove the wagon off the ferry. "Let's go!"

"No! We'll never make it!"

Ann pointed the gun at the ferryman's face. "That's the man I love over there! Start pulling or I'll put twenty bullets in you!"

"No you won't!"

Faster than he could duck, Ann shot three holes through Vincent's hat. "Now, or the next seventeen will continue the line to your belly button!"

Vincent set right to drawing the rope. Ann dropped the gun back into her dress and pulled with all her might. She had to move away before Roscoe could get back and drag her off the ferry. Sally and Roscoe heard the shots and dashed back. Ann yelled, "Get far away from the river!"

Sally demanded, "Get back here!" then saw the perfect row of holes from the top of Vincent's hat to slightly above the brim. She notified Roscoe, "Ann was the one shooting."

"It's not like her to be so reckless." Unable to stop her, Roscoe stood beside Sally and watched Ann move into the treacherous river. *I'm going to hate God if he lets anything bad happen to her or Noah.*

The empty boat bounced wildly in the current. Ann fell to her knees. Vincent grabbed her arm. "I told you we shouldn't make another trip!"

"We're more than halfway. Keep going." Ann got to her feet and yanked the rope.

They arrived at the eastern shore as Frog Bayou spilled over its banks and onto the causeway. Noah screamed at Ann, "You should have stayed over there! How dare you risk your life like this!"

"This man wasn't coming back for you! You can't get a mile back across this causeway in time, so don't yell at me!"

"Get on quick!" The ferryman lowered the gate and jumped off to help Noah hurry the remaining animals onto the boat. "If all three of us pull, we might get over before the water's above the support line."

Noah didn't have his gloves. He yanked the rope anyway. *I guess this is how Ann feels when I do something dangerous.* They moved away from the wooden boards, which were already submerged. The front of the boat rose on a wave. The pulley lifted above the line. The animals tried to stay on their feet when the ferry surged back down. The swells grew ferocious. Once again, the pulley rose and then slammed back onto the line. Its wooden core cracked. "Is it still rolling?!" Ann called out over the roaring of Frog Bayou.

"Seems to be, if it falls apart, we're stuck!

Pull, because your life depends on it! I told you we shouldn't cross again!"

"I'm not letting my husband die! At least we have a chance this way!" Ann suddenly understood Noah's need to take chances. She pulled with all her might.

The rough pull line abraded Noah's hands. He colored the rope red with his blood. He ignored the pain, gripped hard, and tugged. The far shore drew nearer.

The boat rose. Both pulleys jumped the rope and then smashed to pieces upon impact with the hard, wrought iron. The hemp pull rope drew to one point on the iron line. "Try to pull!" the ferryman ordered. With much effort, they barely moved an inch. A twist of the rope frayed as the bayou threw them about. The ferryman exclaimed, "That's it! We're dead!"

Ann turned to Noah, "Your love has been worth everything."

Noah took Ann in his arms. "Yours too, my wife." Over Ann's shoulder, Noah saw Sally on the shore. "She's waving her bow. Everybody, get to one side with the animals."

They cleared a foot-wide opening along the lower side of the ferry. Sally shot an arrow. It flew past the boat. The attached line landed inside. All three on the boat lunged. Vincent nabbed it before the line slid away. They pulled until they got ahold of the thick rope that Sally had tied to the lighter line. Quickly, they secured the rope to the front of the ferry. Ann waved her arms.

"Now, Roscoe!" Sally called out.

"Thank you, God!" Roscoe directed sixteen of their largest animals hitched together in the two harnesses. "Forward pull!"

Vincent hadn't expected to survive. Now, he thought they might. "Keep the pull-rope moving, or the iron line will cut it, and we'll be gone!"

Ann saw Noah's hands. "I'll help you. My husband needs to steady the animals."

King, along with the other mules and donkeys, strained as they struggled to drag the ferry against the rush of water and the friction of the rope. The boat slowly moved along the line. Sally pulled too. It made no difference, but she couldn't just stand there. They drew near. "Keep pulling my ferry! You owe me! Get my boat out of the bayou!"

The boat touched the land. Noah told Sally, "Run and tell Roscoe to pull out the ferry!"

Vincent lowered the gate. It wasn't only the people thrilled to be at the steady land. Eyanosa and the other animals dashed off the boat. "May I get off now?" Vincent asked.

"Yes."

"You're not going to shoot me?"

Ann hugged Vincent. "I won't. I really appreciate you." When she let him go, he released the rope that held the boat to the iron line. Soon, they had the ferry well above flood level.

They remained beside Frog Bayou for four days, learning how to and helping Vincent make new pulleys. Vincent was thrilled with the replacements. "On this side of the Bayou, there's no edible grass for a long way, and it's very marshy. You've seen my barns are full of hay and oats. If you get stuck, you won't be able to get back to buy animal food."

Noah told his family what he had learned on his way to Harmony the previous spring. "There may be quicksand ahead. The more rain, the deeper it will be. I'd like to move on. We can test the road as we go, but we should bring all the hay and oats we can fit into the wagons, in case we do get stuck."

Ann agreed, "I'm pretty sure we'll get more rain, so it'll only get worse if we wait."

"The goats can walk," Sally said, "Let's fill it up."

They loaded the empty farm wagon until hay pressed against the top of the canvas cover then purchased every bag of oats they could fit in the empty spaces of the conestoga wagons. They confined all the unharnessed animals between Roscoe's two wagons before they tied the lead ropes of the animals pulling the farm wagon to the rear. Noah held the reins of the first wagon. Bound together, he, Roscoe, Ann, and Sally walked in front of the caravan to test the road.

A cattle egret sat on the back of King as they rode away from Frog Bayou. They didn't encounter any quicksand pits able to hold them, but the wet sandy road made it very hard to pull the wagons. In the humidity and heat of the day, the squishing and drawing of feet out of the sand became almost unbearable. They pushed on and finally got beyond the sands of the bayou. In the last rays of light, they stopped in the lush Arkansas River Basin grass and unharnessed the mules.

Ann looked around. "There isn't a way to set up a temporary corral. With all this grass right here, the animals have no reason to go anywhere."

Sally's boots were full of muddy sand, and her trousers were soaked. "I want to get dry. We should sleep inside the wagons."

Just as tired, wet, and miserable, Roscoe nodded, and Noah agreed as well.

## FORTY SEVEN

The animals had not stayed where put. Roscoe wasn't happy. "I hope they didn't cross the creek. Let's spread out and search."

By the time they had located all their missing livestock, the morning had passed. Roscoe tied on the last mule. "We need to contain the animals when we get out on the prairie. They could be miles away and all over the place by morning."

Sally thought about the problem. "How could we do that? There won't be trees, and we can't make a space big enough with only a few wagons."

395

Ann offered a suggestion, "We can park the wagons far apart and tie a rope between them."

"Probably can't do that. We'd be too exposed, but we don't have to worry about it yet." Noah started the caravan moving.

At Flat Rock Creek, they discovered it didn't matter how long it had taken to gather the animals. There was no ferry, and the water was too high to cross. They set up camp and then heard the jingling of a wagon harness. Noah went into protection mode. "Get the animals into the woods. I'll signal if it's safe."

They still had the animals tethered on ropes. Roscoe and Sally untied the ends of the lines from the wagons and led them into the dense pine forest. Ann hid in the woods with her rifle trained on the man approaching her husband. She was an expert rifleman. She wouldn't miss if the situation went bad.

A dark-skinned traveler walked up the road. He called out to the person who sat alone at a fire with two large wagons, one smaller wagon, and nothing to pull any of them. "I means ya no harm! I's just a travelin' man!"

396

Noah returned the greeting. "Welcome. I can offer you coffee."

"Much obliged, masta."

Noah pretended to get a cup out of the back of the wagon. *The man won't know it was already warm before I filled it.* He poured coffee into the cup then into his own. Noah sipped the hot drink. The new arrival did the same. After many minutes of conversation, both men had decided the other was safe.

As if it was nothing out of the ordinary, Noah commented, "I'm sure you noticed I don't have animals to pull these wagons."

"An I gots not one thing with me."

"A person might think a man may be protecting his family."

"I sure 'nough would."

"I'll get mine if you want to invite yours over. We won't tell a soul we ever saw anybody."

"We won't tell nobody neither.

Noah gave a salute toward the woods. The man turned and let out a loud whistle. Ann ran deeper into the woods to tell Sally and Roscoe to come back.

When they had been at Fletcher Creek, Noah and Ann had pretended to be slaves escaping to freedom in the west. This day, a real family of escapees arrived in a wagon pulled by two oxen. A woman sat in the seat of a cart that was barely staying together. Three little heads peeked out the opening of the wagon cover.

Ann, Sally, and Roscoe came back. More and more animals returned to camp. One of the children assumed anybody who owned that many animals must be a plantation and slave owner. "Masta, where your plantation be?"

"We don't own land." Roscoe helped the children get out of the wagon. He and Sally noticed the dearth of provisions. Slaves on the run couldn't walk into a store and buy what they needed for two primary reasons. First, they were afraid of being captured and returned to slavery. Second, they had very little money.

Sally offered the family a meal. "We were about to start supper. It'd be rude to eat without inviting you. Please join us."

*Won't make it, if we don't 'cept every bit a help.* "That's kind. We'll eat with ya," said the man.

The woman unharnessed their cows and then milked them with the help of Ann. Ann knew by the ribs of the animals that they were traveling too quickly, and not allowing the animals enough time to eat. They put the cows into the grassy field with the other animals. "We'll have bread, honey, cheese, and smoked ham." Ann climbed into the wagon and handed food to everybody, except Noah and the black-skinned man. Neither of whom was willing to be unable to operate the rifles they casually kept ahold of.

Sally handed a gallon of honey to the middle child. Roscoe passed a wheel of cheese to the oldest child. Ann gave two loaves of bread to the youngest child and a whole smoked ham to their mother.

The runaway slave, trying to get his family to freedom, introduced himself. "I's Solomon, this be Hannah, an' our chil'n, Moses, Asa, and Eleazer."

Noah pointed to himself then his family members. He stated their aliases, "Abraham, Lily, Nancy, and Theo."

After the meal, Ann said, "We have too much weight in our wagons. It'll kill our animals. They can't pull this much, going as fast as we need to travel. We need somebody who can give their oxen plenty of time to eat to help us get the load down, and we need to get rid of the remains of this supper."

Noah joined in. "We also have a wagon we need to dispose of." The animal wagon sat empty and cleaned after the one short time the animals had been inside while being ferried across Frog Bayou.

Hannah believed they probably wouldn't survive the attempt to find freedom as they were, but she and her husband had decided it was better to die trying to stay together as a family than to be alive as slaves and sold apart by their drunken, gambling master, who was losing his father's plantation little by little. Before Solomon could refuse, Hannah piped up, "We'd be tickled pink ta help. How long a cow need ta rest?"

Sally jumped to her feet. "Wonderful! Let's see what you can help us get rid of."

Roscoe explained how to travel long distances and keep oxen healthy while Sally handed out sacks of rice, beans, flour, dried apples, sugar, coffee, and tea. Ann gave the children saleratus, cinnamon, rosemary, cloves, molasses, salt, and pepper. Noah and Roscoe took off the removable backboards and rolled out a barrel of pickles, a barrel of bacon packed in bran, and the barrel of eggs packed in cornmeal.

Ann said, "We still have too much. Don't you agree, Abraham and Theo?"

Noah nodded. "We need to get rid of this jug of honey, a keg of vinegar, and the rest of that wheel of cheese. We've got too much smoked bear, goose, and elk, and a lot of this bear fat has to go."

Roscoe followed along, "Also, two gallons of linseed oil for wagon wheels. And for medicine, let's pour a gallon of whiskey from Nancy's keg into an empty honey jar."

Ann decided they should also lighten their wagons of some of the items from Hank's attic. "Drat, we're still too heavy. There are pockets sewn into the wagon cover. Find a set of summer and winter clothes and shoes that will fit and pack them in the pockets." Solomon, Hannah, and Moses found clothes and shoes that fit. "I'm sorry that we don't have anything that fits your youngest two. Hannah, take these clothes and this sewing kit. You can alter these for Asa and Eleazer."

As items were given, Solomon, Hannah, Moses, Asa, and Eleazer helpfully packed the supplies the other family desperately needed to give away. They filled up the pitch-coated farm wagon that had a new linseed oiled canvas cover with pockets, a recently installed brake, and a double tree and falling tongue that could be removed and installed at either end.

Roscoe also gave them a bag of citric acid. "Mix it with sugar and boiled water." As he had when Noah had first arrived at Bacon's Trading Post, Roscoe described in gory detail what would happen if they didn't consume enough of the mixture.

Because she wanted to share something she enjoyed very much, Ann also gave them five peppermint sticks. Candy was an unheard of luxury for a slave. Hannah carefully packed them away to save for a special occasion.

Ann insisted, "You have to try some." She got another stick, broke it up, and handed pieces to all nine people.

Eleazer exclaimed, "Give me more!"

His father rebuked him, "Don't go askin' nobody to give ya nothin'."

"I have plenty. Here's more." Ann held out the broken pieces in the handkerchief. Eleazer grabbed the whole handkerchief and ran into the woods before anybody could stop him.

Ann started to cry. Misunderstanding and expecting his son would suffer the treatment a slave caught stealing would receive, Solomon begged, "I'm sorry, misses. Don't whip em. I'll gives ya everythin' back."

Ann clarified, "I'm not mad. He reminded me of some people I miss very much. Let him eat the candy."

Sally held her sister in her arms and patted her on the back. "I miss them too."

Solomon still planned to have a talk with his

son's backside. Eleazer needed to learn never to do such a thing again. As they sucked on peppermint, Noah and Roscoe explained to Solomon how to work the brake and make the wagon reverse.

The next day, they disassembled the runaway slave's wagon. They put its old cover over the canvas with the pockets that had already been on the farm wagon. They attached two of the wheels, one axle, the double tree, yoke, and falling tongue on the outside of the cart. They also put the kingpin into the jockey box with all the other needed tools that were already in the box. The other two wheels and axle they attached to the wagon that carried the dynamite.

To keep Solomon from hearing, Hannah whispered, "I sees what ya up to. Bless ya for helpin'."

Ann explained, "God puts us where He wants us. He shows us what He wants us to do and gives us what we need to do it."

Sally added, "And we have plenty of reason to want to."

Most of their food was out of their wagons and into the sturdy cart that could deliver Solomon and his family to the west. Noah and his family had enough food to get to Van Buren where they could buy what they needed to get to Fort Gibson. There, they could completely resupply. They all believed Solomon and his family had enough to make it to California if God helped them.

After two days of waiting, Solomon decided to move forward. Noah warned them, "The water is still too high."

"We gots ta move on. We gots to get over them mountains I heard 'bout 'fore winter."

They prayed together for both families, asked for safety, thanked God for the blessings He gave, and for the freedom to live their lives with the people they loved.

Just before they left, Roscoe whispered to Moses, "Can you keep a secret?"

"Course, I no baby."

Roscoe handed Moses a small bag with ten one-dollar silver coins and four ten-dollar gold pieces. "Give this to your mother at Fort Smith, not before, and give it to her in private."

Moses climbed into their new wagon and forded the creek with his family. On the other side, Solomon called back, "Tol ya!"

"God bless!" Hannah waved as she and the children looked out the back.

Ann waved too. "God be with you! " She turned to her family. "They didn't have any problem crossing."

"I think we can go," Roscoe concurred.

Noah gave the final go ahead, "So, let's get ready."

They arrived in Van Buren after a short five-mile trip. "Shall we stay only long enough to buy what we need?"

The vote was unanimous. They resupplied and then left town through the thick cane undergrowth beside the Fort Gibson Road. They traveled over stony ground on the hills and fertile bottomlands in the lower regions.

Even though the water was still higher than usual, they forded Lee's Creek with no problem. Before crossing into Indian Territory, they stopped for the day. "Will we be at your home tomorrow?" Sally asked.

"Home is still far to the north," Noah replied.

Before the sun went down, Solomon and his family arrived at Fort Smith by the Poteau River. He went into the store to purchase the axle grease, candles, and lantern oil that Roscoe had told them they would need to cross the Great American Desert. Moses gave Hannah the bag of coins.

"You steal this, boy?" his mother asked.

"No, Mama, Masta Theo gave it. He tol me keep it til we here, find ya alone, an' give it."

"Yous a good boy ta do just as Masta Theo tol ya." Solomon didn't need the money yet. Hannah hid the coins under her new winter clothes in her pocket of the wagon cover. When they left, Solomon went south to follow the trail beside the Canadian River. A day north, Noah camped beside the Arkansas River. Both families hoped and believed they would be successful.

# FORTY EIGHT

When Noah crossed Skin Bayou, he had finally returned to Indian Territory. However, if they hadn't known they were far away, they would have believed they walked the thinning woodland of post oaks and hickories around Harmony. Once again, they arrived at a waterway at the end of the day. Noah informed them, "This is Sallisaw Creek."

"Since the water is flowing gently today, should we follow our usual plan and cross?" Ann asked.

Roscoe stated his opinion, "It looks stony over there, and I don't see much grass. Maybe we should let the animals graze over here tonight and cross in the morning."

Noah looked at the clear sky. "We'll let them get a good meal tonight. By midday tomorrow, we'll be in the grass of the prairie."

God blessed them with good weather. The next morning, they stopped at every small patch of grass and allowed the animals to eat what was there before moving to the next.

Halfway through the day, a family with one wagon and four oxen disembarked from the large ferry that had brought them across Vian Creek. Once out of hearing, Noah said, "They probably can still get enough grass."

Roscoe calculated. *We have only two wagons, and it looks like they keep the ferry on the other side. We should get everything over in three crossings. I'll get the man to lower his price.*

After much haggling on Roscoe's part, he doled out three dollars. "I'll take Sally, one wagon, and half the animals."

The ferryman returned. Noah paid his share and rode with Ann. He tried to strike up a conversation. "I heard there're salt flats around here."

The ferryman replied, "It's a mile further up. You can't miss it."

"How can we not miss it?" Ann inquired.

"You'll see," was all they got out of the man. Noah had already known about the salt flats. He had only wanted to be friendly.

Ann walked onto the white lake so monstrous, that she couldn't see the edges. "It's probably not very deep." She swung her hatchet.

An hour of pulverizing and suspending salt in the air dried them as they breathed. Sixteen inches and not at the bottom, Roscoe pried out the two-foot-wide block he had hewn out. "I'm giving up."

Sally continued to hack at the sea of salt. "We gave all our salt to Solomon. We all need to get a chunk as big as Roscoe's."

Noah stopped her. "We have more than we gave away, and we can't keep breathing this salt. We need fresh air and gallons of water."

"All right. Did you notice this salt tastes better?" Sally loaded the fourth block of pure salt. A dusting of salt covered every blade of

410

grass in the area. They traveled until the land and air became salt-free then stopped. Everybody, including all the animals, gulped the clear, refreshing river water.

Lack of grass was not a problem the following day. They traveled through first-rate bottomlands and crossed small creeks beyond the Illinois River. Late in the day, they splashed across Manard Creek and beheld a carpet of prairie flowers and grasses, covering the gently rolling hills. Noah remembered his trip going the other direction. "Fort Gibson is just ahead."

The sun had sunk before they arrived at the stockade of large, vertically-mounted logs situated immediately before the roofs of the wooden buildings inside. Noah informed them, "The soldiers came here to keep the peace between the Cherokee and Osage Indians. We Indians shouldn't be fighting each other."

Guards looked down on them from one of the two corner blockhouses, protruding just beyond the fort's perimeter and positioned diagonally across from each other. It was a dangerous place. For self-defense, the soldiers shut themselves in at night. Once the large gates closed, they didn't open until first light. The gates were already locked, and the guards weren't opening them.

## FORTY NINE

The gates opened on Sally's birthday. On June 23rd of 1840, the very attractive fifteen-year-old-girl walked into Fort Gibson. The barracks, officer's quarters, commissary, bakery, and hospital sat in the central courtyard.

"Where you folks headed?" the commissary master asked when Noah handed him his list of needed supplies.

Noah named the vague area to which they planned to go eventually, "The western sea."

The man offered advice to the two men. "You'll need to get everything for the entire trip now. If you're out of everything already, you

413

used your supplies too quickly. You'll need to learn how to ration better, or you'll never make it."

"We've learned that," Roscoe replied. He didn't add that he had learned the lesson twenty years earlier.

"I see you have a Bible on your list."

"I hope you have one," Noah replied.

"We have a chaplain, but I don't think he has extra Bibles. Polk Preaching Station has some for the Indians. Maybe he'll give one to white folks too."

"Much obliged. We'll check."

Before he went to gather the items on the list, the storekeeper stated the cost. "Twelve sacks of flour - thirty-six dollars, two hundred and twenty pounds of cornmeal - ten dollars, three hundred pounds of lard - fifteen dollars, four hundred pounds of bacon - forty dollars ... That comes to two hundred, eighteen dollars and fifty cents."

Roscoe motioned for Noah to join him across the room. "That's high. I would have charged three-quarters of that amount."

414

Noah reminded him, "It costs more because this is the last place to get supplies."

Roscoe strode over to the man. "I ran a trading post for twenty years, and I know this is too high."

"Mister, those supplies were brought by steamship as far west as the Arkansas can be navigated, which is only Fort Smith. Then, they were loaded on wagons and transported the final sixty miles to Fort Gibson. This is the last place you can restock, so you either pay this price, or you don't get the supplies."

A person could purchase almost anything at Fort Gibson. It was the primary depot for supplies in Indian Territory. The commissary master had no doubt he would sell what was in the store. He had no inclination to lower his price. Noah handed the man two hundred and twenty dollars. "Add another two and a half pounds of garlic and another gross of matches."

When the supplies were in the wagons, Noah changed his focus to the last item on their list. "Roscoe, I'm going to ride to the preaching station and try to get a Bible. See how Ann and

Sally are doing at the bakery." He rode away as Roscoe walked to the bakery where Ann and Sally were supposed to be buying fresh bread. Roscoe entered the bakery and discovered a dozen men surrounding the two women.

"I'm married. I only want to buy some bread. Don't touch me." Ann backed into the corner with Sally behind her.

"What about her?" one of the men asked.

"She's my wife, so you better back away!" Roscoe commanded the men.

The soldier who had asked if Sally was married said, "She's awfully young for you."

"It's not up to you to decide who she marries. Let them out." The privates were twelve altogether. He was one old man. They didn't move. Roscoe tapped the Lefaucheux revolvers in his gun belt, "Twenty bullets each. I suggest you move."

A soldier stepped aside. "I don't mean no harm. We don't have many women here, and certainly not women as beautiful as these two."

As Roscoe ushered Ann and Sally toward the door, Sally said, "Love, I still want the bread."

416

"Give me what they asked for," Roscoe ordered the baker.

The baker wrapped several loaves of bread in paper. He handed it to Sally and then put a dozen pastries in a box that he passed to Ann. "Twenty cents."

Roscoe gave the man two dimes. "Let's go, honey." He took the women to the wagons. The three of them waited for Noah to get back, hopefully with a Bible to replace the one that had remained with Eli and Stephanie.

As soon as she saw his face, Ann spilled out everything that had happened. Sally confirmed the story. "I don't know how far they would have gone if Roscoe hadn't come in."

"That is totally unacceptable. I'm going to talk to the commanding officer." Noah stormed over to get the matter straight. He knocked on the door. A young soldier answered and then stood there and looked at Noah. Noah informed him, "I need to speak with the commanding officer."

For his commander, who sat out of view inside the room on the other side of the open door, the soldier inquired, "What's your business?"

"The behavior of his soldiers."

The commander stood up. Under his breath, he muttered, "Not again." He told his sentry, "Send him in." Noah entered the room. "State what happened." Noah related what his wife had told him. Colonel Howland informed him, "I need to speak with the women."

"I'll get them."

When Noah was out of the building, Colonel Howland commanded the soldier outside his door. "Bring over the usual group."

When Noah returned with Roscoe, Ann, and Sally, the colonel had assembled the men he had repeatedly ordered to not molest the women who came to the fort. The colonel stood in the front room with his men. The commander was a man who gave orders. "Tell me what happened," he barked at Ann.

She pointed at the men. "Those men came into the bakery and asked if I was married. I told them I was, but that one kept touching me. I told him to stop. He didn't until my sister's husband arrived."

418

"Where did he touch you?"

Ann pointed, "My arm, my shoulder, and my hair."

"And you?" Colonel Howland looked at Sally.

"The same thing, only that one touched me. He touched my back, my neck, and my face as well."

"Which other men were there?" he asked.

Ann pointed out the other men who had come into the bakery. "They only asked if we were married."

Colonel Howland asked the first accused soldier, "Private Dennis, what do you have to say?"

"I asked her if she was married. I didn't touch the girl," replied the soldier who had molested Ann.

The colonel looked at the other accused soldier, "Morris, what's your story?"

"Guilty as charged. It's lonely out here, and she's gorgeous. But I wasn't planning on anything, unless she was willing."

"Yes, they are lovely women, but that

doesn't matter. I've told you both to leave the women alone."

He then asked the other men, "What do you men have to say about his?"

One of the soldiers said, "We asked if they were married. I didn't see anything else." He knew exactly what had happened. However, soldiers didn't tell on each other. One day, your life might depend on the willingness of others to guard your back. He looked at Ann and Sally. He felt bad about accusing them of lying. "But I wasn't looking." The other soldiers also didn't see anything.

"For molesting these women, after repeatedly being ordered to leave women alone, every two hours from reveille to retreat today and tomorrow, both of you will walk back and forth in front of the guard house with a fifty-pound sack of rocks on your back." He turned to the man Ann had accused. Colonel Howland had heard the same complaint too many times. Not only from women passing through but also from the women who were at the fort more permanently. They had all said that he had touched their hair. "For lying to your commanding officer, you have forfeited your personal rations for the week."

Because of eating mostly salt horse and hard tack, many of the soldiers suffered from scurvy. This year, Colonel Howland had ordered the soldiers to plant vegetable gardens. Individual rations issued to the soldiers consisted only of coffee, sugar, and whiskey or spruce beer.

The man forfeiting his most coveted rations remembered Noah from his visit the previous year. He thought he could get even. *At least, I can force them out of the safety of the fort.* "I remember that man. He was here last year. He's an Indian."

White people could remain inside at night. Indians could come into the fort during the day, but they had to leave before they closed and barred the gates. Colonel Howland had spent the last few years negotiating treaties and trying to keep the peace with and between the Indians. He didn't care if a person was white or Indian. Some of his officers even had Cherokee lovers. "Thank you for informing me. If any of you harasses or molests a woman again, you will do extremely long, hard labor. Do you understand?"

They all replied, "Yes, sir," and meant what they said, at least at that moment. However, they were at the most westerly-located United States Fort and frequently went months without women around. That made it difficult to resist talking to them when they had the opportunity. The problem was that they touched them.

The colonel said, "Please accept my apology. Would you join the officers for dinner tonight?"

Noah looked at Ann for her opinion. It was Sally's birthday, so Ann wanted whatever Sally preferred. She glanced at her sister. "We accept."

"Wonderful." The colonel returned to his office.

His attendant said, "Formal dress. Eighteen hundred hours."

"We'll be here promptly."

It would be hours before dinner, so they decided to go back to the store. While they looked around, a couple entered the store. "We wonder if we can trade two spinning wheels and two looms for supplies." The man held his wife's hand and silently prayed that the storekeeper would say yes.

It wasn't the first time people stood before the storekeeper, hoping to redeem bad choices. "Let me see them." He walked out of the store with the couple. When they came back into the store several minutes later, the couple had smiles on their faces as they carried the spinning wheels into the store. The storeowner gathered the items the couple should have chosen at the beginning of their trip.

Just before eighteen hundred hours, Noah, Ann, Roscoe, and Sally dressed in formal evening clothes from Hank Butterfield's stolen booty. They walked to the officers' mess hall. It was quite hot when they passed the exhausted men still marching back and forth in front of the guardhouse. Even though they should not have touched her or Sally, Ann felt bad for the men. "May they have water?" she asked the officer leading them to the dining hall.

"Nobody's going to help them and also get labeled as a troublemaker."

"They look like they're about to pass out." Ann walked to the well and drew a bucket of water.

Noah took the bucket and the water dipper from his wife. He dipped out a ladle of water and offered it to the man who had confessed. "My wife is very soft-hearted. She wants you to have water, but I'm telling you, if you ever touch or badger either of these women again, you will have a very short life."

The man handed the ladle back. "Tell her, much obliged, and I'm sorry. I apologize to you too. They are lovely and kind women. You're a lucky man."

Noah filled the ladle for him again. "I'll tell her."

After the soldier drank it down, Noah gave a dipper full of water to the second man. After the man had received his second draught, he returned to his sentence without saying a word. Noah heard the man's snide comment. "Oh, I'm so grateful for water after making me about die of thirst, and by the way, you're going to have a very short life too."

The man who had apologized informed the other, "You're an idiot."

Noah ignored him. He took the bucket back to the well and hung the dipper on the hook.

In the officers' dining hall, they took their seats among the officers. Colonel Howland sat at the head of the table. His first officer discreetly examined the two very attractive women who had just arrived at the fort. From across the table, the officer's eyes swept over Ann and then lighted on Sally. He jumped up. "Where did you get that?!" He leaned forward, planted his hands on the table, and glared.

"What?" Sally cowered under the furious intensity of the question.

"The necklace."

"It was given to me."

The officer shrieked, "That necklace was not given to you!"

Sally defended her statement, "I swear, it was given to me by Edwin Snow."

Noah and Roscoe took Sally and Ann by their hands and moved them away from the table. "Let me explain." Noah stepped in front of them.

The commander also recognized the necklace. "Explain well, or you'll all be in jail."

His officer went silent then sat. Noah motioned for Roscoe, Ann, and Sally to retake their seats. While they ate supper, helped by Ann, Sally, or Roscoe, Noah told the story of Roy and Hank Butterfield.

"I believe you about the Butterfields, but you can't keep the necklace," Colonel Howland informed them.

Sally explained again, "It's my necklace. A man who loves me gave it to me. It has his kiss right here. It's there for whenever I need a kiss."

"My previous First Lieutenant and his wife had their traveling trunk stolen when they boarded the steamboat at Fort Smith. That necklace and that dress were in that trunk. They didn't realize it was gone until they were back east."

The officer sitting across from Sally said, "I distinctly remember Elizabeth sitting right there last year wearing that dress and necklace."

Sally continued her explanation, "I took the dress out of the trunk, but the necklace didn't come from there. It may look like the necklace Elizabeth wore, but it didn't come from the trunk."

Noah said, "May I speak with Sally in the next room?" The colonel nodded then motioned for an impartial officer to accompany them.

"Privately," Noah requested.

"Don't leave," the colonel ordered them.

In the other room, Noah told Sally, "All along, you've known the necklace was stolen property. The chance these people were connected to the necklace was tiny, but it happened. It has to be returned to the owner."

"Take it," Sally told him. Noah unclasped the latch. It dropped from her neck. She left, even though ordered not to. For her birthday, she had lost something very significant.

Noah walked back into the room and handed the necklace to Colonel Howland. "The law states if stolen property is not claimed by its rightful owner within six months, the person filing a claim for possession becomes the legal owner. You know the rightful owner is Elizabeth." He waited for the colonel to state the woman's last name.

"Saunders."

"Elizabeth Saunders had six months to come here and look for her necklace. Sally Williams will be submitting a claim for possession in fifteen minutes." He turned, motioned for Ann to follow, and then walked toward the door.

Ann rose from her chair. "Thank you for your hospitality and the delicious meal."

So the soldiers couldn't leave before Sally submitted her claim, Roscoe remained seated.

As if he didn't know what he had done, Ann informed Noah, "You told him Sally's real name."

"If Sally wants to own the necklace legally, she has to use her real name."

"We can't wait for six months and then leave in November."

"If Tom had been in Harmony, we could have gone. We can't go this late. We'd get to the Rocky Mountains during the winter. Now, we can't even leave before March, unless we carry hay and oats."

At the wagon, Noah directed his sister-in-law, "Sally, get paper and a pen and light a lantern."

Sally had lost her kiss from Edwin. She wiped tears from her eyes. "Why?"

"You're filing a claim for possession of the necklace. If Elizabeth Saunders doesn't arrive in six months, it will legally be yours, and they'll have to write you a legal order of ownership."

"But she may get here, and we won't be here in six months." Sally rummaged for a quill and the ink.

Ann lit a lantern. Noah looked through the index of the case law book from Murray Strong's library. "I read about this after Edwin got all of Roy's possessions. I didn't have to know exactly how to request them for him. I'm sure we have to be completely and precisely correct this time. Here it is."

Sally handed Noah the paper, ink, and pen. He wrote the claim of current ownership and the request to retain possession of the necklace and the dress. Sally signed the paper. The three of them went back to the officer's dining hall. "Colonel Howland, when did Mrs. Elizabeth Saunders leave this fort, and when did she arrive home and look for her trunk?"

"They left this time last year and arrived in New York during September."

"How did you know her trunk had been stolen?" Noah inquired.

Colonel Howland noticed that Noah was holding a large book. "What have you got there?"

"This is a book of case law. I believe we can establish ownership of the necklace and dress right now if you're willing."

All eyes fixed on the colonel. He commanded, "State your case."

"Will you answer the question I asked, please?"

Colonel Howland stated what he knew. "Lieutenant Saunders wrote a letter saying they had hired a man to bring their trunk on a wagon and then load it on the steamer. They saw a trunk loaded by that man, but didn't look closely. They paid the man for his services and went home on the steamer. When they docked, their trunk wasn't there. Only then, did they realize the man must have delivered a decoy trunk at departure. He stated that Elizabeth was distraught about losing her favorite dress and the ruby necklace that had been given to her by a previous suitor, but they would not be able to return to look for the thief. However, he was an average height man with brown hair, brown eyes, and a mustache."

Noah opened to the relevant page and read. "For the owner to recover involuntarily transferred goods, he/she must not be negligent in protecting them, and for inherently identifiable goods, search for said goods should be diligent and timely. The statute of limitations begins to run when the owner discovers or should have discovered the loss of her/his goods. For the buyer to retain the goods, the owner must have been negligent and the buyer must have received the goods by good faith sale or gift."

"Give me the book." The colonel held out his hand. Noah handed it over. The colonel looked at the cover and then the title page. "I'm going to look through this tonight. I'll let you know tomorrow." He left the room with the necklace and the book. The evening of gaiety had been ruined. Noah, Ann, Roscoe, and Sally exited right behind him, followed by the rest of the soldiers.

Sally apologized, "I'm sorry. I should have known better. But this is exactly the kind of event to display a beautiful necklace."

Ann assured Sally, "It's not your fault. I also wore jewelry from the Butterfield loot."

Sally suggested, "Maybe you should apply for ownership of your jewelry too."

To which Noah replied, "Let's not complicate this by adding more pieces of stolen property."

"We always have the worst possible outcome from court cases. I'm going to lose the necklace and probably the dress too."

Noah explained his reasoning. "It's not a court case at this point. If the colonel sees that you have the right to have it, maybe he won't make us go to court."

The bugle blew retire. The two soldiers who had attempted to molest Sally and Ann were utterly exhausted. They took off their burdens and found their beds.

Noah heard the bugle and remembered the message he had been asked to deliver. "Private Morris apologized to us, and he asked me to tell you."

## FIFTY

Sally slept fitfully. She went to the commander's office when the gates opened. With a degrading look, the officer who had accused her of stealing the ruby necklace informed Sally, "He hasn't finished his investigation. He'll send for you when he's ready."

Very sweetly, Sally replied, "Much obliged. Thank you for passing the message."

They made their way to the post chapel, prayed, and read their new Bible for hours. Then, until late afternoon, they strolled around the fort. They looked at the new stone structures the soldiers were building to replace the original log buildings and avoided the two soldiers carrying sacks of rocks.

The officer, who had spoken to Sally that morning, went to the gardens where the accused necklace thieves looked at the vegetables. "Colonel Howland will see you now." He purposefully walked them past the two men accused of molesting the women then continued to the meeting with Colonel Howland. Once in the building, their escort knocked on the office door.

Colonel Howland told the officer, "Send them in." The man opened the door and allowed the four people to enter.

"Sally Williams, you filed a claim for possession of this ruby necklace, which you claim you received in good faith as a gift from a lover, and you filed a claim for possession of the red dress you wore last night on the grounds that you found it in an abandoned building without owner identification?"

"Yes, sir," Sally replied.

"Last night, you told us that you knew the

house was owned by a person then deceased, so you took the dress and other clothes, most of which you later gave away to a needy family."

"Yes, sir."

"As to your claim for the dress, I grant that you have the right to keep it. Elizabeth did not come here to look for it, nor did she send money to pay for shipping to retrieve the dress if we found it. I'm sure a court of law would consider it abandoned."

"Thank you, sir."

"As to the necklace, I don't think there is a statute of limitations as to the amount of time Elizabeth has to recover her stolen jewelry. However, according to the law as stated in this book, the original owner is required to take reasonable measures to protect their possessions and when discovered to be lost or stolen is required to make a diligent and extensive search to recover the object.

"The buyer or current claimant is required to show that they bought or received the object in good faith, believing the title of ownership was clear. A man named Edwin Snow gave the necklace to you as a gift, representing his love for you. You had no reason to believe it was stolen jewelry when you accepted it. You received the necklace in good faith, assuming it was legally given.

"Elizabeth did not take adequate measures to protect these rubies, and she did not engage in any reasonable attempt to find her jewelry. Therefore, she is not entitled to recovery.

"I believe a court of law would also award this necklace to you. Since that would require traveling, time, and expense, I'm going to let you have it and write you a statement of ownership as determined by a military court."

He handed the necklace back to Sally. "Lieutenant, write up the appropriate document for me to sign."

Red-faced and upset about giving his friend's necklace to another person, he did not write the order. "That necklace belongs to Elizabeth, and you know it."

"Yes, I do know it belonged to Elizabeth, but the law has requirements to recover stolen objects, and Elizabeth didn't meet those requirements. Now, write the document."

"Make me carry sacks of rocks and take my rations. I'm not giving her necklace away."

The colonel walked to the door. He waved over another soldier. "Confine Lieutenant Jackson to the stockade, and tell Olson to come here."

The soldier reached for the lieutenant's arm. Jackson jerked away. "Don't touch me. I'll walk."

The two men left. Lieutenant Olson arrived shortly after. "Olson, write a statement of ownership of the ruby necklace and the red dress that Ms. Williams will bring over, so you can accurately write its description. When you have it ready, bring it to me for my signature."

"Yes, sir." The man opened a drawer. "Let me see the necklace, and get the dress."

The soldier hadn't been at the dinner the night before. It didn't matter, everybody in the fort knew about the conflict over the necklace, the incident in the bakery, and the punishment. Sally and Roscoe went for the dress. Noah and Ann stayed to watch over the necklace. Neither Noah nor Roscoe was letting either woman go anywhere, without being accompanied by one of them. After only a few minutes, Sally and Roscoe returned with the dress. The soldier completed the paper then took it to the colonel.

Smiling, Sally walked out of Colonel Howland's command building as the legal owner of the necklace and the dress. "I can't believe this. It's about time we found an honest man in the legal system."

"Yes, but I bet we don't get invited to dinner tonight," Roscoe joked. If any of them had taken that bet, they would have lost. The colonel maintained order, upheld the law, and commanded respect. He had already done the first two. He couldn't do the last if he rubbed the faces of his men in their defeat by inviting the Williams to eat with them again. He didn't.

It was late in the day, and the soldiers in the fort were upset with them, so they decided not to wait until morning to leave. Roscoe stood beside the soldier instructed to feed their animals with the food they had brought with them. "How much hay and oats do we have left?"

"Only a little over half. You have a lot of animals." As ordered by Colonel Howland, the soldier asked, "I'm sure you won't need to carry food away from here. The grass is thick. The army would like to buy what you haven't used."

Roscoe didn't see any reason to make the animals pull the weight. In addition, they would have to come to Fort Gibson every month to look for Eli and Stephanie. He thought it would be a better plan not to further alienate the men stationed there. "I'll sell it for the same amount I paid to acquire it."

The soldier agreed. He paid the money and started unloading the hay. By the time Roscoe and Noah had the wagons hitched, the animal food was gone.

# FIFTY ONE

On the other side of the Neosho River, they took the Shawnee Trial north toward the Santa Fe Trail. Noah told his family, "We're only in the very eastern edge of Indian Territory. We should be safe on the road, but it'll be better if the people watching us can see that I'm an Indian." He went into the wagon and got out the Quapaw Indian clothes he'd had on when he had left his home to find James Williams' farm. He put them on for the first time since he had left Harmony to track the Butterfield Gang.

The wagons were full. Therefore, the goats walked. That slowed them considerably, but they had no problems traveling along the well-maintained road. In the afternoons, thundershowers drenched them. Even with the rain, they had no problems as they crossed the shallow, muddy, sluggish waters of Flat Rock Creek, Cat Creek, Brush Creek, and then Cole Creek. They easily traveled fifteen miles each long summer day. Noah checked off markers in his head: Choteau Creek, Pryors Creek, Wolf Creek...

Seven days later, they left the road and crossed the Neosho River right below its confluence with Spring River. With eager anticipation, Noah told his family, "When Grandmother was young, our tribes claimed hunting rights over a vast amount of land in Arkansas. Your farm was on that land. The chiefs during those times sold all the land for eighteen thousand dollars. That's when our tribe moved here. Most of our people starved coming here. Our current chief is Kehekahtedah. His name means 'handsome bird'. Most people call him 'Lame Chief'. He doesn't live in our village."

442

On the east side of Spring River, they traveled through the Wyandotte then the Shawnee and then the Peoria lands before they arrived at the tiny four-hundred-and-eighty-five-square-miles of land and water at the edge of the Ozark Mountains that was assigned to the Quapaw.

A few miles into Noah's homeland, Sally asked, "How much farther?"

"It's right across Five Mile Creek, but I don't want to get there this late in the day. We need plenty of time for everybody to meet you and hear our story."

Ann squirmed with anxiety. "I'm nervous about meeting your parents."

Noah assured his wife, "They'll love you. Grandmother will too."

# Acknowledgments

Chance and Choices Adventures are made possible by the creative inspiration of my Heavenly Father, who has used a flawed person, Lisa Gay, to tell a story.

## Cover

Kasumovic, Jason. *Rancher and Carriage.* Modified Digital Image. Shutterstock.com. 8 August 2018.

Kaytoo. *Pioneer Wagon.* Modified Digital Image. Shutterstock.com. 6 August 2018.

Aphotostory. *Marsh boardwalk in autumn, located in Sun Island Park of Harbin City, Heilongjiang Province, China.* Modified Digital Image. Shutterstock.com. 25 July 2018.

Gray, Jimmy. *Walking the Boardwalk at Congaree National Park.* Modified Digital Image. Shutterstock.com. 23 July 2018.

Bruce, Robert D. *Grand Canyon cowboy riding horse.* Modified Digital Image. RobertDBruce.com. 6 August 2018.

## Chapter Heading Illustrations by
W. R. Michael Mattingly

**Did you like this story? Please write a review!**
https://www.amazon.com/dp/1945858109

**Chance and Choices Adventures**

**by Lisa Gay**

Pray for Justice

Choose Your Consequences

No Remorse

Means of Escape

Torn Hearts

Xida People

Stone Cold

Goodbye Hideout

Along the Way

The Western Sea

Sally's Sketchbook

**Books by The Traveler**

Provence: a land of lavender and olives

www.ingramcontent.com/pod-product-compliance
Lightning Source LLC
Chambersburg PA
CBHW070542030726
47505CB00001B/129